Nellis Gray

By

Rick Stiller

For all that's right
& true

Rick S

ISBN – 978-0-9892702-9-8

Visit www.rickstiller.com

For those brave enough to stand
for all that's right and true

Nellis Gray

Mama Louise, plump black cook for the Spratlin family, stepped through the kitchen door onto crumbling gray pavers in the courtyard and called to the children in a voice that melded mandates into melody, "Come here, girls, I've got something for you."

She handed each sister a sack lunch and hugged them in turn, "It's such a beautiful morning, I'm absolutely positive that you're going to have a fine first day at school and I'll have cold milk and warm chocolate-chip cookies, fresh out of the oven, when you get home."

Sissy, a little blond sprite with fawning green eyes, squeezed her third mother's hand, whining, "I don't want to go to the public school and why can't Mr. Charles drive us?"

Louise leaned to whisper, "You're starting third grade, so you're old enough to walk to school. It ain't that far and Mr. Charles has other things to attend to, besides driving you girls all over tarnation. He's puttin' on the auction this afternoon and he still has to chauffeur your father down to the plant. Now go on or you'll be late."

Samantha took her younger sister's hand to walk down the drive from the stately manor past the shuttered pool house on the left. The open doors of the garages on the right revealed a baby blue VW bug and a chopped Harley-Davidson straddling either side of a lustrous black Fleetwood Cadillac. Purple martins chirped at the girls and soared from stacked houses on long poles, protected by the eaves of the red barn that was home for a dozen prized horses and ponies until last spring.

They turned down a lane, an allée of immense pecan trees, heavy with nuts, between open fields golden with a second planting of feed corn ready for harvest in a few weeks. "We can cut across the bridge over the creek and sneak through the Gray property."

"Why don't we just walk around? I'm scared of that old man and all those dogs barking and yelping like wolves."

"Ah, don't be a scaredy-cat. We can save ten or fifteen minutes instead of walking all the way around to the bridge on the highway. Besides, the traffic scares me more than the dogs."

"Alright, but I'm not likin' anything about today."

Samantha stopped and knelt down, brushing waves of auburn from glistening dark eyes, "Look, Father's having a hard time and I don't think he can afford to send us to the Academy anymore. He told me that, when things get straightened out at the plant, we can go back, if we want."

"I don't understand," whined Sissy.

"He doesn't have the money to pay for the tuition and books and uniforms and all the rest."

"Is that why they're selling all the furniture that was in storage?"

"Probably."

"I wonder what he's going to sell next?"

"He said they're only going to sell things that aren't being used anymore. It's not like they're selling the dining room table or our beds," laughed Sam. "I'm actually looking forward to going to the new school and meeting new people, who don't look down their noses when you don't wear the latest clothes or have the coolest stuff. I'd like to get to know some normal kids, who do normal things."

"I guess," said Sissy, following reluctantly, as Sam cut through the woods down to the old red footbridge over Crow Creek, a lazy brook trickling through a winding channel of rough sandstone blocks under majestic old sycamores, oaks, and cottonwoods.

Sam started across but Sissy stopped before she touched the rail, "I'm scared of those dogs."

Her elder sister grabbed her hand, "If we're really quiet and run real fast, we'll be through the fence before they even know we've been there. Are you ready?"

"I guess."

"Okay, let's be sneaky."

Sissy stared straight ahead, afraid to even glance down at the running stream, and scurried across the worn planking to duck behind the vegetable gardens. Long rows, lush with corn, squash, tomatoes, and peppers, surrounded fallow areas glowing with the lime green sprouts of new plantings that would provide fresh produce well into winter. They peered around the corner of the old gray barn and charged through a thicket of chickens, that squawked and scattered in a flurry of feathers, raising the dogs, who barked and howled from the porch of the weathered farmhouse across the yard.

The girls squeaked through a gap between fence posts, just wide enough for fox or possum to enter or escape, and charged down the lane, as old man Gray yelled, "You damned kids get off my property!"

Nellis settled into his rocking chair, snickering to himself. At his age, being cantankerous and rude, with a pack of noisy dogs, a cranky potbellied pig named Chester, a countrified accent, and a rusty cockeyed 'No Trespassing' sign hanging on a locked steel gate kept strangers and inquisitive neighbors at bay. The original homestead had been whittled down through the years to pay the hospital bills and a funeral for his wife, Nanny, then, his daughter Ashley's tuition and a wedding. There was still twenty acres of pecan groves bounded by another forty of sparse forest and open meadows that he rented out to Chuck Stern for grazing a small herd of cattle.

He spent most of his years out there on the road and found, too late, that the real purpose of his life was right here in this old farmhouse all along. He finally came home to look after two teenagers, who hardly knew their father, after Nanny succumbed to a lonely battle with cancer and died in the back bedroom. She concealed her disease, during his brief visits, until it was too late.

Her ghost haunted the house to this day, turning lights on and off, opening and closing doors, and moving things around during the night. In fact, he was fairly sure that she was sitting close by, chastising him for being so unkind to those little girls. He snickered and rocked, reaching for a smoke and hearing her voice in his head, *"Will you stop smoking those damned things before they kill you?"*

"I know you're right but maybe they'll bring us together that much sooner. Besides, I still don't smoke inside the house, because you hated it so much."

Blue jays raised a ruckus in the big elm behind the house, a sure sign that the red-tailed hawk was trying to thieve eggs from a nest. The huge bird passed over the farm every morning, sometimes alone but more often with his mate or young, feeding on squirrels, rabbits, rodents, or a water snake from the creek. Whether desperate or lazy, he occasionally foraged through the canopies of the huge trees for eggs and the local birds fought back with loud desperate dives to drive him away.

Nellis scanned the headline in the newspaper reporting another lame remark by a newly nominated vice-presidential candidate, whose only skill or talent seemed to be fitting a size-eleven wingtip into his mouth every time he faced the press. "How is it possible that they nominate complete morons to run for every public office?"

He stroked the warm ears of his old Irish setter, Brandy, and wiped his brow with a red handkerchief. "It sure is humid this morning and we both know it's gonna get worse."

There was also Mamasan - the German shepherd matriarch of the pack, ChaCha - the Chow who maintained an aloof aristocratic independence, and young Gracie – an overcharged mix of sass and playfulness. A shaggy black stray appeared a few weeks back and settled right in as playmate for Gracie. He named her Cody and only had to chase her down once, when she went after some noisy teenagers, before she picked up on the game of bark on command…but do not leave the porch.

He took a sip of lukewarm tea and a puff on his Winston, when an advertisement caught his eye concerning an auction of antique furniture at two o'clock this afternoon on the grounds of Spratlin House, the estate just north of the homestead. Spratlin ran Stanton Enterprises, as his father before him, distilling oil derivatives in a sprawling complex on the other side of the river. Surely the oil crisis and recession had not brought ruin to an enduring business that employed half the town and a family known for generous philanthropy in the community?

"I'd best run by there to see what they're sellin'," he mused.

~

Nellis noticed a downed section of fencing in need of mending, along the far end of the lane out to the main road, as the old Ford pickup slowed at the stop. He engaged the brake and hopped out to inspect a strand of barbed wire, cut clean with shears. Two sets of motorcycle tracks meandered across the meadow, matched by a pair leading back out onto the road. "Damned kids," mumbled the old man, shielding his eyes to scan the pasture, pondering the intentions of a pair of renegade beer-swilling teenagers. "Ain't much out there 'cept cows, a couple of horses, and my privacy."

The city was slowly swallowing the countryside, a puddle of rancid syrup oozing around the last of the farms and ranches. A few stubborn natives would stay until the end but the city was growing relentlessly and open pastureland was cleared, contoured, and ready for construction.

A new development of identical houses stretched a mile along the south fence line and bulldozers were clearing a portion of the Jenkins' place of every tree and shrub in sight. Rich fertile farmland was being transformed into a desert hiding under winding strips of asphalt and uninterrupted acres of Bermuda lawns. He shook his head in disgust, checked the highway, and turned north, muttering, "Sure gonna be a lot of critters looking for new homes. Progress ain't pretty."

A flurry of shadows rippled across the windshield, as a wedge of geese honked their way into a damp southerly gale to spend a warm afternoon feeding in the marsh around a little lake on the Perryman property. The sun was high in the sky but the previous night's horse feathers pointed due west, where frothy white thunderheads were bubbling up along the horizon. "There's weather comin'."

He braked for a young fox trotting along the shoulder of the road at the junction with Maple Ridge Boulevard, a meandering country lane that snaked along the ridgeline, past secluded mansions and manor houses before dropping into Cameron in the valley below.

The town was named after an aging Scottish escaped convict, Ben Cameron, who hopped a train, after clearing Ellis Island with forged papers, and headed west. Within a year he struck oil, started a company, made a fortune, and built the town to accommodate his workers. After he died, his kids sold out the production to Gulf Oil and old man Stanton bought the plant. His son-in-law took over, after his death, and his son succeeded him.

A large sign at the gate of the Spratlin property proclaimed, 'ANTIQUES SALE, 2 – 4 PM', and a procession of cars lined the lane into the property. Nellis pulled off the pavement, across from the entrance, and wandered beneath a massive arch, bearing a large burgundy crest with an ornate 'S' sculpted between a pair of noble lions embossed in gold, then along the winding drive through a thicket of yews and rhododendrons that screened the house from the street.

He spotted a few serious buyers, amid a stream of curious bargain hunters, and stumbled over a buckle in the pavement, as the manor came into view. A few tiles were missing from a slate roof draping the stately Country French villa surrounded by azaleas, dogwoods, and Japanese maples under huge oaks, sycamores, and maples offering the first tinge of autumn gold and crimson.

He passed under a portico into a large courtyard, opening to the back of the house. Paint was flaking from the soffits and window frames, pavers were cracked and in need of replacement, and, where, once, mums might have bloomed in profusion, there was only a smattering of yellow pansies that would struggle through winter to show first color in the spring. A white curtain fluttered in a window on the second story and tortured eyes in a pallid face stared, for a long moment, then vanished like a wisp of smoke in the gentle breeze.

A crowd of more than one hundred browsed through a houseful of large furniture pieces arranged with lamps, pottery, bookcases, figurines, paintings, leather-bound books, and a treasure-trove of accessories from the far corners of the Earth.

Nellis studied many subjects, during his years on the road, to satiate a lifelong curiosity that itched incessantly inside his brain. While his bandmates recovered from hangovers, he padded through museums, galleries, and antique shops. He always considered a piece of art or furniture or a musical composition in relation to the events, occurring in the world at the time, that might have spawned or inspired their inception. Overly ornate Louis XIV pieces looked garish and frilly next to an elegantly simple English cabinet or a rustic desk crafted before the American Revolution, yet each represented the finest craftsmanship of their periods.

A full set of Britannica Encyclopedias caught his eye but the publication date was 1965. A stout black man, in dark suit and bow tie, leaned over with a smile, "They're completely up to date."

Nellis looked up, "But it's published in sixty-five."

"They publish updates every year and I, personally, inserted every one, every year, so these youngsters couldn't claim they'd been misinformed."

The old man held out his hand, "Nellis Gray."

"They call me Mr. Charles. I've been Head of Household since the Spratlin's got married almost thirty years ago." He tipped his driver's cap, "Say, you're not the Grays who live across the creek are you?"

Nellis smiled sadly, "I guess I'm about the last of us but, yeah, I'm still keeping the place up."

Charles clapped him on the back, "Well, I'm pleased to finally meet you, neighbor. Is there anything you're looking for in particular? The auction's gonna start in the little while but I'd be happy to show our next-door neighbor around."

Nellis scanned the furniture, "I'm not really looking for anything in particular, probably can't afford it anyway, but I live in a small house, so whatever it is would have to be on a smaller scale than most of these pieces."

Mr. Charles' teeth glowed like the Cheshire Cat, "Do you play games?"

"What kind of games?"

"Chess, backgammon, cards…games like that."

"I used to play chess and backgammon with my children on occasion…when they were young."

"Let me show you my favorite piece in this whole collection." He walked across the drive to a small, simple table with a green felt top that lifted off to reveal a chessboard on the reverse and a backgammon board inside. A traverse drawer opened on each side, for game pieces and chips, and slender legs tapered into brass sabots. The boards and details were tastefully inlaid with contrasting strips and panels. "Mr. Spratlin's father told me that this table is actually a late Louis XVI piece made of walnut and tulipwood. I taught each of the children to play these games on this table, so I've always been fond of it."

Nellis ran his fingers across the chessboard, "It's beautiful and so…restrained. This must have been made as the French were ramping into social revolution. Ostentation was an invitation to the guillotine."

Mr. Charles grinned, "I thought you were just lookin'?"

"Actually, I don't have anyone to play with but I'd hate to see something this fine end up where it isn't appreciated. How much you want for it?"

The houseman crossed his arms and leaned back, stroking his chin thoughtfully, "Tell you what, you'd be my first sale, so how 'bout one-hundred dollars?"

"You could get more than that in the auction."

"I could but I wouldn't know that it would be well-loved and cared for, as something this fine should be. I only use lemon oil on it, twice a year on every surface except the felt."

"I think I could afford that," said Nellis, reaching into his pocket to produce a small wad of twenties. He peeled off five bills and handed them to Mr. Charles. "Thanks, I promise to look after it."

"You want some help carrying it out?"

"No, thanks, I can see that you've got plenty to do," replied the weathered man, gazing around at the crowd. "Things kinda tough in the oil patch?"

"We're just clearing space in the garages. We've got one son, Brad – the veteran, living in the pool house and another, Bruce, has installed an art studio in the loft over the barn, so, rather than the family shrinking, they seem to be expanding into every available space on the property."

Nellis nodded knowingly, "I guess we live in different worlds, don't we?"

"Different realities, maybe?"

"And obligations," said Nellis, reaching to shake the man's hand. "I sure appreciate your generosity."

"Just bein' neighborly, brother. You take good care of her for me."

Nellis hoisted the little table and started through the crowd, glancing up to the curtain billowing from the empty window, before toting it back down the long sweeping drive to the pickup.

~

A deafening clap of thunder sent a terrified Sissy running for shelter under a sprawling elm, as a brilliant flash of lightning exploded in the upper branches of a giant sycamore, spewing flaming torches tumbling to the ground. The storm broke to a momentary calm under towering thunderheads roiling eerie green overhead. In the distance, a wall of dust roared across the fields, flinging debris from construction sites and wrenching enormous trees to the ground.

Sam grabbed Sissy's hand, dragging her along the gravel track leading into the Gray property. "C'mon, we can make it home, if we run fast!"

Huge droplets splattered in the mud, followed by the clatter of hailstones hammering the path. The girls raced along the drive, through the gap in the fence, around the barn to the little bridge over a raging creek. Rushing rapids lapped at the planks and the whole frame shuddered violently. A tangle of blue lightning snapped across the treetops, traced by a staggering boom rumbling up the channel. Samantha grabbed the trembling handrail and stepped onto the strut, as a huge branch surged over the bridge, shattering the planking and twisting the steel banister. Sissy screamed, her plea barely audible in the torrent, "Stop, it's too dangerous!"

A calloused hand grabbed Sam's shoulder to pull her back and a grizzled face leaned close, "There's no bridge to cross, darlin'. C'mon, there's shelter in the barn!"

He wrapped the girls under his slicker and trotted to the door through a tangle of squawking chickens, a small herd of goats, five dogs prancing around the girls, with Chester the pig nuzzling in for a scratch, and countless cats peering down from the rafters amid a flutter of doves and pigeons. Nellis heaved the heavy door closed and shook off his tattered hat and parka. Wind and rain battered the old barn and a salvo of hail hammered the metal roof. He offered a dry horse blanket, shouting above the racket, "Sorry, I don't have any towels out here."

Sissy hid behind her sister, as Sam dried her face and hair with the rough cloth, "It's okay, you don't have to hide."

"Are you sure?"

Little rivulets of water dripped from curly waves of salt and pepper hair down the old man's craggy cheeks and prominent nose. His scruffy flannel shirt and dirty jeans were soaking wet, sagging around his lean frame, but Nellis cracked up, "Do I really look that scary?"

Sissy peeked out, considering the ragged straggle of gray hair and several days' worth of stubble on his worn and weathered face, "Yes."

Nellis's blue eyes crinkling into merry slits, as he laughed and laughed, "Who are you girls?"

"I'm Sam and this is my sister, Sissy. We're Spratlins."

The old man held out a rough hand, "Pleased to meet ya', I'm Nellis Gray but most folk, young and old, call me Nellis."

"Thanks for giving us shelter from the storm," said Sam.

"That's what neighbors are for," said Nellis, reaching to flip the switch of an old dusty radio on a shelf.

The speaker crackled but announcer's voice was urgent, "Residents living south of Cameron should be on the lookout for tornadoes. Several wall clouds have been spotted to the southwest and they're headed our way. Take shelter immediately in the northeast corner on the lowest level of a sturdy structure. Should a tornado approach, leave your vehicle and take shelter in a ditch or low-lying area until the storm passes. This is a tornado warning, take precautions now!"

The farmer scratched his head, "Well, if the creek don't overflow, we might be okay in the tack room. Grab some blankets and let's get settled."

The girls dragged several blankets from the stack and followed him to a closet crowded with saddles, bridles, and harnesses. Nellis hauled in a pile of hay bales and stacked them into a cave with a small breach close to the north wall. "Crawl in there and cover yourself with those blankets."

Vicious thunder chased crackling fits of lightning and a raging southwesterly gale rattled the rafters of the old barn. The old man peeked through a crack between the wallboards to find the creek boiling over its banks but the surging tide rushed downhill through a ditch along the back of the vegetable garden.

The wind died and the rain slowed to a drizzle but the damp momentary hush reverberated with a low tremor approaching from a distance, the snarl growing louder and more menacing.

Nellis called Chester and the dogs and slid into the gap between the bales, pulling them closed, "Let's just settle in here for a few minutes and see whether this monster might just pass us by."

The stout pig honked and the dogs snuggled into the tiny cave but Sissy whined, "I'm scared."

"It's okay to be scared, I am too," said Nellis, gathering the girls close and grabbing the strapping binding the bales over their heads. "You just hold on tight and don't let go, no matter what."

A massive growl, the deep churning rumble of an approaching locomotive, rattled the barn from the weathervane to the foundation. A barrage of debris, Mother Nature's artillery shells, crashed through weathered wallboards and splintered hundred-year-old oak beams with the ease of a sharp ax through kindling. The shrill whistle of the furious funnel peeled the roof back from the southwest corner, ripping metal into slashing shards, shredding boards into shattered slivers, and nails into lethal darts, while sucking the contents of the barn out to feed the pungent fury of the tempest.

The overwhelming roar of Mother Nature's rage drowned out the girls' screams, as timbers tumbled onto the frail wooden storeroom, which collapsed around the hay bale cave with a final guttural groan of surrender. After two minutes of howling frenzy, the sisters' cries suddenly seemed shrill in the silence that followed the storm.

The dogs sat up, sniffing, and Nellis looked at his two young charges, "Are you alright?"

"Is it over?" whimpered Sissy, trembling with fear.

"Yeah, it's gone," said Samantha.

Chester honked and cuddled against Sissy.

"Let's see how bad it is," said the old man, pushing on bales, wedged in place under a pile of shattered timber, until one moved. He crawled through the breach and heaved some jagged planks out of the way. "You can come out now but be careful, there's busted boards, twisted metal, and rusty nails everywhere."

Sissy and Sam followed a snorting Chester and sniffing dogs through the gap to find the south and west walls of the barn piled up around the tack room, the north half of the corrugated roof peeled back, and the rest completely gone.

Cats, goats, and chickens appeared one-by-one, baaing and clucking in dazed confusion. The younger sister started crying, "Your barn's gone."

Nellis guided the girls outside and knelt down to console Sissy, "We're alive, that's all that counts. I can build a new barn but I can't build new lives." He hugged the two girls and stood up to watch whirling clouds charging off to the east, trailing a wake of rubble and destruction, shimmering in a streak of blazing sunlight spillign under the back of the storm to the west.

A long black Cadillac pulled up to the steel gate and Mr. Charles stepped out, took off his driver's hat, and shook his head in disbelief, surveying the devastation and the three survivors, surrounded by a herd of dogs, cats, goats, chickens, and a stout pig, next to the remnants of a once sturdy barn.

Nellis unlatched the gate and the girls ran into his arms, "I was so worried about you and I'm sorry I didn't get to you in time. I was going to pick you up at school but I got delayed at the auction. Are you okay?"

Sissy looked up at him, "Nellis saved us from the storm."

"Yeah, but his barn got blown away," added Sam.

Mr. Charles walked over to shake Nellis' hand, "I...we could never thank you enough."

"As you said, that's what neighbors are for," said the old man, gazing around. "The house's okay and my two horses are out to pasture in the south forty, so they probably survived."

"Yeah, but this is a mess."

"Ah, I helped rebuild it when I was a teenager, I can certainly do it again."

"Anything I can do for you, before I take these children home? I 'spect the family's a might anxious."

"You go on, they've been through enough for the first day of school."

"I'll say," smiled the black man. "Thanks again."

"No problem," said Nellis, as Mr. Charles held the door and the girls climbed into the back seat of the car.

Chester and the dogs gathered around Nellis to rub against his legs until he knelt down to pet each in turn. "I'm real proud of all of you for protecting those little girls. The barn's a mess, let's go see what else got ruined."

They moved through a maze of rubble into the vegetable gardens. The tall crops - corn, pole beans, and climbing tomatoes - were all flattened, their stalks pointing southwest. The ground crops were damaged by gravel and debris from the runoff but the broccoli, cabbage, lettuce, spinach, onions, and carrots would survive to produce.

The herd trudged over the little ridge to survey acres of sunflowers in the west field, which was nestled in a hollow surrounded by ancient gnarled oaks, statuesque sycamores, and molting cottonwoods. A triangle of flattened stalks pointed northeast but the rest of the field was undamaged. He pulled off his old hat and brushed his hair back, "That damned storm went right between this field and the house...but it surely took out the barn. Someone's lookin' out for us, guess we should be thankin' Nanny."

He burrowed into a row between the standing flowers to inspect a well-disguised grove of bushy green marijuana that was ready for harvest. The old man pulled a loupe from his pocket to peer at glistening red fibers on a fat bud. "Damn, you're ready for harvest and I've got no barn to hang you to cure. Ain't that the pits?"

The plants were interspersed between rows along the northern edge of the field and appeared undamaged. "Guess we'll have to figure out some alternative…and quick."

~

At eight o'clock the next morning a large flatbed truck, marked with 'B&B Lumber' on the doors, pulled up to the gate and the driver honked.

The dogs barked ferociously but Nellis calmed them and ambled over to the truck, "Can I help you?"

"You Mr. Gray?" asked the heavyset driver, leaning out the window.

"Yeah, that's me, what's it to you?"

"I got a load of lumber for you."

"I didn't order no lumber."

"Hey mister, it says on the delivery to bring it to this address, signed by my supervisor. If you don't want it, I'll take it back."

Nellis scratched the stubble on his chin, unlocked the gate, and walked around to the back of the truck to inspect the load. The driver got out with the form, "You got two stacks of twenty-four foot 12 X 12's and four bundles of 4 X 12's and it looks like there's 2 X 12's, roof trusses, and shingles coming later."

"Who sent this?"

"I have no idea," replied the stout courier. "I just deliver it where they tell me."

Nellis pointed, "Over there by that heap of trash that used to be a barn."

"Looks like you'll have all the materials you need to put it right."

"Maybe so."

The driver off-loaded the beams and boards and drove away.

At ten o'clock another truck pulled up to the gate, followed by a small crane and two flatbeds heavy with materials. Nellis walked over to unlatch the gate as an athletic young man in a Stanton-blue uniform climbed out of the cab.

"You Mr. Gray?"

"Yeah, who're you?"

"I'm Anthony Higgins, maintenance foreman down at Stanton. Mr. Spratlin sent us along to give you a hand getting your barn back in shape. I guess it's his way of saying thank you for saving his daughters."

"Well, I'll be damned."

"You may be but, if you want some help, I've got a crew who know what they're doin' and a crane to place those beams."

"Bring 'em on in," yelled Nellis, rolling the gate out of the drive.

By the time the black Cadillac pulled in at three-thirty, the crew had hauled most of the debris away and new beams and struts were being installed with assembly-line efficiency.

The girls jumped out of the car and ran to hug Nellis. The old man took off his floppy hat and knelt, "I never expected...anything...let alone all of this..."

Samantha pursed her lips, "We would have died out here, if you hadn't saved us."

"That's what's important," said Nellis.

"And so's this," said Sissy pointing to the barn. "It's important to you."

Mr. Charles opened the rear door and a tall man in a dark tailored suit strode confidently into the yard. He had broad shoulders that drooped slightly, perhaps under the weight of his station, a mane of white hair, and a slight grimace etched into handsome, aristocratic features.

Nellis stood to greet him, removing his hat and offering a calloused hand, "You'd be Mr. Spratlin?"

"That I am," said the man with weary dark eyes and a small grateful grin. "And I am most pleased to have the pleasure of your acquaintance, so I might thank you, personally, for saving my daughters during the storm. My children are everything to me." He gazed around at the construction, "I'm very sorry you lost your barn."

"Well, your daughters didn't have anything to do with that part of it. It fell down without any help from them," joked Nellis. "I don't really know how to thank you for the materials and this crew of guys. They're crackerjack!"

"They're my best men, they only do things one way…the right way." The industrialist looked around at the tattered ruins of expansive vegetable gardens behind the barn, bounded by curving beds full of flowering shrubs and perennials shielding a tired gray farmhouse nestled under enormous black walnuts, red oaks, and maples. Rows of pecan trees marched across a meadow to the south. "How much land do you have?"

"Oh, there's 'bout sixty acres left but it's startin' to feel like suburbia all around."

"Do you have family?"

Nellis shook his head, "No, my wife died of cancer, a few years back, and my children moved away."

"So, you're lookin' after sixty-acres all by yourself?"

The old man cackled, "There's one thing to be said for working for yourself."

Spratlin leaned expectantly and Nellis grinned, "You can't blame no one else, if things don't go the way you planned."

"Amen to that. I know exactly what you mean, except, when I make a decision, it affects thousands of people."

"Same problem, bigger scale."

Spratlin extended his business card, "Again, my sincere thanks for saving Samantha and Sissy. If there's anything I can do for you, please do not hesitate to call. This is my direct line."

"With the help of your crew, we'll have this buttoned up before the next system rolls through."

"Let's hope for rain without the pyrotechnics," said Spratlin. He turned to Mr. Charles, "Will you collect our young ladies? I have to be back at the office shortly."

"Yes, Sir, Mr. Spratlin." Mr. Charles marched around the side of the barn to find the girls standing in the outline of the demolished tack room with Chester.

Sissy looked up from petting the pig between the ears, "This is where we were hiding under a straw fort!"

The driver lifted his hat to wipe his forehead with a handkerchief, "You're lucky Mr. Gray is a wise man. Now come along, your Papa needs to get back to the plant."

"Alright," whined Sissy, patting Chester gently before grabbing Sam's hand to trot around the barn. The girls hugged Nellis and climbed into the Cadillac.

Chapter Two

John Malcolm and Fred Jameson rose with Mr. Spratlin, as the union representatives, Dobie Johnson, Roy Stiles, and Mitch Mitchell, were shown into the conference room by Katherine Kennedy, Spratlin's personal secretary.

Spratlin walked around the huge table to shake hands, "Dobie, Roy, Mitch, I appreciate your time, won't you have a seat?"

The men settled into comfortable leather chairs and Mitch asked, "What's this about?"

John Malcolm, treasurer for Stanton Enterprises, cleared his throat gruffly, "Gentlemen, we have a problem and we need your help to find a solution."

"What problem's that?" inquired Roy.

Fred Johnson, Vice President, interrupted, "Workers and management have been partners in this enterprise for more than one-hundred years…"

Before he could continue, Dobie broke in, "That's management talk, give it to us straight."

Spratlin stood, "Gentlemen, the pension fund, along with a substantial portion of my personal holdings, were heavily invested in the stock market. As you know, the market turned south on us during the crash last spring and the value of our principal investments declined dramatically."

Roy jumped up and slammed his fist on the mahogany table, "That's our money, you bastards! Who's responsible for this?"

Malcolm raised his hand, "You'd have to blame me, for I was the one who was trying to grow your investments into something more substantial, which, ultimately would have reduced worker's contributions over time."

"Hell, I'd be satisfied just to get back the money I put in," said Mitch. "How much is left?"

Stanton raised his hand for silence. "We're working on a plan to invest the balance in more secure vehicles for the short term and the company will dedicate a fair portion of any profits to compensating the fund until it's balanced." He paused, "I understand your anger and frustration but there only seem to be two choices here. The first is that we work together, you hire or appoint an accountant and an attorney to represent your interests and to work with John to make sure that every person who is retiring over the next few years gets full benefits, while we rebuild the fund."

Dobie, Roy, and Mitch stared at the president of the company with anger and suspicion. Mitch snapped, "And the second option is that we go on strike, until you find a way to make up the difference!"

Malcolm responded, "I'm afraid that a major strike, at this moment, would doom not only your pensions but the future of the company."

"That's blackmail," shouted Dobie. "You bastards are living fat off our backs. The men aren't going to stand for this!"

"Mr. Johnson," replied Spratlin, "if we do not find a solution to this dilemma, there will be no Stanton Enterprises and we can all stand in line at the soup-kitchen together. Those are the choices."

"So, now, you're sayin' the company might go under?" roared Mitchell.

"I'm saying that I am divesting myself of all extraneous assets and expenditures to support this company through a very trying time. We borrowed heavily to expand the plant two years ago and, you know as well as any of us, with the recession, diminished demand for our products is dragging the bottom line. The company will go into forfeiture, if we do not meet our obligations."

He scanned from one to the next, "You all know me. We grew up together. Your fathers and many of their fathers, before them, worked for my father and grandfather. We grew this town together and I hope to pass my obligation to all of you on to the next generation." He paused, "We've been through tough times before and we pulled together to overcome the ravages of floods and tornadoes, the hardships of wars and recessions, and the personal losses that every family in the community has shared. We can solve this problem if we stick together."

The three men glanced at each other, before Dobie asked, "What do you want from us?"

John Malcolm replied, "Help us save all our jobs and the future of this city. Simple as that."

"What do you want from us now?" asked Stiles.

"Let's get the union to hire an accountant and an attorney you can trust," said Fred Jamison. "I'd suggest Jules Schreiber. He's an accountant and an attorney and a union man from way back. I bet he'd come out of retirement to lend a hand."

"Is that Ethan's grandfather?" asked Dobie.

"Yeah, check him out. He's been through countless union battles, so you know he's sympathetic to your cause. On the other hand, he knows his stuff and he's a realist, who can guide you to the best course of action or inaction, as it may be," said Malcolm.

"He's a solution guy not a rabble-rouser," added Jamison. "What do you say?"

"I'm not lookin' forward presenting this to the men," said Mitch Mitchell, shaking his head solemnly. "No, they're not going to like any of this."

"I'll call a general meeting, if that would help," said Spratlin.

"No, this screw-up needs to be handled right or you'll have riots at the gates," said Roy Stiles. "Give us a couple of days to sort this out among ourselves and get in touch with Ethan's granddaddy."

"Fine," said Jamison. "We'll meet again on Monday."

The union men rose and sauntered out of the room, grumbling to each other.

"That went better than I expected," said Malcolm.

"Don't get your hopes up," said Jamison. "They haven't agreed to anything."

"I'm afraid they hold the future of the company in their calloused hands," said Stanton Spratlin, as he gathered his papers and strode from the room.

~

Sibble Savage, a tiny ageless waif, who nannied this generation and Stanton and his sister, Ruth, before them, trudged up the wooden stairs to the loft above the barn and knocked gently on the door at the top. "Master Bruce, are you decent?"

The door opened a crack, "It's ten o'clock in the morning, what could you possibly want at this hour? And, no, I haven't been decent since I was twelve years old."

"Is that any way to treat your second mother?" demanded the little black woman in a gray uniform with a spotless white apron. "D'you think these ol' bones need to be standing out here in the cold on these stairs."

The door eased open and Bruce stepped back to allow her to enter a long studio, glowing with north light from a skylight cut across the roof. Enormous gloomy canvases, portraying the most base and vile human excesses, leaned against the walls but, opposite the windows, an unfinished white square surrounded a solid red sphere with an iridescent green eyeball staring out from the center.

Sibble glanced around the room, "I don't pretend to understand art..."

Bruce grinned, rubbing a two-day growth of beard, "I don't pretend to understand what I'm doing either. It's just what comes out of the brush."

"No, it comes out of your mind," scolded his nanny, "and I'm not sure who put what in there, while I wasn't lookin'?"

"None of us could have asked for more love or affection than you gave us."

"You always were quick with the sweet response but I know you better than that!"

"Can't argue there. What'd you want anyway?"

"Oh, Missus Spratlin asked if you'd stop in to see her, after Dr. Selfridge leaves?"

"She won't be conscious after he gets through with her."

"That's no way to talk of a doctor," said Sibble. "You should show some respect young man. He's only trying to help her get better."

"He's a quack and we both know it. He's pumping her full of Lithium and Valium and topping it off with white crosses to keep her from going into a coma!"

"Now, now, she's a sick woman."

"She's a hypochondriac."

"She's also your mother. So, get yourself cleaned up and go see her, before I bring her lunch up at noon, or I'll go find a switch to lash your skinny butt, just like I did when you were a scrawny kid."

"I'll do it for you, not her."

"Just do it. Things are hard enough for everyone around here," said Sibble, opening the door to clutch the rail as her block heels thumped down the stairs, one at a time.

Bruce knocked gently on his Mother's bedroom door and peeked in to find her propped up in bed, surrounded by plump pillows and crisp linen sheets embroidered with pink floral bouquets. She wore a Chinese silk gown, open to reveal more than a glimpse of cleavage, and flicked on the lamp, which made her blond hair and porcelain complexion glow in the darkened room, but makeup and lighting could not conceal her torment. "I'm so glad you came to see me. I get so lonely."

"I came by a couple of days ago, remember?"

"Oh, yes." Her words were slurred but she smiled, reaching to take his hand, "You know I never get enough of my favorite son."

Bruce stepped closer and stared for a moment. She had been a beautiful woman in her youth, before pills and liquor drained the color from her skin, the life from her bloodshot eyes, and the spirit from her soul. His father loved her with all his heart but, after Sissy was born, she retired to this bedroom, never venturing into the rest of house or the grounds again. As far as he knew, they had not slept together since. "How are you feeling?"

"Better, now that the doctor refilled my medications."

"Between the quack doctor and the good Reverend Billy Joe Hardman saving your soul, you should be all set."

"They're both fine men, just like you," snapped Marjorie.

"I'm a faggot because you trained me, remember?"

Her lips pouted, "You're my beautiful boy, would you help me feel better? Please?"

"Mother, do we have to?"

"I need the human touch and yours is so gentle." She pulled back the sheet and took his hand, "Please?"

His fingers found the heat between her legs and massaged gently, as she unzipped his jeans to fondle him, whimpering, "I produced this beautiful organ and I want to put it back where it belongs."

"No! Besides, you made sure that I'll never fuck a woman again."

"We'll not talk of that."

"It's no secret!"

"She's my sin, not yours."

"Miraculous conception."

She shuddered, "I've seen your models, they're all beautiful young men. Don't you paint women too?"

Bruce smirked, "I'd rather play with boys."

"Don't share this with anyone else, it's mine," moaned the woman, as violent waves of ecstasy exploded through her body.

Bruce backed away and tucked himself in, as she dabbed at her lipstick with an embroidered hanky. A knock at the door interrupted and Sibble swept into the room with a bed tray, "Here's your lunch, Mrs. Spratlin. Can I get you anything else?"

"No, I'm sure Mama Louise has prepared far more than ten men could consume."

Sibble nodded, "That's probably true but you eat what you can to build your strength, now, and I'll be back for the tray in a little while."

She turned to Bruce, as she left the room, "There's a turkey sandwich waiting for you in the kitchen."

"Why, thank you," replied Bruce, blushing.

"Thank you for coming to see me," said Marjorie. "I so enjoy your visits."

"I know you do," said her son, kissing her forehead and turning to leave.

"Come back soon."

He did not reply but closed the door quietly.

~

Nellis shielded his eyes to watch a young peregrine falcon hovering on a southerly breeze, sharp eyes scanning for a foolish rodent out in the open or any bird that might take flight. Frustrated, he tilted the tips of his wings and soared a hundred feet straight up to bank hard right, circling the yard four times before he disappeared over the pecan grove.

He sauntered up the path to the house, "That's just pure magic, that is. Sad part is that his huntin' ground is being gobbled up by tract housing lined up on an endless green lawn with nary a tree or a shrub in sight. Maybe he'll take a likin' to the ol' homestead."

He was just settling in with a cup of hot tea, when the dogs perked up, as Sissy squeaked through the gap in the fence and skipped across the gravel drive to the house. She stopped on the step, as Chester and the dogs crowded around to lick and sniff, pointing to the game table that Nellis had set up on the porch, "I'm so glad you got that table. It's very special to all of us."

"It's a story within a story, isn't it?" replied Nellis pointing to the chair opposite. "Checkers?"

"Sure."

"Red or black?"

"Red, of course!"

"Where's Sam?"

"Oh, she went to check on my brother Brad. He's a mess." Sissy looked up, as they laid out the pieces, "Two questions."

"Okay."

"Why did you bring the table out here?"

"Because it doesn't look right for a grownup man to have an unescorted young lady in his house," replied Nellis, carefully.

"Why?"

"Because people always think the worst of everyone else, first, and ask questions later. Let's just say that I like the breeze and Chester and the dogs would get hurt feelings if they couldn't hang out with you. What's the other question?"

"Oh, you said the table is a story within a story. What did you mean?

Nellis smiled, rubbing rough fingers across the intricate banding inlaid in the board, "Do you have any idea of where this came from?"

"I think Mr. Charles said it came from France," replied Sissy.

"Very good but from what part of history?"

"It seems very old. I don't know, a hundred years?"

Nellis smiled, "I'm guessing that it was made around the time of the French Revolution in 1789. Before that, the furnishings were lush and gaudy, covered with gold leaf as a note of ostentation. As the revolt approached, cabinetmakers refined their styles to produce wonderfully understated pieces like this. The craftsmanship is superb. How do suppose they cut each of these little rectangles and interlaced this tiny strip of ebony in between each joint?"

"That is fairly amazing. They must have had good eyes," laughed Sissy.

"A steady hand and great patience."

"But you said there's a story inside the story."

"Well, let's imagine that a cabinetmaker spent the better part of a year making this little table. He had to find exactly the right woods for these slender legs and the delicate top, with strong straight grains to support the heavy leanings of inebriated patriots and provocateurs."

"What's inebriated?"

"Drunk," laughed Nellis, moving a black chip to counter Sissy's move.

"What about provacatator?"

"A patriot is someone who defends their country or their beliefs. A Provocateur is someone who causes trouble, in this case maybe a revolutionary who wanted to bring down the king and the government. And that's the beginning of the rest of the story, isn't it? Think about all the people, probably influential people of their times, who sat at this table of an evening, imbibing on a stout brandy or a bitter ale, while they played cards or backgammon and discussed the political future or the latest social gossip or, maybe, they traded contacts to expand their fortunes. Needless to say, this table didn't reside in a house like mine, more like yours probably."

"So they would have been rich people?"

"Yes, most certainly. No commoner could afford a fine piece of frivolous furniture like this, that's what brought about the revolution. Society was divided between the Bourgeois, the wealthy merchants and industrialists, along with the nobility and the leaders of the Church, and the little people, who resented the gentry getting rich while the workers starved. The crops failed and the peasants couldn't feed themselves, while the privileged hosted grand parties for thousands of guests, serving endless courses of foods and wines from all over the world, certainly flaunting their wealth and extravagance."

"Do you think that people plotted the overthrow of the King over this table?" asked Sissy.

"Could very well have happened," said Nellis, jumping two of her pieces in one turn. "You might wanna pay attention to the game, girlie."

She jumped three of his men and landed on his side, "King me!"

"Yes, Ma'am!"

"So, I wonder where it went from there?"

"And how'd it get here?"

"If only it could tell us."

"Well, we do have some clues."

"Like what?" asked the little blond.

"Well, for one thing there are two labels on the bottom of the table."

Sissy took two more of his pieces and leaned under the table, "Really?"

"Really. One is a weathered shipping label addressed to Sir Cyril Ritchard, at an address in London. The other is a price tag from a gallery in New York that looks like it might have been printed in the teens or twenties."

"Who's Cyril Ritchard?"

"Sir Cyril Ritchard was a famous Australian actor, who is most celebrated for his magnificent portrayal of Captain Hook in the original Broadway production of Peter Pan. He is a 'Sir' because he was knighted by the Queen."

"I saw the film of that on television. He was really funny, especially when the crocodile was around," laughed Sissy. "I wonder what conversations he had over this table?"

"I'd love to have been a fly on the wall, he was a very gifted man."

"That's the first clue, maybe we could find out its secrets somehow."

"Worthy of a little research," mused Nellis, inspecting the sparse collection of black pieces surrounded by red kings. He jumped two stacks to get his crown.

"You don't give up easy, do you?" smirked the young sprout, jumping two more of his men. "It sure is nice having the bridge up again."

"Yeah, Tony Higgins brought in a couple of his welders, who put that together in an afternoon. Talented guys."

"Looks like the barn is almost done."

"Yup, finish up a few details and whitewash her and she'll be better than new. I sure do appreciate all the help from your daddy and his men."

"I think you saved his daughters and he found a little joy in repaying your kindness."

"Sounds like things might not be going so well over at your place," said Nellis quietly.

Sissy's grin vanished, "Oh, it's not so bad."

"Which means it's not as good as it was."

"Well, Sam told me that Father doesn't have the money to send us to the Academy this year and Mother's been sick in bed since I was born. Then there's my brother, Brad, who got wounded in Vietnam, so he's drunk and crazy mad all the time, and Bruce, who's decided he's an artist, so he can act as weird as he wants."

"And how's Sissy coping with all of this?"

The little girl looked up, tears welling in her eyes, "I wake up every morning hoping that it's all just a bad dream and bright sunshine will make it all better."

The old man leaned back in his chair, "Sometimes, life isn't kind…or fair, for that matter. You are not responsible for fixing these problems or making your family members better. Each of them has to overcome their own demons and heal in their own ways and all you can do is do your best to be who you are…a charming little imp with an enchanting and devious smile."

"What's devious?"

"Sneaky!" laughed Nellis.

Chapter Three

Nellis wiped his brow, gazed up at hundreds of golden-green plants hanging from the rafters of the new barn. He savored the sweet aroma and grinned, "There's gonna be a happy Christmas for a lot of folks this year."

He jumped as the old phone jangled and retrieved it from the hook on a post, "Hello."

"Hey, Nellis, it's Jazz. How ya' doin'?"

"I'm hanging in there, man. Downside is that my barn got knocked down by that twister a couple of weeks ago. Upside's my neighbor sent over a crew of guys, who built me a new one."

"Shit, it goes and it comes, if ya' know what I mean?"

"Sometimes the gods just make fun of us," smirked Nellis. "I'm grateful for the help."

"Hey, listen, I'm playin' the Church tonight and wondered whether you'd like to sit in on a couple of tunes?"

"I haven't played much since I got back here. Somehow, real life and sixty-acres gets in the way of doin' what I love best."

"Well, shake off the rust and get your ass in gear. I've got a hot band and we'll be cookin'. Come on down!"

Nellis hesitated for a half-a-second, "All right. I'll cruise by there about ten."

"Lookin' forward to it," laughed Jazz.

Jason Taggart, Jazz to his friends and fans, grew up in the country ghetto, on the other side of the river. He and Nellis had rival bands through high school. Jazz was always playin' heavy stuff like Hendrix and Zeppelin and burning up the stage with wild theatrics, while Nellis hooked up with a laid-back bunch, performing original tunes that ranged from psychedelic blues jams to sentimental pop tunes that always made the girls cry. Their styles were drastically different but they shared a mutual admiration and love for the instrument. Jazz took off for Los Angeles, chasing fame and fortune, while Nellis traveled the blues circuit from Chicago to Memphis and across the cotton belt.

He wandered into the back bedroom, pulled the well-traveled case from beneath the bed, and strapped on his 1959 Goldtop Les Paul. His knuckles were stiff and once hard calluses on his fingertips were soft and tender, as he worked through little riffs and stretched a note here and there. His lips curled into a grin, "Lucy, girl, I'm sorry I've neglected you all these months but, I promise, we're gonna start cookin' again."

~

The Church was resurrected by a tribe of hippies, after it was abandoned following a gas explosion that leveled most of the dilapidated neighborhood. Gutted and restored as a sanctuary for rock-n-roll, blues, and red-dirt country, the new tenants installed a huge stage with a staggering sound system, a killer light show, stained-glass windows with idyllic scenes from nature, and antique pews surrounding the dance floor.

The parking lot was full of hogs, hot cars, and battered pickup trucks with gun racks in the rear windows. Nellis eased into a space near the back of the building, grabbed his case, and strolled past a group of kids toking on a joint in the alley and a couple making out in the shadows. Two bikers were lounging on chopped Harleys and a hulking guy with a burr cut and a mean scar across his cheek yelled, "Hey, little man, where ya' think you're goin'?"

"Who's askin'?" smirked Nellis, thinking, *Do we really have to run this reel one more time?*"

"I am, asshole!" replied the young thug, staggering to his full six-five to lunge at Nellis, who sidestepped the brute, extended his left foot, and dropped the inebriated punk facedown on the pavement with a knee between the shoulder blades...and Lucy's case never touched the ground.

He looked up at the drunk's companion, who was stretched out on his bike, shaking his head with a broad grin. Nellis asked, "You hip to Jazz?"

"Yeah, man, that cat can play," said the other biker.

"Taught him everything he knows," said Nellis. "You oughta come inside and listen, we're about to tear the house down."

He hauled the drunk upright, grabbed his arm, and shoved him up the steps into the Church. "You're gonna dig my music or I'll knock your ass down again."

Heavy guitar and bass reverberated through the building and the crowd of hippies, bikers, and country hicks danced and stomped to the beat. Nellis worked his way around the edge of the throng to slip through a door backstage and strapped on Lucy.

The song ended and Jazz glanced over to the side of the stage with a big stony smirk, "Ladies and gents, we're gonna slow things down just a little bit and I'd like to introduce an old friend and living legend, Nellis Gray!"

The crowd clapped and cheered as he plugged in and tuned up, then sauntered over to a mike. "Good evening, I'd like to thank Jazz for inviting me down to play a few tunes for you." He scanned the crowd and grinned, "I see a few folks who might be old enough to remember some of these songs. How 'bout we start off easy with 'Sunday Morning Sunshine?'"

He turned to the band, "Y'all remember this one?"

They all smiled and nodded, as he started the descending riff and eased up to the microphone,

> *Up with the sunrise, wipe the sleep from my eyes*
> *Surrounded by the sweet scent of you*
> *Warm taste of coffee, the papers, the news*
> *Sunday morning, sunshine, and you*
> *Sunday morning, sunshine, and you*

He and Jazz traded slow moody licks, stretching each note, each phrase into a mellow wail. Nellis turned back to the mike,

> *Into the garden, smell the roses in bloom*
> *The birds sing their song for you*
> *Take my hand, for it's moments like these*

Sunday morning, sunshine, and you
Sunday morning, sunshine and you

Several young ladies at the foot of the stage, certainly younger than his daughter Ashley, gazed up adoringly with tears streaming down their cheeks. The crowd applauded and the drunk biker raised a beer bottle in appreciation, clapping his buddy on the back.

Jazz leaned over, "You've still got the magic, old man. Let's play another!"

The band charged through a dozen songs, building the tempo and the intensity into a frenzy, and ended the set with a barnburner called, 'Too Much of a Good Thing'. Nellis cranked up his Southern growl,

Living in a house
Full of beautiful women
Blowin' through my life
Like a storm.
A cold wind blowin' south
You know what I'm talking about!
Too much of a good thing
Lord, save me from myself.

The house was rockin' and the audience was dancing up the aisles and hanging from the balcony.

Fell for a vixen with velvet eyes
Said I was her reason to live
Loved me, left me
Took all I had
Now I got nothing left to give, nothing left to give
Too much of a good thing
Lord, save me from myself

Rolled the dice
And hit it twice

Now Uncle Sam
Wants a slice of my life
It ain't right
Too much of a good thing
Lord, save me from myself!

The crowd clapped and cheered. Nellis took a bow and walked up to the mike, as drunks raised a ruckus in the shadows at the back of the house with glass shattering and bodies flying. He shielded his eyes but couldn't see through the glare of the stage lights. "You've been a terrific audience and I'd like to thank Jazz and the rest of these incredible players for lettin' me sit in tonight. Y'all take care now."

He hugged Jazz, high-fived the players, and trooped off the side of the stage, as the band cranked up a heavy metal version of Sly's 'Dance to the Music'. Rather than getting hung up in a sea of fawning drunks, he stashed Lucy in her case and slipped out the side door into the parking lot.

A voice barked, "Hey, old man, where the fuck do you think you're goin'?"

Nellis shook his head, as the totally smashed biker staggered across the parking lot, supported by his buddy and a skinny blond with big tits and white hair that looked as if it had been bleached with Clorox one too many times. "So, what'd ya' think?"

"I think you play that thing like you're makin' love to it."

"Well, thanks. We've been together for a long time."

"I oughta break your fingers for that trick you pulled on me earlier but I took it out on some stupid hippie kid instead."

"I guess I should thank you," smiled Nellis, "but I won't. I'm guessin' you were military, you should know better."

"Yeah, Nam." The drunk extended his hand, "I need to thank you for saving my little sisters a couple of weeks ago. I'm Brad Spratlin."

"Small world," replied the guitar player, shaking his hand. "They're nice girls and I was just being neighborly."

"That was more than bein' neighborly, brother," stammered the drunk, as his wardens dragged him over to the Harleys.

Nellis strolled over to the truck and eased out of the parking space, braking as the two bikes and a corvette peeled out of the lot onto the highway. "There's trouble waitin' to happen."

~

A cold rain rode a north wind and the dogs, along with Chester the pig and most of the cats, decided that staying dry on the porch beat all other options. Nellis pitched a couple of small logs into the wood stove, wrapped a blanket around his legs, and opened the paper. He reached for a smoke and a cup of coffee, scanning the headline,

'STRIKE LOOMS AT STANTON PLANT'

In spite of round-the-clock negotiations, Workers' Union representative Dobie Johnson, leaving the latest round, said that misappropriated pension funds must be restored, before further talks can continue. "The workers will strike at midnight unless our ultimatums are met!"

John Malcolm, Chief Financial Officer at Stanton, is quoted as saying, "We've made every effort to find a sound fiscal solution to this tragic dilemma and the workers have been warned that a prolonged strike could prove catastrophic for the company. Management requests that they return to the bargaining table with a willingness to find a resolution that is feasible and acceptable to all parties in these talks."

The Union maintains that a major portion of the pension fund, administered by Stanton Chief Financial Officer John Malcolm, was lost during the market collapse last year.

It is believed that management has offered to replenish the fund over the next few years but the most recent annual report revealed a steep decline in overall sales, in spite of a major expansion a few years ago.

The union rank and file are demanding more than promises to resolve this conflict and a midnight work stoppage appears certain. Considering the financial obligations of Stanton in a soft market, an extended strike might well force the company into default.

"That explains a lot," thought Nellis. *"That poor bastard might have millions stashed away someplace but it sure ain't gonna be enough to dig him out of this hole."*

He savored a sip of coffee and a puff on his smoke, *"Funny how, when you're not in the middle of it, you can see both sides. If this gets outta hand, it's gonna hurt the whole town. Most everybody depends on the plant and the workers to spread those dollars around to keep everyone else goin'. Maybe we could get 'em all to come together at a little benefit concert. It sure is hard to be pissed off when you're listening to good music, watchin' pretty ladies dancin', and enjoying a cold brew."*

He walked inside, picked up the phone, and dialed, "Hey Jazz, it's Nellis."

"You were cookin' last night brother," replied a groggy Jason. "I looked for you, after we finished, but you were gone, man, like a freakin' white ghost."

"I'm just not up for wading through a crowd of drunks, if you know what I mean. Just been there too many times over the years and I ain't got the energy to go out partying all night anymore."

"Been there, done that?" laughed Jazz. "I mean it man, you still got it."

"Yeah, I dug the gig last night, man, and I want to do it again, only bigger. How long you plannin' to stick around?"

"Well, my Mama's plannin' to keep me around through next weekend and I've been on the road so long, I could use a little break and some home cookin' for a change. What have you got in mind?"

"Seen the paper this morning?"

"Naw, man, you woke me up. I should be pissed."

"The union guys are going on strike against Stanton."

"That sucks for the whole town...fucking grocery stores and restaurants and gas stations, hell, everyone depends on that money machine."

"You're right. Seems the pension fund got squandered in the last market crash and the union guys are pissed."

"Rightly so."

"Yeah, but...everyone's gonna suffer if this goes down. The company says that they'll go out of business, if the strike doesn't get resolved. So, I got to thinkin' about how to get everyone together and I thought maybe we could put on a little benefit concert, to get everyone in the same place at the same time. Some good music and few beers and folks become more reasonable. What d'ya think?"

"We both know that a drunk crowd can go just about any which way, except where you expect, but I'm in."

"Cool, but I think, considering the crowd and our purpose, we might want to keep things mellow."

"Aw, no pyrotechnics?" whined Jazz.

"No, man, we gotta do this right. Get with your guys and see what you can work out and I'll call a couple of other people and see if we can't turn this into something that everyone's gonna want to experience."

"When and where?"

"To be worked out," replied Nellis. "Wonder whether we could get the armory on a Saturday night?"

"Fucking racist rednecks."

"Hey, they're our rednecks and good ol' boys and whatever. If they can provide the stage and we don't have to plunk down a deposit, we can turn over the proceeds to feed the kids or something."

"Call me back when I'm awake," said Jazz.

~

At midnight, a mob of strikers, brandishing banners and placards under flaming torches, blocked the entrances to the plant, chanting, "No one in, no one out!"

The executives and chief engineers remained inside to place each operation into maintenance mode, until the hostilities were settled. Stanton Spratlin stood alone in the darkened window of his office, watching his employees marching against everything they had built together. Their chants and cheers could well be the death knoll for the company.

Spike heels clacked a strident cadence in the hallway and the inner door to his office opened quietly as his secretary, Katherine Kennedy, entered the inner sanctum.

"I told you to leave with the rest of the employees," said Stanton.

"I'm staying," replied the willowy brunette, walking around the desk to rest her hands on his shoulders. "I'm so sorry this is happening."

He turned and wrapped his arms around her, "We've survived through three generations of challenges and we'll survive this. The pension trust will be refunded as our output increases. They must understand that."

"I'm surprised that Jules Schreiber let things go this far. I thought he was a cool head."

"I did too," sighed Stanton. "I trust that he's the voice of reason being overruled by an angry mob. The sad part is that I don't blame them for their anger, I just have to figure out how to convince them that we have to find a solution or we'll all go down together."

She hugged him, "It won't come to that, everyone has too much to lose."

"It shouldn't have come to this," said Stanton, pointing out the window to a giant bonfire just outside the main gate. "This could get out of hand real quick."

"Should I call the police?"

"Yes, I believe you should. Ring up the chief and let me talk with him. I don't want them making things worse." He admired her sensuous rhythm, as she strode into her office to make the call.

The intercom clicked, "I have Chief Billings on line one."

"Thank you," said Stanton, picking up the receiver. "Joe, how are you this evening?"

"I'm fine, Mr. Spratlin. How can I help you?"

"Well, the men have gone on strike and they've barricaded the entrances to the plant. They've built a big bonfire in the street and I was hoping that you and your men might make sure that this doesn't turn into a riot. I don't want anyone getting hurt nor can we tolerate destruction of property."

"I've had two cars outside your plant since eleven o'clock to keep an eye on things but I'll call in two more, just to make our presence known, if that would help?"

"I'd really appreciate that and tell your men that we don't need anymore trouble than we've already got."

"I'll make sure, sir," replied the chief, an old country gentleman, who knew everyone's business and made sure things remained calm and secure in Cameron.

"Give my best to Sally."

"I'll do that and I'll let you know what I know."

"Thank you. I'll remain inside the plant, so you can reach me at my office number."

"Can do."

He hung up the phone, as Katherine appeared with two steaming cups of tea. He accepted the offered cup gratefully. "Thank you."

"You're welcome. Have you eaten?"

"Not since lunch," said Stanton, staring out the window.

"Dorothy made up enough box lunches to keep the skeleton crew going for days. Shall I go fetch one or two?"

"I'm alright for the moment."

"You won't be, if you don't eat. I'll be right back," said his secretary, marching out of the office.

Stanton crossed his arms and stared out the window, "It's going to be a long night."

~

Mitch Mitchell and Roy Stiles managed to temper the zeal of the strikers, until two company tankers approached the gates at dawn and the protesters surrounded the rigs, shouting, "No one in, no one out!"

The union leaders pushed through the mob, screaming, "Stop! Those are our men!" but, consumed in the crush, their pleas were drowned out by a chant of, "Scabs! Scabs!" Several strikers clamored onto the hoods and started bashing the windshields with ax handles until the glass crinkled. They tore the windows from the frames, hauled the drivers out onto the pavement, and started pummeling them.

Two police cars pushed through the crowd with sirens wailing and lights flashing. Four officers emerged to retrieve the battered drivers and escort them from the scene. A wave of workers started rocking the trucks, until one rolled over on its side, spilling a small flood of diesel across the pavement. The protesters edged away when someone tossed a flaming Zippo into the puddle and orange flames rippled across the asphalt to the upended rig. The initial blast consumed the tanker and the fuel tank erupted with a thunderous orange ball that rose straight up in the air, illuminating the entire plant.

"This is totally nuts!" yelled Mitchell.

"No Shit!" replied Stiles, "We've gotta get these lunatics under control!"

"It's going to take more than the two of us. Go call the office and get Dobie and Schreiber down here!"

Roy ran across the street to a pay phone at the gas station to make the call. Mitch marshaled a small squad to push the protesters back and grabbed a bullhorn, "I want everyone to back up slowly! Come on, back up and spread out!"

His helpers pushed the crowd away. "This is not what our strike is about! You know it and I know it! I want all nightshift strikers to go home and I want this half of the day shift over here on the right to come back at noon."

A sullen "Boo!" echoed through the throng and a few of the rowdiest started pushing and shoving.

"I said that will be enough!"

A voice yelled, "You're supposed to be negotiating to get our money back!"

"I can't be negotiating if you morons are beating up our own guys and destroying the equipment. We're here to protest, not start a riot!"

"If they won't listen, we'll burn the place down," hollered another.

"And who wins? Not you or me or them or anyone else in this town. We all depend on each other! Where are you going to find another job, especially a job that pays you even half of what you're making now?"

Dobie Johnson's dark blue Ford pulled up behind him and Jules Schreiber climbed out of the passenger seat shaking his head. He scanned the anger and frustration in the faces surrounding the burning truck, walked over and took the megaphone, "Gentlemen, may I have your attention?"

The crowd quieted.

"You are here to demonstrate our determination to be treated fairly. Your actions reflect directly on whatever leverage we have in our negotiations with Stanton Enterprises and I have to say that incidents like this make our job that much harder. We gain nothing, nothing from brutal acts of vandalism and destruction of property. Do I make myself clear?"

A reluctant 'yes' rolled through the crowd. "I want you to do as your leaders have instructed. Those of you assigned to the gates may remain, the rest of you Go Home Now!"

A resigned murmur rumbled through the horde and small groups started peeling away in all directions, until the last bunch of strikers broke up into crews to man the gates as two fire trucks pulled up to douse the fire.

Mitch turned to Jules, "Thanks! The voice of reason was dearly needed."

"I am in complete sympathy with their anger and frustration but you absolutely must control your men. We don't want the governor and the National Guard showing up to score political points. This is your fight, so do it right."

"I agree with everything you've said," replied Roy, scanning the smoldering truck. "This could have been worse."

"There can't be an encore," said Schreiber. "There's too much to lose and nothing to gain."

"Those words sound familiar," grinned Mitch.

"I'll defend your right to strike but I will not participate in or support wanton violence. I was enjoying a quiet retirement and I would gladly return to playing with my grandchildren without a second thought, if you gentlemen do not keep your workers under control."

"We'll make sure things stay on the up-and-up," said Dobie.

"Score one for the naïve not being prepared."

Chapter Four

Katherine picked up the phone at her desk, "This Katherine Kennedy, Mr. Spratlin's secretary. How may I help you?"

"Miss Kennedy, this is Nellis Gray. I'm a neighbor of Mr. Spratlin's."

"Oh, yes, you're the man who saved Samantha and Sissy, aren't you?"

"Well, yes Ma'am, I am and Mr. Spratlin was kind enough to send some of your men over to help rebuild my barn. He also gave me his card and said that if I ever needed anything to give him a call."

"As you know, we're in the middle of a strike at the plant. Perhaps, there's something that I could help you with?"

"Well, it's more like I want to help you. See, I'm a musician and I've organized a benefit concert for Saturday night with a whole bunch of local celebrities helpin' out. The thing is, it's going to benefit the kids of the workers, who aren't workin', and the Union's agreed to call off the protest for a few hours, so their folk can let off some good-natured steam. We were kinda hopin' that the executive staff would honor our invitation to join in the fun and, maybe, use the festive atmosphere to have some private conversations without lawyers or rabble-rousers or whatever. Just guys, who've known each other since they were kids, enjoying a cold brew and some good tunes."

"That is an interesting proposition, Mr. Gray. Could you hold the line for a moment?"

"Certainly."

The line went dead for several minutes before Miss Kennedy returned. "Mr. Gray?"

"Yes, I'm still here."

"I've talked with Mr. Spratlin and the office staff will gladly accept your invitation."

"Great, we'll be crankin' up the music about eight o'clock at the Armory and I look forward to meeting you."

"You too. And thanks," replied Katherine, as she replaced the handset.

Spratlin appeared in the doorway, "Do you really think this is a good idea?"

"I don't honestly know but I do know that something has to give to get everyone talking again and, maybe, this is the opportunity we've been looking for."

"I want to argue the legal points but I know you're right."

~

The band took the stage to cheers from the crowd, eager for a night away from the picket lines and the stress of unemployment. Nellis walked up to the mike, "How y'all doin'?"

Claps and whistles.

"I'm Nellis Gray and we've got a super lineup for you tonight." He grinned, "Some of you old timers might remember me, and my good friend, Jazz Taggart, and his Band of Merry Men from back in the day. We've also got Sunny Lynn singing a few country ballads, Jeff Haley doin' some Big Bopper, and Mr. Joe Jackson singin' the blues the way the blues is supposed to be sung, if you know what I mean?"

Cheers and applause.

"There's only one rule for this event."

"Yeah, what's that?"

"Have a good time, get crazy if you need to, but I want everyone to look around at everyone else. We've got union workers, we've got engineers, and we've got management, who all need a night off from the craziness down at the plant. There will be no arguing or confrontations or any other nonsense or we'll shut this thing down in a flash. We're here to have a good time and raise some money for the kids. Am I understood?"

The crowd gazed around, suddenly aware that almost every employee of Stanton was in attendance, as well as their families and people from the rest of the community. There was a reluctant murmur of, "Yeah."

"I look out at all these faces and I see kids I grew up with, friends, neighbors, and a few of you I hoped I'd never see again."

Laughter.

"The point is, we're a community and we've gotta stick together. So buy your friends a brew, you can hassle with each other tomorrow but we're gonna have a good time tonight!"

A huge cheer went up as the band launched into Nellis' 'Too Much of a Good Thing'.

After an hour set, the dance floor was packed and everyone was sweltering but smiling. Jazz walked up to a mike, "We're going to take a short break and then we'll bring out Sunny Lynn."

The crowd applauded.

As the musicians were filing down the stairs from the stage, a pale, pudgy man in a blue pinstriped seersucker suit appeared and climbed up to stand at a microphone, "Ladies and gentlemen, it is my privilege to have a moment to talk to you, my constituents. In case any of you don't know me, I'm Curtis Hall, your Representative to Congress."

Mild applause and a few catcalls.

"I just wanted to say that I find the treatment of the Stanton union employees abominable and I want you to know that I stand with your right to strike and our obligation to stand up to management's shady financial dealings with your pension fund! The press is all over your story and our voices are being heard across the country!"

A few people cheered. Stanton, Miss Kennedy, Malcolm, Jamison, and the rest of the executive staff stood to leave.

"I need your support, so make sure you vote for me in the election next month, so I can open an investigation into the investment practices of Stanton Enterprises and propose a bill to the House of Representatives to end company management of employee pension funds!"

Nellis appeared at the other microphone, looked up at the soundman and ripped a finger across his throat, "Now, just a darned minute, Mr. Representative. I'm pretty sure we didn't book a comedian for this show and I'm fairly certain that you were not included on the guest list. In case you're too ignorant to notice, this is a community benefit for needy children and I'm absolutely certain this celebration doesn't need your input or your opinions." He turned to the crowd, "This is a family matter and, if you don't mind, I'd like to ask a few of you boys in the crowd to show this moron out."

The Congressman stammered, "Do you know who I am?" but the audience cheered and clapped as two rather large fellows climbed onto the stage to escort Mr. Hall out the back door.

"Do I know who he is? Hell no! But I'm damned sure I won't be voting for that fool, come November. Now, where were we?"

"Partyin'!" yelled a petite blond, sloshing her glass of beer in salute.

"Right on!" replied Jazz, strapping on his Stratocaster.

"Listen, that reminds me," said Nellis, scanning the faces peering up from the floor, "Dobie, Roy, and Mitch, why don't you buy your bosses a beer?"

Mitch Mitchell saluted and the trio carried a couple of pitchers and a stack of glasses over to a corner table.

Stanton stood, as the men approached and offered his hand, "It's good to see you guys under these circumstances."

"I'll agree with that," said Dobie, taking a seat next to Katherine. "Hell, if you bring Miss Kennedy along, I'll probably agree to just about anything!"

Spratlin raised his glass in a toast, "Here's to finding an agreement."

"Amen," said Roy.

"I've said it before and I guess I need to say it again. Without all of you, there is no Stanton Enterprises. We might as well lock the gates and walk away."

Dobie was slightly drunk and raised his glass, "And without you and the suits, we wouldn't have jobs. Hell, the whole community could just dry up and blow away."

"So let's find the solution to the problem that's fair to the men and, at the same time, doesn't put us all out of business."

∼

At four o'clock on Monday afternoon, the black Cadillac appeared in the lane and the girls climbed over the gate before Nellis could close up the barn and cross the yard to unlatch the chain. Sissy and Sammy hugged him, as Mr. Charles ambled up the drive to shake his hand. "Looks like you might have saved the Spratlins again."

"What are you talking about?"

"Somethin' happened during your little concert the other night, somethin' good, and Mr. Spratlin asked me to deliver this note to you in person," replied Mr. Charles, handing him a buff envelope with an embossed 'Stanton Enterprises' and his name written in beautiful script.

The girls smiled up at him, as he carefully unsealed the message.

"Well, let's just see what your Daddy has to say." He read the note aloud.

> *Dear Mr. Gray,*
>
> *I believe that I am, once again, in your debt, as the Union and Stanton Enterprises seem very close to an agreement. Your benefit concert to bring the two sides together was most ingenious and we, all of us, enjoyed your banter with Representative Hall. You should consider running for office. I, for one, would make a generous contribution to your candidacy and, for a change, I believe the Union leaders would agree.*
> *Again, my thanks and sincerest best wishes,*
> *Stanton S. Spratlin*

Nellis lifted his hat to brush his gray hair back, "I'll be darned. I just got some friends together to play for a good cause for some good people."

"You're a special man," said Mr. Charles, "and I'm thankful for all that you've done for this family. We're all in your debt."

The old man cracked up, "I already got a new barn, so I don't think I need anything else!"

Samantha said, "You helped a lot of people find a way out of a big argument. Let them be thankful."

"Yeah, you deserve it," added Sissy.

He looked down at the little blond, "Does this mean I get to start with an extra King the next time we play checkers?"

"No, it means I won't beat you as bad as I did the last time."

~

Nellis settled on the porch with the dogs and Chester, as the sun nestled into the trees to the west casting long shadows that framed licks of brilliant yellow stealing through the vegetable patch to light up the new barn. He took a sip of hot tea and sniffed the first buds of Jamaican Blue. "Ah, what a wonderful bouquet."

He crushed the sticky flowers into a small tray and rolled a perfect cylindrical joint. "Let's see what you're made of, sweet lightning." The flame from his Zippo flashed and the tip glowed orange as he inhaled…then exhaled a giant cloud very slowly and grinned, "Now that's what I'm talking about!"

The phone jangled and he stubbed out the roach after his third hit, trotting into the kitchen to pick up the receiver, "Nellis Gray."

"Yeah, that's who I'm callin'," laughed Jazz. "How you doin', man?"

"I'm recovering. The life of a rock-n-roll star is for younger folk. They can maintain a permanent buzz, so they don't feel the pain!"

"Hell, you're rock solid, man. I loved that groove you laid on that Representative dude. What an asshole."

"Yeah, someone had to show him the door," laughed Nellis.

"Hell, I'm headin' out of town tomorrow, got gigs in Chicago and Detroit, but I wanted to tell you that I got a thank you note, hand delivered, from Mr. Spratlin himself and it's signed by the whole crew. I don't think I've ever received a formal thank-you note for playin' before."

"Yeah, I got one too and he even suggested that I run for Congress against Curtis Hall."

"Hell, man, you oughta do it. You'd beat his ass."

"Yeah, right, me running for public office? Like I need those headaches? I don't think so."

"At least think about it. Hell, if nothing else, you could get a giggle out of it."

"Fine, as long as this stays a joke," replied Nellis sullenly. "Hey, I do want to thank you and the guys for helpin' out. We raised almost five grand and it's all going to feed poor kids."

"That's cool man, save the children from freaks like us!"

"You've got one hot band, man, you should be recording."

"Yeah, I'm lookin' for a new contract and I don't even care if they put us up as a come-back group. I just can't stop playin', I'm addicted."

"I know what you mean but part of that addiction is the lifestyle and we both know it."

Jazz laughed, "Well, there's always a willing chick and free dope and another party, so I guess it ain't all bad."

"You be safe and smart and holler the next time you're comin' to Cameron."

"Can do, Mr. Representative!"

The line went dead and Nellis wandered back out to his chair. The tea was lukewarm but sweet and the effects of the Jamaican Blue were coming on. He gazed out into the yard, ablaze with the last shards of sunlight skimming the shadows, and smirked. *Really good visuals, nice mellow cerebral high, and the pain in my back is completely gone. I'm thinkin' our harvest is definitely going to make some people happy.*

He stroked Brandy's ear, lit a smoke, and leaned back into the cushions. *I wonder whether they drug test Congressmen? I'm sorry, Representative Gray, you smoked a doobie in the last thirty days, so you can't serve your constituents.*

~

It was well past midnight, when an old panel truck pulled up to the gate and doused its lights. Nellis quieted the dogs, shooed Chester out of the drive, and unlatched the chain. The van pulled into the barn and Ned Perkins, a beanpole of a man with long straggly rusty blond hair and a full beard, crawled out of the cab to wrap Nellis in a bear hug, "Shit, it's good to see your ugly face."

"Guess I could say the same," laughed Nellis.

"Listen, I don't mean to be rude or anything but I need to be on the road before the bears wake up. I've got miles to go."

"No problem. I've got two hundred pounds boxed and ready."

Ned pulled a briefcase out from behind the seat and flipped it open. "Fifty grand, all faced and bundled in thousands."

Nellis thumbed through a bundle, scanning for sequential serial numbers and fakes, then another, at random, for a quick count. "We've been doin' this since we were punk kids, so I know you're on the money. When do I get the balance?"

"Two weeks. One batch is going to Nashville and another to Atlanta. I'll make the round trip and be back on your doorstep on schedule, geared up to boogie again."

"Good, I'll have the next batch ready to go."

"Cool, let's load this ol' girl and I'll be on my way."

"Can do!" replied Nellis, stashing the case in a stall and wheeling out a dozen sealed brown boxes.

Nellis put a kettle on the stove and stumbled out to the gate to collect the newspaper. The chickens flocked around his legs demanding breakfast before he got bogged down, with his nose buried in the Cameron Gazette for the next thirty minutes. He sauntered through the barn to grab a pail of grain to scatter like flecks of gold across the path to the glee of the chattering hens, and filled the bin for Chester, four tins for the cats, and five dishes for the dogs. The horses were down in the south pasture and he'd gather them up after breakfast.

He found the paper on the gravel path inside the gate but noticed a brown manila envelope taped to the crossbar addressed to Nellis Gray in a familiar and beautiful script. Calloused fingers pried back the silver wings of the clasp on the back to retrieve a stack of paper bound with an oversized clip. The cover page was typed:

> Dear Mr. Gray,
>
> Enclosed, please find a dossier on Congressman Curtis Hall that you might find illuminating.
>
> I believe I speak for a great many of us when I say that I've been a dedicated Republican, since I could vote, and I have worked enthusiastically to support our candidates through these many decades.
>
> Unfortunately, the traditions and values, that made our Party worthy of election, have been hijacked by a mob of racist radicals, who ply the ignorant and the illiterate of our society with propaganda that is both terrifyingly hateful and blatantly false.
>
> We are not in a position to expose the truth but it is our hope that once you understand what we are up against, you will reconsider your position on running for our Congressional seat.
>
> Sincerely,

The letter was unsigned but he sensed a hint of Chanel No. 5. He wandered back to the porch fumbling the newspaper, envelope, and loose pages. The kettle whistled a shrill note and he charged up the steps, dropped the papers in the chair, and hustled into the kitchen to kill the flame and pour the remaining water through a filter full of freshly ground beans into a carafe. The aroma was rich and earthy and he sipped carefully as he wandered back to the porch, tapped out a fresh Winston, and straightened the papers in the file.

The second page featured an eight-by-ten black and white image of a slightly younger Congressman, dressed in the white robes of the Ku Klux Klan, standing in front of a flaming cross planted in the yard of a burning shanty with his eyes ablaze and his mouth twisted in a primal scream, as he hoisted a Confederate battle flag aloft in triumph.

Nellis shook his head, *"I don't know that I need to read much more of this, I already know the guy's an asshole."* But he scanned more than a dozen pages, listing associations with radical wingnut organizations across the South, each peddling campaigns blaming Blacks, Hispanics, Asians, Catholics, Jews, and Liberals for all sorts of fictional offenses, which morphed into long-winded essays proving that the government is coming to take your guns away, or your land, or your children, or your life. The propaganda was specifically targeted to taxes, or government excess, or abortions, or gun rights, but every appeal misquoted scripture to prove that God would absolutely justify their perverse form of patriotic bigotry.

The final pages listed campaign donations, including sizable contributions from conservative political committees around the country and the usual right-wing hate groups, but there were also individuals representing several national corporations that might benefit by his vote, a right-to-life congregation in Mississippi, and the National Rifle Association. Of note, a fairly staggering personal donation from Cameron's own Reverend Billy Joe Hardman, who counted on the congressman to protect his right to spew a twisted Gospel over the airwaves and solicit contributions from tens of thousands of true-believers around the world. There was big money in that game and it seemed likely that it would not take much to prove that Congressman Hall was sharing in the bounty.

He wandered into the back room and returned with a small drawing board and some basic art tools. Twenty minutes later, he finished a simple graphic layout with text above and below the portrait of Curtis Hall:

Meet Your Congressman
CURTIS HALL

You elected him.
You can fire him!
VOTE!

A smirk crossed his lips, *"I always knew those summers I spent in Uncle Charlie's sweltering print shop, would pay off someday. Look at me now, designing political posters that'll probably change the course of the election."* He laughed to himself, *"Or get me killed, one."*

The phone jangled and he limped into the kitchen to grab it, "Hello?"

"Mr. Gray?" inquired a female voice.

"Yes, who's this?"

"Katherine Kennedy, Mr. Stanton's secretary."

"Oh, yes, how are you?"

"I'm fine. I just wanted to make sure that you received the package that I left for you."

"That was you, huh? Yeah, I got it."

"Interesting material."

"I didn't make it past the second page, with that photo, before I got the message. In fact, I've designed a little poster that I'd like to hand out but I really don't want to be personally associated with having a commercial printer reproduce it, if you know what I mean."

"I most certainly do," replied the secretary. "If it's not too big, I could print copies for you on our Xerox machine. It will print up to eleven-by-seventeen."

"That's plenty big enough," replied Nellis. "Think you could print up a couple of hundred on some sturdy stock?"

"Sure, that's no problem at all. I'll make sure I have the paper."

"Great. I'll drop by this afternoon, if that's okay?"

"Sure, I can print it while you wait," replied Ms. Kennedy. "I'll be in my office all afternoon and I'll leave word at the front gate to have you brought directly to me."

"Thank you. I'll see you in a couple of hours."

~

Nellis was escorted from the gate by a genial guard, who enjoyed the music at the Armory and was happy to be back at work. After climbing an enormous staircase from the lobby, he stood before Ms. Kennedy's desk in a paneled anteroom at the entrance to Mr. Spratlin's office. The tall, lanky, and stunningly beautiful brunette stood to greet him. Piercing dark eyes and the subtle hint of Chanel No. 5 reminded him that she was also the articulate, educated, and in-charge woman he spoke with on the phone. She reached long graceful fingers to shake his hand, as the guard left the room. "Thank you for coming in."

"This is some complex you've got here. I'm impressed," said Nellis, holding out a brown envelope, "The layout's ready to print, it should fit your paper perfectly."

She withdrew the design and smiled, "You're a man of many talents, this is as professional as any I've seen put together by the ad agency for the Company. I'd rather hire you!"

"Thanks, but I know just enough to keep myself and my designs out of trouble and not much more."

"Well, this should have a dramatic impact, if it gets distributed in the right places."

Nellis grinned, "I'm sure you'll hear about it when it happens."

Katherine led him to a large storage closet with two massive copiers nestled between stacks of boxes of office supplies. She wiped the glass of smudges and dust and laid the little poster on the glass bed. A moment later the machine spit out a perfect copy. She held it up, "How's this?"

Nellis held the page up to the light and squinted, then he turned it upside down and cocked his head slightly to the right. "It's not quite straight. Let me move it just a smidge and we'll punch up the contrast a tad to clean up the whites."

Another print appeared and they admired it together, "That's better."

"I can't believe that tiny nudge made so much difference in how it feels," added Katherine. "That's fairly amazing. Two hundred?"

"Yes, Ma'am."

"I guess I should explain that Mr. Spratlin is out of town and asked me to deliver our clandestine package to you in the dead of night and, I must say, that is a long dark lane leading into your property."

"If I'd known you were coming, I would have met you out at the road."

"I'm just teasing," laughed the secretary as the sheets started stacking up in the bin. "I couldn't see much but I'll bet your place is beautiful."

"You should come by during daylight and I'll show you around. It's a last bastion, for wild critters and cantankerous old men, on fertile land that's slowly being gobbled up by suburbia."

She smiled, "I'll take you up on that."

"Your boss suggested that I run for Congress, twice, and I'm afraid he might be disappointed to find out that I've been a dirty dog Democrat, since I was born, and always will be. I've always been a one-for-all and all-for-one kind of guy."

Katherine's laugh was deep and genuine, "I honestly don't think party affiliation has anything to do with his opinion of you, it's simply a matter of respect for your character."

Nellis blushed, "I'm a simple man who does what seems right at the time, even if other folks don't see things my way. Sometimes that works out fine and others, maybe, not so much."

"We are, none of us, perfect but I've always thought that we ought to judge each other on the contents of our hearts and yours is, obviously, in the right place."

"Why thank you."

She handed him a box full of posters, "I mean that very sincerely, Mr. Gray, and I believe Mr. Spratlin does too."

~

Sissy sprinted up the hill and bounded the kitchen steps for a hug from Mama Louise and an after-school snack. Samantha turned off the drive to knock on the sea green door to the pool house. Floor to ceiling drapes and storm shutters blocked a magnificent view of a once gorgeous garden surrounding a perfectly maintained pool that had not seen a swimmer or a noisy party in years.

She could feel loud music thumping through the door and slipped into total chaos. Steppenwolf was howling 'Born to be Wild' at sonic decibels through a dim blue haze, the floor was littered with empty Budweiser bottles and greasy pizza boxes, and the air-conditioning was cranked down to frigid. Her hulking brother was curled in a fetal ball, in the middle of a bare filthy mattress on the floor, with sweat pouring off his muscular body, as if he was running a marathon through the tropical jungles of Vietnam. Wild eyes darted around the room, searching for danger lurking in the shadows, as he dropped a loaded Colt 45 on the mattress when she moved into view.

"Brad, are you alright?"

"No, they're coming, I know they're coming," shouted the veteran above the music.

Sam walked over to press 'Stop' on the cassette deck. "Who's coming?"

"The Cong, they're not done with me. They want revenge."

"You're at home and the war's long over. No one's going to hurt you and you never have to go back," replied Samantha quietly. "I'm here to make sure."

"Will you hold me?" whispered Brad.

"Sure," said the girl snuggling on the mattress to wrap her arm around his broad shoulders and rest her head on a roaring dragon tattoo crawling up his bicep. She kissed the ragged scar on his cheek and mopped his forehead with a grungy pillowcase. "You're home and you're safe with me."

"You don't know what I saw, what I did," screamed Brad. "You'd hate the person they made me into, I'm the monster that every mother warns their children about!"

"You were a soldier in an awful war but you survived and you're here now, not there. It's all going to be okay, promise. That's not real anymore but this is."

He squeezed her ass, "You know how to make me feel better. You're my angel."

"I'm here to help your head and your heart," replied Sam, struggling to free herself from his grasp.

He forced her hands into his crotch and pulled up her shirt, "You don't even have titties yet but I'm going to show you how to make it better."

"You're drunk and that's not going to solve your problem," shouted the girl, "now, let go! I'm your sister and I'm too young!"

"Just help me out," said Brad, unzipping his shorts to wrap her slender fingers around his erection. "Get me off or I might not be able to stop myself from taking my beautiful little sister's virginity right now!"

Sam darted for the door with tears streaming down her cheeks, her hair a tangled mess, and her plaid shirt torn from a khaki skirt twisted around her waist. Brad staggered after her, pulling up his shorts and shielding his eyes against the blazing light outside the door, "Come back here girl, I was just foolin'!"

She turned to look back and ran smack into Reverend Billy Joe Hardman on the path, whose portly body tumbled over onto the lawn with her on top. Sam struggled to untangle herself from his flailing hands, which were fumbling for a rumpled check that wanted to flutter away in the breeze behind her back.

"Let me go!"

"My dear, are you alright?" replied the minister, who, lying flat on his back, or as flat a fat man could lie, finally focused on the girl's tear-stained face, as she wriggled off his belly and ran off into the barn.

A moment later, a huge hand reached down to lift him up but the two men struggled in a strange two-step for several moments before Billy Joe was upright and steady enough to notice that young Brad's shorts were buttoned but not zipped and barely contained an enormous erection.

He laid his hands, still clutching the check, on the young man's broad shoulders and stared into his eyes. "I can see how you're suffering under the weight of your fight with the devil and I think I can help you, son, if you'll let me? The Good Lord has given me powers to mend the wounded and heal a tormented soul."

Brad shook his head, straining to focus on the fat man's pious expression and sympathetic stare that slowly dropped to the bulge straining to escape his shorts, "I don't know Reverend, I've lived the other side. I know the devil on a first name basis."

Fixated on Brad's erection, he mumbled, "Let me help you as I've helped your mother."

"Helped my mother?" Brad reached down to clutch the crotch of Reverend Hardman's linen slacks and squeezed his balls and a tiny erection, until Billy Joe's eyes watered and his jaw dropped open, then the vet grabbed the check, stuffed it into his mouth, and chewed it up. "We all know what my mother needs to save her soul and you're taking money for that? You're a fucking hypocrite, you know that, brother? We both know the answer, so I'm tellin' you to stay away from this house or I'll cut your tiny weenie off with a machete!"

He released his grip and the Reverend gasped for breath. "And, if you ever say anything about this to another living soul, I'll swear to everyone that you got down on your knees to beg me to let you suck my big dick, right there in the pool house. Now get the fuck out of my sight."

"But my…check?"

Brad spit out a soggy wad and shoved it in the Reverend's gaping grimace. "Now git!"

The overweight minister staggered up the drive to climb into his black Lincoln and roar off around the house.

The inebriated veteran stumbled across the pavers into the barn, hollering, "Sammy, I'm so sorry honey, please forgive me. I promise I'll never touch you again, angel. I'm so sorry, you've gotta forgive me or I'll shoot myself!"

Bruce appeared from behind the Cadillac, "Haven't you done enough harm already? You're lucky she got away or I would have killed you myself! What the fuck is wrong with you, man? I know we're both nuts but even you wouldn't hurt your own sister."

Brad fell to his knees, bawling, "I promise, I'll start taking my meds again and I'll go to my therapy. I can't live like this anymore, man, I'm living nightmares, even when I'm awake. Everyone would be better off if I just ended it."

Bruce wrapped his arms around his older brother, "This family is really screwed up but, at least, we have each other when things don't make any sense."

"Nothing makes any sense, man, nothing."

Sissy ate the last bite of her strawberry ice cream cone, sitting alone on the kitchen steps, watching waves of drama unwind, and weeping for the pain her family took such pleasure in sharing with each other.

~

Cars jammed the gravel road and crowds wandered in and out of the fairgrounds, off the highway on the west side of the river, an aging complex of racetrack and rodeo ring surrounded by a dozen weathered red and white barns in various shapes and sizes. A ballpark anchored a patchwork of dusty playing fields that also served as parking during events and catch basins for torrential spring rains.

The buildings spent most of the year empty and unattended until the beginning of baseball season, when dirt track racing and the rodeos started coming through town. Maintenance crews and volunteers did their best to spruce things up a bit, as each event approached and, gradually, the entire grounds were as good as they were going to be for the opening of the State Fair the last week of September. In spite of the effort and yearly expense, the Town Council would not justify investing in improvements, so, fifty years of history and memories would slowly crumble to neglect.

He pulled up to the security gate and rolled the window down. Joe Billings, the Police Chief, leaned in, "Are you playin' tonight?"

"Naw, I'm just dropping off some fliers at the main stage. I hear they're lettin' the political riff-raff have a turn tonight."

"I'd much rather listen to you play. You go on through but keep it slow, this place is full of fools, who ain't payin' attention to nothin' but their corndogs and cold beer, if you know what I mean."

"I promise not to run over any children," laughed Nellis. "Drunk adults are fair game."

"I'll find you a good lawyer," laughed the Chief, as the truck pulled around behind the midway to the back of the main stage.

Four teenagers clustered around the driver's window and the tallest boy said, "Hey, Nellis what's up."

"As I told Henry on the phone, I've got a little job for you boys, if you're willin', and I'll pay ya' ten bucks each for fifteen minutes work."

Marty jammed his hands in his pockets, "Sounds dodgy, what do want us to do?"

"Just hand out some posters and invite people to come by the main stage to hear their Congressman's speech, simple as that. You hand 'em out and take off when you're done."

Henry turned to his pals, "C'mon you guys, it's ten bucks for nothing."

Marty nodded, "I can't make that much in a day working for my daddy in the fields, so I'm in."

Mike stepped closer, "What's on these posters?"

Nellis grinned and held one up for inspection, "What do you think?"

"I think I wouldn't vote for that asshole," said Jamie.

"Well, a whole bunch of folks did and he got elected. I'm thinkin' maybe it's time to un-elect him."

"Hell," said Marty, "I'd just about do this for free but I sure could use ten bucks to buy more film for our movie."

"You guys are making a movie?"

"Yeah," grinned Henry. "It's a send-up of high school life called, "Is This All There Is?"."

"Great title. I want to see it when it's done." Nellis hopped out and handed fifty sheet bundles to each of the boys, "Now listen, I want you to wait until you see Congressman Hall approach the stage, before you hand these out. Don't let anyone see them until I give you the signal, okay?"

"You want us to make the posters follow him in?" asked Jamie, his dark eyes wide under a soft afro and a creamy chocolate complexion.

"That's exactly what I want," replied Nellis. "Each of you set up in one of the four lanes that spit out at the stage and, once we start, don't be afraid to let the folks know what you're sellin'!"

The boys accepted a ten spot and touched hands with mischievous grins, before heading out through the crowd. Nellis perched on the tailgate, waiting for the portly Congressman to appear. He was scheduled to speak in twenty minutes and, within moments, the pinstriped seersucker suit waddled out of the crowd, headed for the entrance behind the stage. Nellis scanned the crowd for the boys and held up a thumb.

Henry started hawking, "Make time to hear your Congressman! It's time to know who you elected! He's giving a speech in five minutes on the main stage, don't miss it!" He held out the posters to several passing people, who accepted them from the nice young man, only to react with revulsion and outrage when they looked at the placard.

"Is that really Curtis Hall?" asked a matronly woman.

"That's your Congressman," replied Henry politely.

"We'll just see about that," snapped the woman, as she marched her husband into the tent to find chairs in the front row.

Within minutes, hundreds of anxious people rushed into the seating area waving the posters above their heads, chanting, "Curtis Hall! Curtis Hall!"

Without waiting for an introduction, the Congressman strolled triumphantly onto the stage with a big smile and a wave for the cheering crowd and took a bow, before he looked up to recognize the photograph on the posters that were fluttering and flailing above angry faces screaming obscenities and worse.

Nellis grinned, as he started the old truck and idled along the service path to the front gate. The truck slowed to a stop, "I don't know for sure but you might want to send security down to the main stage. There was some sort of ruckus goin' on and it didn't look pretty."

The police chief stared for a long moment, then smiled discreetly, "I know you didn't have anything to do with it but I'll send someone directly and thanks for the tip."

Nellis tipped his hat as he pulled away, "Just trying to make sure everyone has a good time but entertainment comes in many forms. You take care now."

~

The sun was just peeking through the trees by the time Nellis finally settled into the old chair on the porch to sip his coffee and inhale that first drag of the day. He opened the paper to find the headline:

Sheriff Quells Riot at Fairgrounds

above the photograph with the caption:

Congressman Exposed!

Before he could begin reading, the phone rang in the kitchen and he hobbled through to answer it, the ache forecasting another front coming. "Hello?"

"Mr. Gray?" inquired a warm female voice.

"Miss Kennedy?"

"Have you read the paper this morning?"

"Actually, I was just getting to it. Had to feed the critters before they'd let me sit down with a cup of coffee."

"I'd really like to see your place sometime."

"You say when."

"Okay, I will, but, in the meantime, the main story mentions the crowd waving black and white posters with a scandalous photograph of the Congressman. Evidently, the Chief of Police arrived just as the mob was about to drag the poor man off the stage to lynch him."

"Lucky Joe got there when he did."

"Yes, I'd have to agree," replied Spratlin's secretary. She paused, "I'd have to add creative and devious to my description of that man with the big heart."

Nellis laughed, "Coincidentally, I told the Chief just the other day that entertainment comes in many forms."

"I wouldn't be surprised to see a resignation shortly, once the Congressman gets past denying that the photograph was actually of him."

"'Instant karma's gonna get ya', as John Lennon sang."

"Well, I hope that yours is spectacular," laughed Katherine. "Mr. Spratlin is due back this afternoon and I'm sure that he'll be impressed with your response to his letter."

"I hope he's pleasantly amused."

"We'll be in touch," said Miss Kennedy.

"Thanks for callin'," replied Nellis as he placed the phone in the cradle. He wandered back to the porch, grabbed his lukewarm coffee and half-smoked butt, and settled in with the paper again. Before he could put on his reading glasses, Chester snorted and the dogs started yelping as a mud-brown AMC Pacer slid to a stop on the gravel outside the gate in a cloud of dust. Curtis Hall extracted his portly self from the tiny car, holding up the torn remnants of a poster, screaming, "I saw you, you son of a bitch! I know you're behind these damned posters! You're the one! I saw you there!"

The dogs pranced around the porch, until Nellis released them to charge into the drive. He leaned against the door jam, puffing on his Winston and shaking his head. The Congressman fumbled a target pistol with a long barrel out of his pants and discharged a round towards the howling dogs.

Nellis grabbed the twelve-gauge and marched out to the gate, "Just what the fuck do you think you're doin', you moron? Get the fuck off my property before I shoot your ass!"

"You done it, I know it was you!"

"What makes you think I had anything to do with whatever you're yellin' about?"

"Because I saw you sittin' on the tailgate of your truck outside the main tent, yesterday, and you had that little smirk on your face, just like at the Armory when you had me evicted by those two goons! Then you just disappeared, like a ghost, so, it had to be you!"

"I was there to round up my nephew and his buddies, simple as that."

"You're gonna pay, just you wait and see," said Hall, waving the gun above his head.

"Congressman, I suggest that you put the gun away before someone gets hurt or I will have to shoot you because I feel that I am in imminent danger. Put the gun in the car and do it now!" said Nellis, leveling the shotgun.

Congressman Hall started blubbering, staring at the gravel, and let his hand drop to his side for a long moment. He looked up, bloodshot eyes darting around in panic, and pointed the gun at his own forehead.

"What are you doing?" yelled Nellis, reaching to unlatch the gate and racing to grab the pistol.

"What's the point? You ruined everything." A tiny hole appeared in his forehead before the concussion of the shot exploded near Nellis' ear and the portly Congressman toppled over backwards.

He grabbed the gun and tossed it into the grass, then leaned over fixed staring eyes and a steady trickle of blood flowing down his cheek. There was no pulse.

Nellis called Chester and the dogs away and marched back into the house. He dialed the Police Chief's direct line.

"Chief Billings, how can I help you?"

"Joe, it's Nellis Gray."

"Hey, Nellis, how ya' doin'?"

"Not so good, actually. Listen that fool Congressman showed up at my gate this morning, waving a gun around, blaming me for destroying his life."

"So, what happened?"

"That damned fool shot himself in the head with his own gun!"

"You didn't help him out with this, did ya'?"

"Honest, I was racing to try and stop him. I still can't hear outta my right ear, from when he pulled the trigger. Half a second more and I might have saved him from himself."

"Alright, I'll head out there, after I call the coroner."

"Thanks, Chief, I sure appreciate ya'."

Nellis was perched atop the closed gate, smoking a cigarette and contemplating the ignorant arrogant fool lying on the gravel, when two squad cars sandwiched the coroner's wagon in a steady procession down the lane followed by a long cloud of dust. He was thankful there were no lights or sirens nor anyone from the press and hopped down, as the Chief got out of the car.

Billings was big man and the holster and accessories, hanging from the broad belt cinched around his girth, creaked as he lumbered over to inspect the body. He took off his broad rimmed hat and wiped his brow before he stood up, "We'll let Doc Kelly do his thing but I'm bettin' that's a twenty-two round dead between the eyes."

"I've been through some weird stuff in my day, Chief, but a guy commitin' suicide because he's pissed off at me is a first. More often than not, they wanted to roast my ass and probably with good reason!"

"If that hole was just a smidge larger, I don't think I'd believe you but I know you wouldn't defend yourself with a twenty-two. You're a twelve-gauge kinda guy and our dearly departed Congressman would be missing his face."

"I guess I should say thanks."

"I'd rather you tell me how the hell this happened."

"I was sittin' up on the porch with the dogs, drinkin' some coffee and reading the front page of the paper, when this jackass climbs out of that little bitty car and starts yelling about how he knows that I'm the one who sabotaged his career. Then he takes that fancy target gun out of his pants and fires off a shot at the dogs. I went out with the shotgun and told him to put the gun away but he kept ranting and waving the gun around and, all of sudden he looks up and his eyes are really weird, and he points the gun at his head. I unlatched the gate and ran to stop him but I couldn't get there in time and the gun went off in my ear. I tossed the gun into the grass over there. That's all there is to it, honest."

"We both know you distributed those posters at the fair last night and put an end to his career," said the Chief. "So, whether you pulled the trigger or not, his blood is on your hands."

"But...?"

"I can't charge you with anything and I won't share this with the press or anyone else, but you know and I know, just so there's no misunderstanding."

"I appreciate your discretion, Joe, and I won't forget your kindness."

"You go back inside, while the Doc gets his work done, and come by the station later this afternoon to give an official statement."

"I'll be there," said Nellis, shaking the Chief's hand and walking back to the house.

Chapter Five

Nellis nursed his second beer, lounging on the porch in a decided funk, when a classic blue Pontiac Grand Prix pulled up at the gate. The horn sounded twice and he lumbered down the steps and across the path to find Miss Kennedy, in a checkered flannel shirt over faded jeans and well-worn boots, leaning through the gate to pet the dogs, who jostled for position but did not bark. "I heard about what happened."

"Yeah, about two steps back from where you're standing and I couldn't stop it."

"Can I come in?"

"Oh, yeah, sorry, don't mean to be inhospitable, although I'd prefer everyone else to think I'm some cranky old miser or something and leave me the hell alone." He unlatched the chain and swung the gate open to allow her car through, then closed it again.

She pulled up next to the barn and climbed out. "Nice barn."

"I'm fairly certain I've got you to thank for some of that," replied Nellis. "C'mon up to the porch and let me get you something to drink."

"Okay," said Katherine, following him up a winding path of crosscut slabs of a large tree trunk. "What kind of wood is this? It's beautiful."

"Black walnut," said Nellis, pausing to point. "Used to be a line of 'em along the house down to the creek, part of a grove that was established years before our folks showed up and started growing pecans. Most of 'em just reached maturity and died off. This ol' place has seen its share of history, in fact what became the Cammy Trail crossed the lane through that little dip just this side of the main road. Indian tribes would trek through here to meet at the Council Tree down by the river and the first settlers followed their path in covered wagons to the fresh water spring."

"That's fascinating."

He marched up the steps, held the door for Miss Kennedy, and whisked up a stack of papers from the second chair, "Here have a seat. I'm having a beer, want one?"

"It's a bit early, do you have any coffee?"

"Of course, coming right up."

He nipped inside to the kitchen and she sat back in an old but truly comfortable lounge chair to survey a magnificent view of the yard from a wooded rise on the west, across an expansive vegetable garden that was still overflowing with produce in spite of the damage, to the new barn and a grove of pecans stretching off to the east along the south side of the lane. Bare tangled branches in the tops of several trees were stark reminder of the storm that passed through the yard only weeks ago. A loud 'Caw!' brought her out of the chair as a large red-tail hawk dove to chase a rabbit darting through the veggie patch.

Nellis reappeared with a silver tray bearing a sterling pot of coffee, with cream and sugar, two China cups with saucers, silver teaspoons, and linen napkins. "You need to come by more often."

"Why do you say that?"

"Because you give me an excuse to use these beautiful service pieces that have been sitting in the cupboard since my wife died."

"Treasures this beautiful were made to be used," replied Katherine, taking a steaming cup.

"Cream or sugar?" said Nellis, offering a gleaming bowl.

He sat in the rocker, placed the beer bottle on the floor, and sipped his coffee.

"As I said earlier, I'm sorry all this happened. I feel responsible for putting you in that position."

"Ain't your fault. I designed the poster before we ever talked, so you might have planted the seed but I nurtured it and gave it life," said Nellis. "Trouble is, it grew too big too fast, kinda' like what I was saying the other day about doin' what I think's right and how, sometimes it works out for the best and others maybe not so much."

"This has to be a 'not so much'."

"I've been sittin' here pondering the thought that we set out to expose a lyin', cheatin', racist pig but it turned out that he was really just a sniveling little weasel underneath all that bloated bravado. We set a bear trap and caught a rodent, who was so terrified that everyone would find out who he really was, he shot himself in the face rather than fess up. I've been around for a long, long time, traveled all over tarnation, and I've seen my share of weird stuff, but this one's an original."

"I wish I could say that it's not your fault…or our fault, but we made it happen together at the suggestion of my boss, who spoke on behalf of several dozen prominent citizens, who felt the same way. We, all of us, must bear this together."

"I'm thinkin' my political days are over," said Nellis.

"I wouldn't blame you, one bit," replied Miss Kennedy, "although, I think the system needs people like you, who aren't afraid to step up for what's right and true."

"Are you lookin' for a job as campaign manager or what? I'm definitely not runnin' for anything," said Nellis. "Are we clear on that?"

"Yes, Sir. I'm terribly sorry, if I offended you," said Katherine, setting her cup and saucer on the tray and standing to leave. "In spite of the incident earlier today, I still think that you are an exceptional man and I would be proud, if you would allow me to refer to you as my friend."

Nellis stood, "I'm sorry, I didn't mean to drive you away. Please finish your coffee."

"No, thank you. I'm afraid I've overstayed my welcome."

"Then I hope you'll come again, when we can take the horses out to show you around the property."

"I'll take you up on that when things die down a little," said Katherine at the screen door. "Oh, incidentally, rumor has it that there will be a funeral on Thursday, at the Lily Chapel, and Reverend Billy Joe Hardman will be presiding."

"For obvious reasons, I will not be attending."

~

Storm clouds were building in the west, by the time Nellis returned from giving his statement down at the station in the late afternoon. A nap offered hope for temporary relief from an aching back, terminal headache, and a gut full of guilt but he needed to check on Chuck Stern's cattle and the fencing down at the south end, where those damned kids on motorcycles broke in again, after he fixed the break along the lane.

He parked the truck and ambled into the barn to saddle up his favorite mare, Babe, a big chestnut with a mischievous gleam in her eye and a giddy-up gait. He was contemplating running her stallmate, Bessie, down and back just for the exercise, when Chester and the dogs escorted Sissy through the doorway, her fawny eyes glistening with tears. "What are you doin' here, little one?"

"I heard about what happened," said the girl, reaching to hug him around the waist. "I'm really sorry."

"Aw, don't be sorry for me, I'm okay," replied Nellis, squatting. "We should feel sorry for sad people like Mr. Hall."

"How did he die?"

"You really want to know?"

"Yeah, I do," whispered Sissy. "Grownups don't trust kids with the truth."

"I have no way of knowing for sure but it wouldn't surprise me if the coroner's report doesn't come back showing that Congressman Hall was drunk or high on pills or something. Anyway, let's just say he shot himself and it wasn't an accident."

A big tear rolled down her cheek, "My brother threatened to kill himself this morning."

"Are you talking about your oldest brother, Brad, is it?"

"Yeah, it was like a really weird movie."

"I want to hear what you have to say but I have a question first, do you ride?"

"I've been riding since before I could walk," replied the little blond, dropping her eyes. "Our barn was full of horses, until last spring."

"Fine, then, I've got to go down to the south forty to check on some cattle and make sure that bunch of teenagers on motorcycles haven't cut down my fence again. Do you want to ride Bessie down there with me? She sure could use the exercise."

"Sure, let's saddle her up," said Sissy walking into her stall to stroke her soft muzzle. "I'm sure we're going to have a nice ride."

Nellis cinched up the saddle and they rode around the house and along a ridge through a sparse grove of trees.

"So, tell me about your movie."

"Well, it started with Sammy running out of the pool house with her clothes all messed up, screaming like someone was tryin' to kill her, followed by my brother, Brad, who was stumbling drunk, only Sam wasn't looking and crashed into Reverend Hardman, who had been up at the house prayin' with my mother. He fell over on his back like a giant tub of Jello in a fancy striped suit and Samantha was kind of pinned on top of him for a minute, before she slid off and ran into the barn. Then Brad caught up and picked the minister up but they got into some kind of argument and ol' Billy Joe jumped in his Lincoln and sped away, before Brad started wailing about how sorry he was and how Sammy had to forgive him or he'd just kill himself right there in the driveway. My other brother, Bruce, got him calmed down, but this stuff just keeps happening and I don't understand why everything is so weird?"

Nellis stifled a grin, "Actually, if someone filmed that for a movie, no one would believe it."

"That makes it even worse," sniffled the girl, kicking ol' Bessie into a trot.

They pulled up on top of a little rise that opened to a broad pasture with dozens of cows lying in the shade of clusters of trees along the western fence line. Nellis took off his hat to brush back his hair, "See how the cows are all hanging out in the shade under the trees?"

"Yeah."

"They know there's weather comin' and they're already in position to find some shelter, if it gets bad."

"Nothin' stupid about them," sniffled Sissy.

"I know you don't understand why all these things are happening in your life and, if you consider how my day started, you've got to realize that weird stuff just happens and there really isn't anything we can do to control other people or keep them from hurting themselves or each other."

She started crying again, "But...?"

"These are the people you love the most in the whole world but they're just people, fragile souls who have problems and make mistakes," said Nellis gently. He reached to wipe a crocodile tear from her cheek, "But, consider this, they don't have to be perfect to be wonderful. I've always wondered how we can love each other so much, in spite of our failings and weaknesses."

"I do love them all," said Sissy, "but I sure don't understand what's going on with any of them, even Sam."

"How old is she?"

"Twelve."

"So, she's about to be transformed from a young girl into a teenager and that's a really hard transition for boys and girls. The rest of your family is struggling through a really hard time and, from what I can see, just about every one of them is fighting their own battles just to survive. I'm guessin' they're countin' on you to be the joyous sprite who brightens up everyone else's day."

"Yeah, you're right. They all smile when they're around me but it doesn't last."

"Well, maybe it's enough to keep everyone going," replied Nellis. "Listen, I want to ride along the south fence to check for breaks, if that's okay with you?"

"Sure, lead on."

The horses trotted down the hill and across the field to an animal track that meandered east, shielded by a line of trees that almost hid the desolation to the Simpson place. A couple of hundred yards from the end of the pasture, they found a break. Nellis jumped down to inspect the wire, "Cut clean through, again."

"Why would anyone come all the way around here to break through the fence, when they could get in up by the road?" asked Sissy. "Either they're stupid or it doesn't make sense?"

"Pretty much like everything else today, eh?" said Gray, climbing back on Babe, "Let's see where these tire tracks lead."

They followed the trail across the meadow and through the trees to a little spring-fed brook, that emptied into the creek along the north end of the property, where they found the remnants of a bonfire, several soggy sleeping bags, and dozens of beer cans scattered around the banks.

"Looks like someone had a party down here," said Sissy.

"Yeah, least they could do is clean up after themselves. This is a mess."

"If we had some bags or something, we could pick 'em up."

Nellis scanned billowing thunderheads building in the western sky, "I already saved you from a storm once and I'm thinkin' I don't want to do it again. Let's head back and I'll run the truck down here later to mend the fence and gather up this trash."

"I'll help, if you want," said Sissy, "but, meantime, betcha I'm gonna beat you back to the barn."

"Small chance!" yelled Nellis, poking his heels into Babe's ribs.

~

Professing to represent the company at the Congressman's funeral, Katherine greeted business associates and prominent citizens in the lobby before slipping into a pew at the back of the quaint white clapboard chapel. Whether guilt, for precipitating the events that led to the poor man's suicide, or some sad and savage curiosity, in spite of Stanton's protestations, any chance of redemption demanded her attendance.

She was a woman who craved order in her office and in her life. Even the affair with her married boss, Stanton, was tidy and scheduled and methodical. The events of the past few weeks – the tornado, the workers' strike and violent riot, the slightly inebriated easing of hostilities that occurred at the concert, and the campaign to unseat the Congressman that ended in tragedy – pitched her sense of security topsy-turvy and shattered the idyllic and completely bogus bubble of her sheltered reality. Life, outside the confines of her cozy illusions, was anything but orderly and she was having a hard time believing that her own was any better.

And then there was Nellis Gray, who crafted his countrified persona to deflect attention from the wicked intelligence of a sage old owl, who's weathered savage storms to cultivate a wisdom grounded in his own set of rules and principles, with absolutely no regard for what anyone else might think. His music was playful and irreverent and he moved the emotions of the crowd with grace and ease. Yet, as soon as the spotlight was dimmed, he retreated behind a steel gate on that beautiful property and only appeared, like a phantom, at the precise moment when common sense was needed to evaporate everyone else's drivel. She had caught a fleeting glimpse of the character behind the guise and it sputtered and sparked like the fuse of a firecracker about to explode into a rainbow of iridescent colors. Mysteries always tickled her curiosity, especially when she found them ruggedly handsome.

The music from the organ swelled and the congregation rose, as the family strolled down the center aisle with stoic dignity. While several of the Congressman's constituents wailed, not a tear was shed by his wife, three children, or the troop of other relatives. The Reverend Billy Joe Hardman raised his hands and intoned, in a high-pitched tenor that rattled the rafters, "You may be seated."

As Katherine took her seat, she noticed that everyone in the church was white, with the exception of a heavyset black woman sitting in the last row, shepherding four young children, with complexions of creamed coffee, dressed in their Sunday finest. She sobbed quietly, dabbing tears with a white handkerchief under the black veil of a broad-rimmed hat.

The Reverend stepped to the podium and waited patiently for the congregation to settle. "We are gathered here to celebrate the life and mourn the tragic loss of our esteemed Congressman, husband, father, uncle, cousin, and good ol' boy, Curtis Hall."

He paused for the congregation to respond with a rousing, 'Amen'.

"Let no one deny that he served the Lord in a mercurial life that touched everyone he encountered from the homestead to the Capitol

Building in Washington, D.C." He paused, "Not bad for a country boy, who never finished high school."

The audience laughed. The black woman scanned her children and muttered under her breath, "Yeah, that man certainly touched me."

"Nor can it be said that he ever abandoned his core beliefs, the foundation of this beautiful church, this idyllic community, and our great country, in spite of the lies the liberal elite are preaching through the media to brainwash our citizens into accepting restrictions on our rights as God-fearing Americans!"

Several people rose to cheer, with fists raised in the air, screaming, "Hallelujah!"

"Curtis Hall stood up for our rights and our freedoms! He never wavered from defending the sacred scriptures that have been handed down since Jesus Christ walked the Earth!" He held a well-worn Bible above his head, "This is the word of the Lord and it is by his word that we shall break the shackles and chains being cast upon us by pointy-headed intellectual sinners!"

The audience laughed.

"Our friend, our Congressman, had Jesus by his side when he fought the good fight, when he rose up as a righteous voice against our headlong descent from sanity and order into fire and brimstone and sure damnation! God created giants to defend the little people and Curtis Hall embraced his duty to stand against integration, and free love, and mixed marriages, and homosexuals, and the conspiracy to force restrictions on the right of every American to own and carry firearms! The good citizens of this great nation need leaders like Curtis Hall to defend us from our own government!"

Half the congregation jumped to their feet, shouting their approval.

"Let us sing!" screamed Billy Joe Hardman.

The chorus rose and the little chapel reverberated in song:

Amazing Grace, how sweet the sound,
That saved a wretch like me.
I once was lost but now am found,

Was blind, but now I see.

T'was Grace that taught my heart to fear.
And Grace, my fears relieved.
How precious did that Grace appear
The hour I first believed.

Through many dangers, toils and snares
I have already come;
'Tis Grace that brought me safe thus far
and Grace will lead me home.

The Lord has promised good to me.
His word my hope secures.
He will my shield and portion be,
As long as life endures.

Yea, when this flesh and heart shall fail,
And mortal life shall cease,
I shall possess within the veil,
A life of joy and peace.

When we've been there ten-thousand years
Bright shining as the sun.
We've no less days to sing God's praise
Than when we've first begun.

Chorus:
Amazing Grace, how sweet the sound,
That saved a wretch like me.
I once was lost but now am found,
Was blind, but now I see.

(John Newton 1773)

Billy Joe shouted, "I once was lost but now am found, was blind, but now I see! Curtis Hall was a shepherd guarding our flock against another Yankee invasion, this one under the cloak of immoral and unconstitutional laws to suppress our freedoms, destroy our American way of life, and silence evangelical devotion. Our former Congressman believed in the teachings of the Good Book."

The crowd murmured 'Amen'.

"He believed in protecting our country from immigration, from atheism, from commie pacifists and faggots and Jews and Catholics and niggers. He was a lifelong believer in maintaining the purity of the white race and our God-given place as overseers of the inferior subhuman tribes, just as the Good Book demands. If it wasn't for our lineage, a heritage that we can trace all the way back to Adam and Eve, mankind would still be living in caves and chasing wild animals with slings and spears. God anointed the white race first, last, and always!"

'Amen'.

Katherine stood and stepped into the aisle to depart quietly but the Reverend shouted, "Must you leave so soon?"

Startled, she looked up at the fat man in the black robes, standing in a shaft of golden sunlight shining down on the alter, with his fists planted on his broad hips indignantly. "I do apologize for disrupting your service but I'm afraid I must leave before I become ill."

"It is rather stuffy in here, get the poor woman a glass of water," yelled the minister. "But, please, you don't want to miss the eulogy by the Congressman's anointed successor, our own Mr. Miles Brantley! If Curtis was a stanch defender our values, Miles Brantley will rekindle the Civil War to set things right!"

The crowd rose to their feet, yelling, "Right on!"

Katherine turned to leave and the black woman and her children rose and crowded into the aisle.

"I insist that you stay, Miss Kennedy is it? Yes, this is the biggest small town in the district and we've all known each other since we were little tikes. I must compliment you for showing more gumption than your boss, ol' man Spratlin! I assume that he sent you in his place, because we all know that he'd never show his aristocratic face in a humble little church like this. I doubt he'd show up in anything less than a cathedral with a full-blown Bishop tending the service!"

Katherine stood up very straight and said, "Actually, I'm quite sure he would never stoop to your level. I chose to attend this service out of respect for a tragedy that everyone in this community must share but, the more I listen to your sad racist rantings, the more convinced I've become that you do not represent any respectable religion, because you twist and mutilate the word of our Lord to drag these poor ignorant people to certain suffering and eternal damnation. At best, you're a miserable excuse for a human being, who perverts the ministry for vast personal profits. May God forgive your blasphemy."

Ignoring his protests and jeers from an angry congregation, she turned to guide the black woman and her children out through the back of the church.

As they marched into bright sunshine the woman looked up at her, "What's wrong with you, girl, are you trying to get us all lynched?"

"I'm sorry, you didn't have to get involved in this, but I couldn't listen to that pompous moron's hateful nonsense for another minute."

"Well, if you're as smart as I hope you are, you'll hightail it outta here before a mob comes charging through those doors."

"Do you have a car?" inquired Katherine.

"No, we walked from the other side of the river. Even though these are the bastard children of that abusive bigot, he was their father and they should show up for his funeral to pay their respects."

"I'm so terribly sorry," said Katherine. "I'm driving the company station wagon, why don't you let me give you a lift, just to be safe?"

The woman looked at her with disbelief in her eyes, "White people don't give niggers rides in their cars."

"This white woman does. Now let's get out of here before someone in there decides to track us down."

"They surely know where I live and I'm pretty sure they could find your address in the phone book. They ain't the kind of folk to confront either of us in broad daylight. They're more likely to show up wearing white sheets and carrying torches in the middle of the night. At the very least, they'll be wantin' to burn us out, if not kill us as an example for any other uppity niggers or pretty white nigger-lovers foolish enough to believe the law will protect them."

"Is it naïve to believe that's the law of the land?"

"That might be the law on your side of the river, honey, but it sure ain't on ours."

Katherine held out her gloved hand, "I'm Katherine Kennedy."

"I'm Maybelle Brown and this is Daniel, Hubie, Muriel, and Martin."

She shook each little hand in turn, "I'm pleased to meet you."

Maybelle Brown and her children crowded into the back seat and the cargo space, insisting that it would be improper for her to sit in the passenger seat in the front. None of the children said a word, as Katherine drove across the bridge, turned off the highway on an unmarked gravel road that meandered through a forest of post oaks and cedar to a shanty in a clearing next to a babbling brook. There were no telephone poles to carry power and an outhouse and old hand pump outside the front door hinted that the house lacked running water.

The Browns climbed out of the wagon and Maybelle leaned in the passenger window, "I appreciate the lift and I pray to the Lord that you haven't opened up a can of worms that we'll all regret before that white trash is finished getting' even."

Katherine reached into her purse and withdrew her business card, scribbling her private number on the back. She handed it to Maybelle, "I realize that you probably don't have a phone, but here's my information. If they start any trouble or if you ever need my help, just call me…and I mean every word I've said."

"Honey, I appreciate your good intentions but this is the real world out here. Nobody cares if some nigger gets beat up or killed by a bunch of drunk racists. They're just good ol' boys out for a little fun. Hell, that's how I got all these kids. The first time, Mr. Hall and his pals came rolling through here in the middle of the night, after burning down the Jones place up on the hill and killing two children in the process. I came out on the porch to see what all the fuss was about and he staggered up here, called me all sorts of awful things, beat me bloody, and tore off all my clothes. His buddies all started yellin' about what a nice body I had, so he bent me over that banister right there and raped me in front of his drunk friends. He liked the fact that I was a virgin."

Katherine grabbed her hand, "My God, how can people act like that in this day and age. That's disgusting!"

"No, what's disgusting is that he liked it so much, he came back again and again. I couldn't stop him and I was too ashamed and afraid to tell anyone, so I let it happen. When I got pregnant with Daniel, he started giving me cash for food and took me to the clinic when I went into labor. Instead of cutting off his sad little porker, I took the money, so I'm just a stupid whore who got pregnant four times."

Tears ran down Katherine's cheeks, "I think you're a proud woman who survived unimaginable brutality the only way you could. Now you're raising four beautiful children who need you more than ever."

Maybelle turned to watch the children trooping into the tiny house, "I hated everything about their father but I couldn't love any of them more than I do."

"Tell me, do you have any training or have you ever worked?"

"I've never had a real job but I'm a hell of a cook, when I have food to work with."

"I'll keep that in mind." She squeezed the black woman's hand, "I'll see you soon."

Maybelle laughed, "If either of us lives that long."

Katherine drove back across the river and went directly to the supermarket, where she loaded up two carts with enough food to last the Browns for at least a week. It was late afternoon by the time the station wagon returned to the shack. She honked the horn twice and Maybelle and the children appeared at the door.

Katherine got out and opened the tailgate, "I've brought you some supplies that ought to keep you going for a week or so."

"You didn't have to do that. We've got food."

"Well, now you've got more."

The children gathered around to peek into the bags. Daniel smiled, "Look Hubie, here's a box of Oreos and a whole bag of cupcakes!"

"This bag's got three bottles of orange juice," said Muriel.

"Yeah, well, this one's full of milk bottles and there's even chocolate," said little Martin.

Maybelle started to cry, "I don't know how to thank you."

"Don't thank me, take care of your children. Do they go to school?"

"I don't have any way to get them to the public school and back, it's too far for them to walk and they sure ain't gonna send no bus down into this hollow. Sometimes, I can get someone to take them but it ain't often enough."

"We'll see about that," replied Katherine, climbing back into the car. "Cook up a fabulous meal for your kids and I'll be in touch."

Maybelle grinned, "If I can keep 'em outta the sweets until dinner time!"

~

It was well past four in the afternoon by the time she drove into the parking lot at the plant and climbed the stairs to the executive suite. Stanton came out of his office at the sound of her high heels clacking across the tiled floor. His eyes softened with concern at the sight of her mascara stained cheeks and he took her in his arms, "What's happened?"

Katherine started crying again, "I went to the Congressman's funeral."

"That was a mistake."

She pulled away, "I thought so too, until I couldn't stand listening to one more bigoted word from that Reverend Hardman. I stood up in front of the whole congregation and told him what I thought of his version of Christianity, before I walked out of the service. Then, I met Hall's black mistress and four children who live out in a shanty, in the woods on the other side of the river, with no electricity or running water. It's probably good that he killed himself because, after what I've learned he did to her, I'd track him down and cut his nuts off with a very dull knife without any regrets!"

Spratlin gasped, "That doesn't sound like my favorite lady in the whole world."

"I think something's changed in me, since all this started with the strike and the riots and the concert and Hall's suicide. I used to feel rather smug at being so safe and comfortable in our little bubble but there's an ugly world out there and I'm feeling rather guilty for ignoring the obvious truth."

"What truth is that?"

"That what we think of as normal is just gloss covering up a wicked and brutal subculture that's always existed all around us but we refuse to see it for what it really is…"

"It's not that bad…"

"The hell it isn't! Do you realize that we still have Klansmen riding around in pickup trucks in the middle of the night burning down houses and raping black women? Curtis Hall got elected to Congress and his biggest contributor was Reverend Hardman and I can guarantee that some of the rest of those good ol' boys in those trucks were community leaders who were at the service. We all look the other way and pretend it's ancient history. Well, it's still happening and I, for one, am not going to stand for it anymore."

Stanton pursed his lips, "Do you honestly think you can stop racism and bigotry and cruelty and ignorance by sheer willpower?"

"Well, I'm going to start by helping one woman and her four children," said Katherine, wiping her eyes with a lace handkerchief.

"And how do you plan to do that?"

"She claims to be a great cook, do you think Mama Louise could use a hand?"

"I can't take on the financial responsibility for five more people at the moment. Hell, I'm selling everything that isn't nailed down just to prop up the pension fund."

"That's not what I asked! You can take it out of my salary."

He backed away, "The woman, I've known and loved through all these years, left here a few hours ago and came back as a fanatical activist. You honestly don't know what you're getting yourself into but I'll warn you that the dark underbelly of our society isn't going to change just because you want it to. You're trying to take on a brutal culture of fear and bigotry and hate and they wouldn't hesitate to take out anyone who stands against them, including a beautiful white society dame like you. Sure, we know the devil's out there hiding in the shadows and we contribute our efforts to those who stand against them."

She walked over to lean against her desk, "While I was sitting in that church listening to Hardman twist the scriptures to glorify that bastard's ignorance and cruelty, I realized that the Klan got smart. They went out and bought expensive suits and hired public relations firms to write clever speeches, filled with bits and bites that sound perfectly reasonable but they're really just catch phrases for the same old lies and bigotry they've been spouting, since they hid behind white sheets and burning crosses. Nothing's changed, they just dressed it up in different clothes!"

"Societies and civilizations have always been built on the premise that it's us against another group. We're better or more just or more righteous and our leaders and their leaders have always used that lie to bind disparate groups into homogenous cultures to fend off their enemies. Our government uses it all the time, hell, we've been fighting the communists since the end of the Second World War and, if and when they're defeated, we'll have to find someone else to blame for our faults and failings. Having a common enemy is the glue that holds societies together. Unfortunately, no one's figured out how to rally support by reminding people that it's a beautiful day outside or the economy's running smoothly or we've conquered diseases. Cohesive societies need someone that everyone can hate together."

"I'm sorry but that's just wrong. It might have been acceptable when we were tribes defending our hunting grounds but we're supposed to be civilized and intelligent enough to invent a better way. We fight wars to protect the rights of the innocents. We fought the Civil War to free the slaves, we fought Hitler to save everyone who wasn't Germanic from slaughter, but we tolerate the same brutality in our own backyards? That doesn't make sense to me."

"Darling, I adore you with all my heart," said Stanton, "but you're about to take on trouble that we can't afford, at the moment, and

I'm afraid the consequences might be far more dire than you can imagine. It wouldn't surprise me to find that half the men working in our plant support the radical right and we certainly don't need to get them riled up again."

Tears welled in her eyes, "Does everything in our life have to revolve around business and money?"

"That's why we're here, isn't it?"

"Maybe that's not enough anymore," replied Katherine, picking up her bag and marching out the door. The determined cadence of her steps faded down the hallway and then the stairs.

The dogs trotted out to the gate without barking as the panel truck eased to a stop and Ned Perkins leaned out the window, "Hey pups! How ya' doin'? Where's that ol' coot who feeds ya'?"

Nellis unhitched the chain and rolled the steel grate back, closing it after the van pulled through into the barn. Ned uncurled his lanky frame from the driver's seat, "You're a sight for sore eyes, brother."

"You're just a sight, man. You look like you've been on the road too long."

"Well, that's true, drove her all the way through from Atlanta and only popped a couple of white crosses."

"And twenty cups of java, right?"

"Yeah, I'm a tad acidic."

"Well, grab your stuff and I'll cook you some dinner. I kept a couple of T-bones out, knowin' you were coming."

Ned grinned, "I'm bettin' you could probably find me a shot of good whiskey and a doobie or two to relieve my road aches.

"I'm bettin' I could," replied Nellis, reaching behind the seat to grab the duffle and a small suitcase. "I take it this is the important stuff."

"Yeah, my clean underwear is in the case, so be careful with that one."

"You asshole! C'mon into the house."

Ned followed Nellis through the ramshackle porch into a small parlor with deep yellow walls, furnished with antiques and fine paintings, that opened into a kitchen with Chinese red walls, gray cabinets, and white countertops, a gray dining room with subdued lighting doubled as a library, into a small bedroom with soft green walls and a large spool bed.

Nellis dropped the suitcase on the bed, "This was my daddy's bed and it's the second most comfortable in the house."

"Sounds good enough for me."

"Help yourself, the bathroom's next door and I even left clean towels for ya', if you want to get cleaned up. Meantime, I'll bring you a drink and make us some grub."

"Deal," said Ned peeling off his jacket. "I need to scrape the road grime off."

Twenty minutes later, Nellis lit candles in the dining room and served up two platters with beautiful steaks, fried potatoes, and a green garden salad with his magic dressing. "Have a seat."

"You didn't have to get all fancy for me, brother."

"Hell, the closets are stuffed with beautiful objects that never get used, why not share them with the folks I love the most?"

"I've always been sweet on you too," laughed Ned, savoring a bite of medium rare steak. "I'd forgotten that you are one hell of a cook, man. I think I'll hang out for a week or two of your cookin' and maybe I could put on some weight."

"You could put on some pounds, if you'd quit driving twenty-four-seven and eating speed."

"Fuck, I don't have any choice, you got the product and my folks got the bucks and I'm in the middle."

"Yeah, I'm just giving you shit. Everything go okay?"

"Of course, easy in, easy out. I've got the balance and half the next batch in the duffle."

"Cool. We've got enough for one more round, if you can handle it?"

"Yeah, works for me. I can turn it around in two weeks again."

"Done."

"So, what's happening in sleepy ol' Cameron?"

Nellis cracked up, "There ain't nothin' sleepy about this little burg. In the past month, we've had a tornado take out the barn, then a strike and riots down at Stanton Oil, the biggest employer in town. Jazz and I gave a concert and got the two sides to kiss and make up but our fanatical Congressman tried to stir up more trouble, so I printed up some posters with a picture of him, from several years ago, dressed in full Klan regalia with a house and a cross burning in the background, and got them handed out at the state fair, just before he gave a speech. Needless to say, that didn't work out so well and he showed up outside the gate the next morning screaming about how I'd ruined his life. Then the motherfucker pulls a target pistol, about two feet long, out of his pants and puts a round in his forehead!"

"No shit?"

"No shit! And honest-Injun, I never touched the guy. I'm hopin' the Chief sees it my way and doesn't file charges because I didn't kill the bastard."

"So, you gonna run for his seat or what?"

"Why the fuck does everyone want to get me elected to public office? I'd just as soon hang out here with Chester and the dogs in peace and quiet for the rest of my days than get all tangled up in bureaucratic hoopla! I don't need it."

Ned savored his last bite of steak, "You don't need it but maybe they need you."

"Will you stop that, I don't want to hear anymore about it. Are we clear?"

"Yesssssir!" laughed Ned. "So, where's my joint?"

Nellis reached a finger behind his ear under a thick wave of salt and pepper hair and produced a perfectly cylindrical reefer. "I take it you sampled our wares?"

"Yeah, man, it's fine."

"Well, this is like the hash-maker's hash. I've been messing around with hybrids and this is a cross that turned out pretty sweet." He lit the joint and inhaled, passing it to Ned as he sputtered, "Careful, it's burning a little hot."

86

"Yeah, man, nice flavor. I'm getting a little bit of blueberry in there somewhere."

"The high's pretty mellow. I find it makes my backache better and I want to go do something outside."

"I can see that, I'm getting some soft tracers around the lights. I'm thinkin' you're on to something good here. Think you can produce a crop of this?"

"I think I've got enough seeds to do half and half next year. We'll see."

"You could charge a premium for this, man," grinned Ned, slumping back in his chair. "I'm thinkin' one more shot of that Scotch and I'm heading for bed."

"You've been on the road too long, brother. You can sleep as long as you want but don't be surprised if one or more of the dogs comes in to keep you company."

"Just so they don't park their butts between me and the bathroom, we're all square."

~

Ned, warming his hands around a hot cup of coffee, found Nellis picking peas and thinning carrots in the vegetable garden to the west of the new barn, "How do you keep up with all of this by yourself, man?"

"I just start," laughed Nellis. "There ain't no stopping, 'cause there's always something that needs doin' and it's not going to get done unless I do it!"

"I'd say you're nuts to be doin' all this at your age but I look around and it's all so beautiful that I hope you can keep it goin' forever."

"Well, thanks," said Nellis looking around. "Honestly, there's no place I'd rather be than right here diggin' in this dirt."

"I'm just sorry you don't have anyone to share it with 'cause it sure is special."

The big red-tail swooped over the yard, cawing loudly. Nellis grinned, "I share it with him and the rest of the critters that are moving onto the property to escape all the construction."

"I get it, I get it!" laughed Ned. "Listen, I need to get packed up and on the road, if we're going to clear this thing out in two weeks. I just hope I can trust you not to have quite as much excitement in your life while I'm gone this time."

"Believe me, I didn't set out to get in the middle of any of that, it just kind of happened."

"Yeah, well, the ceiling can fall in on you and you don't need to do anything to make it happen."

"There's wisdom in there somewhere but I don't think I'll try to figure it out until I'm much older! Let's get the truck loaded and you outta here."

"I appreciate the hospitality. Think we could do some of your world-famous ribs the next time through?"

"Sure, I'll have 'em smokin' when you get here!"

Chapter Six

Sister Gwen shooed youngsters to their classrooms with a gentle smile and a blessing, as she cleared the hallway of the St. Francis Orphanage, which housed more than a hundred children from all over the state in a safe, clean environment that was terminally under-funded and teetering on financial disaster. She pushed through the heavy front doors and down the steps to collect the mail from the large black box at the curb and cradled a thick stack of bills and legal documents in her arms.

The nun shook her head in frustration, as she flipped through the envelopes, tallying the funds being demanded in each statement, until she came to a plain brown envelope, with no stamps, that bore her name in simple block letters. A faint chill of hope ran up her spine, as she fingered the contents, knowing that three of these showed up each fall for the past two years, a few weeks apart, and the last one contained twenty-thousand dollars in two neat bundles. The gifts literally kept the doors open and she prayed that her secret donor would continue his philanthropy because more homeless children showed up every day.

~

Hank Garrett finished cleaning up the pots and pans, from the breakfast serving at the Soup Kitchen, and dried his hands on a tattered towel hanging from his shoulder. Benny Fisher, his baker, dropped a stack of mail on the counter, "I've got some dough rising in those pans on the stove, so don't let no one go bangin' around in here until I get back, okay?"

"Yeah, man, I'll take care of your dough. Enjoy your break, 'cause I'm guessin' we're going to have a hundred-fifty for dinner this afternoon."

"Hey, it's better than when the plant was out on strike and we had more than three hundred," replied Benny.

"I know, I know, but we both know that we can't make it all work if we're feeding a hundred-fifty hungry mouths two meals a day, every day. Something's gotta give."

"Yeah, but, somehow, we always make it work out and we've never turned anyone away."

"I'm glad you've got faith, man, because sometimes I start doubting whether we'll find the funding to keep it all goin'."

"Keep the faith, brother. I'll be back in an hour."

"See ya'," replied Hank, thumbing through bills and junk, until he came to a plain brown envelope with his name printed in block letters and no address or postage. He tore open the flap to find two bundles of hundred dollar bills and smiled, "Lord, I believe! I don't know who sent this, so I'll thank you for lookin' after all these folks who need our help."

He figured the last package was sent to help out with the influx of workers during the strike and never expected the generosity to continue, but he could feed a lot of mouths with the money and he sure wasn't going to ask any questions.

~

Constance Calhoon only had one rule for the homeless, who showed up every night for a bed and a short respite from living in the elements, be clean and sober or you're sleeping on the street. She showed no patience or sympathy for the drunks she evicted and no qualms about sending the stinky ones directly to the showers. Most didn't argue because they knew the lady with the big heart and the warm hall would welcome everyone, without judging their circumstances or questioning their value.

"It's not about where you came from, it's about where you're going," she'd say to one and all. "This is merely a little detour, before you get on with living the rest of your life. I believe it and I'm going to make damned sure that you believe it too! Once we both know that you're a believer, you get to be on your way, so I can free up space to help someone else."

Sammy Smith, a tragic and permanent resident, suffered brain damage at birth and lived on the streets, fending for himself, since he was abandoned by his mother as a youngster. Constance took him in and found that he was conscientious about little jobs she assigned to him, like hauling dirty laundry downstairs and bringing piles of clean sheets up in the dumbwaiter, or sweeping the front steps every morning and bringing in the mail. Seeing his smile, his pride in being productive and repaying her kindness always warmed her heart.

He finished the steps, put the broom and dustpan back in the closet in the hallway, and headed back out through the foyer to meet Tony, the mailman, at the mailbox under the pink neon cross that flashed 'Welcome' day and night. Sammy marched up to Constance's little office and handed her a pile of mail, "Tony said to say 'Hi' to you."

"Tony's a sweet guy, just like you. Thanks for bringing the mail to me, it saves these old bones a trip."

"Happy to help, Miss Calhoun," grinned Sammy. "I'll be getting the laundry down next."

"I sure appreciate your help, Sammy. You're a very special boy."

"I kinda feel like you're my guardian angel. You always look out for me."

Constance peered over her glasses, "I'm glad we found each other, that's what's important."

"You make me feel like I'm a real person, instead of just a dummy."

"You're no dummy, Sammy, and don't let anyone tell you otherwise. You have a huge heart and you've been through more than your share of hardships in your short life, so you deserve to be appreciated."

"Thanks," said the boy. "Oh, I almost forgot, another toilet started leaking upstairs. I turned the water off and closed that bathroom, but the guests are going to be waiting in line, if we don't get them working soon."

"All it takes is money and we don't have much to spare at the moment. I'll call Teddy and see if I can con him into stopping by to fix it on his way home. I sure can't afford a real plumber or a new john."

"I wish I knew more about it or I'd fix it for you," said Sammy.

"You do enough around here and, besides, that's not your responsibility. I'll figure out how to get it taken care of somehow. You'd best get on with your chores and thanks for bringing the mail to me, I really appreciate your help."

"Aw, it's nothin'," replied Sammy, with a bashful grin. "I'll start moving the laundry."

"Thanks," said Constance, as she thumbed through the mail, piling bills in one growing stack, everything else in a second with the exception of a few personal letters that showed up for the guests. Occasionally, she got to hand something to a resident but, more often than not, they either passed on or had yet to arrive.

She stopped at the brown manila envelope on the bottom with no postage or address, just her name in simple lettering. After a momentary hesitation, she ripped it open to find two stacks of bills, which she knew would total twenty-thousand dollars or four new toilets, a whole lot of repairs to the building, and, maybe even, some new mattresses and bedding.

Tears glistened in her eyes as she thought, *"I don't know who you are or how to thank you but God bless your soul for caring enough about down and out strangers to lend a hand. It means so much to them and to me."*

~

Nellis heaved his aching back into the chaise on the porch with a groan, took a sip of steaming coffee, and lit a perfect joint. "C'mon magic, this old back is needin' some help."

On his third puff, the muscles between his shoulder blades began to relax. He laid the roach in the ashtray, sipped his coffee, and rubbed Brandy's soft ears, "I'm getting too damned old to be doing all this heavy lifting but, best as I can figure, there's no one else stepping up to help out."

The Irish setter turned to rest his head in Nellis' lap, sad eyes staring up at him. "I sure am lucky to have you for a best friend and faithful companion, old fella."

The phone rang in the kitchen, so he peeled himself out of the chair and sauntered in to answer it, "Hello?"

"Mr. Gray?"

"Yes, who's this?"

"I'm sorry, it's Katherine Kennedy. Am I disturbing you?"

Nellis laughed, "Beautiful women always disturb me, lady, especially when they're beautiful and intelligent."

"Now you've made me blush."

"Good! How can I help you?"

"I was wondering whether there might be a convenient time when I could stop by."

"Just so long as you're not bringing me another dossier."

"No, just me."

"When do you want to come by?"

"What are you doing now?"

"I'm taking my afternoon break," replied Nellis. "This old back gets cranky, when I overdo things."

"Why am I not surprised that your body protests?" said Katherine. "You don't strike me as the kind of person who can sit still for very long."

"You're a true judge of character, Miss Kennedy, and dead on the money."

"I'll be by in a little while, if that's convenient?"

"You come on by and I'll make sure Chester and the dogs don't get too riled up."

"I like your pig and your dogs but, then, I like most animals anyway."

"I knew there was something I liked about you."

Twenty minutes later the flashy Grand Prix stopped outside the gate. Nellis led the dogs and Chester across the yard to roll back the fence then, closed it after she pulled through. Brandy and the other dogs pranced around the car, yelping impatiently until she got out and petted each in turn, paying special attention to Chester, who pushed through the pack to rub against her legs.

"They're a friendly bunch, once you get to know them."

"We've got a rule, the dogs can bark their heads off from up on the porch but they don't get to storm the gate unless I cut 'em loose."

"Why does that not surprise me either?"

"Simple, I treat them just like I treat people. I've never doubted that all these critters are just as intelligent as we are. Just because we're too dumb to understand their language doesn't mean they don't understand ours."

"You might be on to something there," said Katherine, as they walked across the yard, "they're certainly more honest."

"On that, we agree," replied Nellis, holding the screen door. "Can I get you something to drink?"

"I'd take that beer you offered the last time."

Nellis looked into her sad tired eyes, "I'm guessin' you don't have to go back to work this afternoon?"

"I'm not sure I'm going back to work at the plant, period. Things have changed."

"Hold that thought and I'll be right back with a couple of cold ones. Have a seat and get comfy."

He reappeared with frosty bottles of Budweiser that he poured into two beautiful steins, "We can pretend the beer isn't domestic."

She held up her mug, "To honesty!"

"Amen!" added Nellis, easing into the rocker. "So, how can I help?"

"First, I'd like to apologize for overstepping my bounds, the last time I was here. You're a very special person and I had no right to try to push you into something that you didn't want to do."

"Ah, don't worry about it. I'm not going to do anything I don't want to do, even if it is at the request of a beautiful lady."

Katherine took a long slug and sat back against the cushion, "I made the mistake of attending Curtis Hall's funeral."

"Big of you to show up."

Miss Kennedy grinned, "I managed to hold my tongue for the better part of fifteen minutes of Reverend Hardman's racist ranting, before I attempted to leave quietly."

"Attempted?"

"Well, he demanded that I stay to listen to the end of his bizarre sermon and a eulogy by the next anointed bigot, who's already running for Hall's seat, but I decided that I should get his black mistress and four children out of there before things got really crazy."

"His black mistress?"

"Yeah, in addition to his pearly white family. I learned later that he and a bunch of white robed Klansmen were riding around drunk, burning down shanties, when they stumbled across Maybelle Brown, an innocent girl who stepped out her front door to find out who was causing the ruckus in the middle of the night. He beat her, stripped her, and raped her in front of his buddies. Then he came back, again and again, for years. She told me, he left money to buy groceries for the kids but she was too scared and ashamed to ask for help and who's going to stand up against the Klan anyway?"

"Bastard was worse than we thought," said Nellis, shaking his head. "It's a sick world out there."

"That's why I came to talk with you," said Katherine.

"Why me, I might be kinda sick too but you have to have your own friends?"

She drained her mug and stared for a long moment, with tears running down her cheeks. "I thought I had life all figured out. I earned my position at the company through hard work but I've been having an affair with my boss for years and I don't see that relationship going anywhere soon. I live very comfortably but, suddenly, everything's out of whack, it's all turned upside down, and I don't know what I believe in anymore. It's like I've been looking into a mirror that reflects a bright fanciful view of life but, now, it's turned into a filthy window and there's an ugly sadistic world outside my little bubble."

"You just stumbled into a different reality," replied Nellis, "but, like it or else, it's always been there."

"I guess I realized that I've always ignored it, because it didn't really have anything to do with me. I was insolated by my good fortune or upbringing or education or status but I can't pretend anymore, that's just not good enough."

"I'm bettin' you missed the Sixties too," laughed Nellis.

"What do you mean?"

"I mean I'm bettin' you weren't out in the streets protesting or staying up all night getting stoned and listening to weird music."

"I was a good student!"

"You missed the most important part!" laughed Nellis. "You were supposed to learn about people, all kinds of people, not just facts and figures that any moron can look up in a book. You were supposed to get pissed off that the U.S. government was sending thousands of boys over to Nam to get their asses shot off, so some corporation could show a big profit. You were supposed to smoke dope and march for integration and women's rights and protecting the environment and stopping the war. You were supposed to absorb the shock wave that rolled through our culture and changed everything. Instead you were a good student, who became a certified Republican and they stole your soul in the process."

Miss Kennedy looked slightly indignant and even more confused, "But…?"

Nellis lit the roach, took a big hit, and held it out to her, "Did you ever learn to smoke dope?"

"I tried it once or twice in college but I didn't like it."

"No, you didn't get it," laughed Nellis. "Here take a little puff and hold it in for a minute."

She took the little joint and inhaled deeply. Her ebony eyes opened wide, as she struggled to hold it in, but, finally, a giant cloud of blue smoke erupted from her lungs in a hacking fit.

"Lesson one, don't get greedy. Take a little puff, you can always take another, if you need to."

"Are you trying to kill me or what?"

"I can honestly testify that no one has ever died from smoking a joint. They might get stupid or lazy or inspired but they don't get dead. Now try it again, only smaller."

She toked again and slowly blew out a thin stream of smoke, "That actually tastes pretty good."

"Yeah, this stuff is sweet and fairly mellow. I'm thinkin' you should just sit back and get comfy and see how you feel in five minutes."

He got up and disappeared into the house only to reappear with an old Martin acoustic guitar and two glasses of iced tea. "Here, I'll play you a little something relaxing."

She closed her eyes and he played a melodic tune that made her think of butterflies and hummingbirds fluttering through a field of flowers, then a little brook trickling over smooth rocks, and finally a great river coursing slowly to the sea.

"That's beautiful," sighed Katherine. "What's it called?"

"River Running," smiled Nellis, taking a sip from his glass. "That's the first time you felt what it's like to be stoned. There's nothing crazy about it, it's just a different awareness, an appreciation of the simple beauty that's all around us everywhere, every day. Oh, and I brought us some tea because I don't want you getting confused inside your head. Being stoned is a whole different experience than being drunk on Budweiser."

She gazed out across the yard, where sunlight shot through the shadows to light up colorful peppers and the last of the tomatoes, like glowing gems on tattered vines in the vegetable garden. She turned to a sharp 'Caw' from the red-tail hawk, who flew in slow lazy circles above the trees searching for dinner, and noticed the chickens over by the barn scurry for cover. "It's like things we take for granted suddenly have new meaning."

"Life has new meaning and it isn't the one they told us about, when we were kids in school. It's way bigger than that."

She looked up, grinning, "Could I use your bathroom?"

"Certainly," said Nellis, leading her into the living room.

She stopped in the doorway, gazing around at the antiques nestled against yellow walls under beautiful artwork. "No one would ever imagine how lovely this is, from seeing the house from the outside."

"Nanny and I were both artistic and neither of us was afraid of color." He opened a closet door that had six squares painted on the inside, each a different and distinct shade of yellow. "We liked all of these, so, after we made a final choice, I never got around to painting out our test panel."

"That's very clever," said Katherine. "Where did you find all this furniture?"

"Some of it was handed down through the families and I managed to bring a few pieces back, when I was on the road. It's always been a work in progress and, after all these years, there's always more that needs to be done."

"Well, it is lovely."

"Thanks," said Nellis leading her through the Chinese-red kitchen and the dining room with the wall of books. "There's a bath just through this bedroom."

He refreshed their glasses of iced tea.

She reappeared after few minutes. Her sad tired eyes were bloodshot but sparkling and a tiny grin hooked the corners of her lips. "This house feels like it just goes on and on, every room is unique, yet they all tie together to make a warm and inviting home."

"It was a great place to raise the kids, when they were little."

"How many do you have?"

"A daughter, Ashley, who's a nurse married to a surgeon in Boston and doesn't come home anymore, and a son, Nathan, who hit the road, when he was seventeen, and never came back."

"I'm sorry," said Katherine, "that's got to be hard on you because you're a caring person."

"I wasn't so caring when they needed me most. I was out there on the road for years, when I should have been here, so I can't blame them for being resentful."

"If they could understand who you've become, I think they'd be very proud of their father."

"Well, thank you, but I doubt that's going to happen."

"What about your wife?"

"She died of cancer, a few years ago, before I finally learned that, if you've got roots, you've gotta be around enough to nurture them through floods and droughts or they die."

"I'm sorry that you've been left alone." She leaned against the sink, sipping her tea, fascinated by the cardinals and the jays tussling at the feeder outside the window. "I think I've changed my opinion of marijuana."

"How's that?"

"I don't know about everyone else, but I feel like I've slowed down enough to pay attention to the simple beauty that's all around. I've spent too much of my life being too busy to notice." She paused, "How often do you feed the birds?"

Nellis smiled, "When the weather's nice and there's plenty of food out in the fields, I only fill up the feeders for my own amusement. When the weather's bad, like ice and snow or a raging drought, I can go through fifty to a hundred pounds of sunflower seeds in a week, easy."

"Do you care for this whole place by yourself?"

"Yeah, most folk'd think I'm nuts, and I probably wouldn't argue, but it's been in the family for three generations and, even though we've been working on it for near a hundred years, it's not even close to being finished. Maybe, if I'm lucky, I'll have things under control before I die but I'm not promising I'll get it all done by then."

"You're amazing, you know that?"

"No, I'm persistent, there's a difference. Amazing makes me think of sparkling childhood wonders and there ain't nothing sparkly about most of the jobs I do around here. They're just plain dirty."

Katherine cracked up, "Well, I don't know much about farming but, if you ever need an extra hand, just let me know. I might be looking for a job."

"I'll take you up on that lady but I promise you won't appreciate the working conditions."

"What, no air-conditioning?"

"Yeah, the great outdoors and the worst of what Mother Nature has to offer."

"I've spent too much of my life inside air-conditioned offices with fluorescent lighting and windows that don't open."

Nellis took a pitcher of tea from the fridge and filled both glasses, "So, what is it you want from me, lady?"

Katherine accepted the glass and sipped, "I think I sensed more than knew, that you might have some of the answers to the questions that I've been asking myself for the past few weeks, since all the craziness started. I'm honestly not trying to be forward by saying that something about you forced me out of my comfort zone. I felt it from the first time we talked on the telephone. It's almost as if I secretly believe that you know something that I'm supposed to learn."

"Let's not get too far out ahead of ourselves here. I'm a flesh and blood mortal, who's made more than my share of mistakes, but I've also seen a different side of life than you have and I'm pretty sure it's more fun than figuring out how to squeeze profits out of every last dollar."

"I wouldn't be surprised if you're right."

"Plus, you learned that you can get stoned and enjoy it and that it probably isn't the scourge that the government's made it out to be. I, unapologetically, use it for pain and I've never found anything that works better, with fewer side effects, including all that crap the doctors prescribe. That shit might kill the pain but it turns my brain to mush, and I have enough trouble keeping track of all the nonsense that's in there already, so I won't take it."

"I don't blame you," replied Katherine.

"So, did a shot of old Nellis help your psyche or whatever?"

"I think it did but I'd be willing to bet that another session might keep me pointed in the right direction."

"Your fancy car seems to know it's way to my gate and I'm here pretty much twenty-four-seven. I've always got too much to do."

"Then I'll come see you again, sometime."

"Bring your work gloves, honey, I usually don't have time to stand around shootin' the bull."

They walked out through the porch and across the yard amid the herd of dogs to her car. She climbed in and closed the door. "Thank you for taking the time to let me vent."

"Lady, we all need someone to unload on, once in a while, and it usually works out better if it's someone who understands how painful life can be."

"Why is it that every time we talk, I feel as if there's another layer of truth about Nellis Gray masking another and another...?"

"You keep your eyes open and your wits about you. Those demons that you've encountered are very real and they don't take kindly to folks like you and me sticking our noses into their business."

"I'll take your advice," said Katherine starting the engine.

Nellis opened the gate to let her out and closed it, watching the car disappear in a swirl of dust. Big drops of rain splattered on the gravel drive and lightning ripped across the sky, "No wonder my back's been aching all day."

He gathered the dogs and trotted over to the shelter of the porch, where Chester had already taken refuge in the corner. He settled into the chaise, lit a Winston, and sipped on the last of his tea. Another clap of thunder brought gusty winds driving sheets of rain horizontally and Samantha and Sissy suddenly appeared at the screen door. Both were soaking wet.

Nellis jumped up to let them in and grabbed an old towel, "We can't go on meeting like this, girls!"

"We thought we could make it home before the rain got here," said Sissy, "but wrong again."

Samantha dried her thick hair with the towel, "Who was that lady in the blue car that zoomed out of the lane?"

"That was Miss Kennedy," replied Nellis. "I think she works for your father."

"I know her, she's nice," said Sissy, "but who was in the pickup truck that was waiting down by the highway when she came out? It pulled in right behind her."

"Pickup?"

"Yeah, a shiny red one," said Samantha.

"How 'bout I give you girls a ride home and we'll see what we find on the way?"

"That sure beats walking home in the rain," said Sam.

"Fine, then, let's go," said Nellis, handing out two slickers that were hanging on a hook behind the door. They splashed through puddles to the barn and climbed into the old truck. He pulled up to the gate, jumped out to open it, and climbed back in to pull through.

Sammy giggled and jumped out when he stopped again, "I'll close it for you, I'm already wet!"

Lightning crackled through wind and rain, as the old truck braked at the main road and turned north. They stopped again at the intersection with Maple Ridge and started to turn west along the ridge to Spratlin House, when Sissy screamed, "There's Miss Kennedy's car in the ditch!"

Nellis pulled onto the shoulder, set the brake, and jumped out. "You girls stay right here, until I find out what's going on."

The Grand Prix was nose down in the gully with a crushed fender on the left rear. Nellis climbed down the embankment and opened the door. Katherine's limp body rolled out into his arms. He gathered her under his slicker and clamored up to the road. Sissy opened the passenger door and he slipped Miss Kennedy onto the seat.

"Is she dead?" asked Samantha.

"No, but she's probably got a concussion," said Nellis inspecting an abrasion on her forehead. "Let's take her by your house, it's close."

The old truck traversed the meandering road, pulled into the drive at the manor house, and parked in the courtyard. Mama Louise and Mr. Charles rushed out of the kitchen, as Sissy and Samantha climbed out, "Are you children alright?"

"Yeah, but Miss Kennedy had an accident up on the road and she's hurt."

Nellis ran around the truck, "She's out cold and I think she's probably got a concussion."

Mama Louise took the girls into the house, "Bring her inside and we'll see what we can do for her."

Mr. Charles lent a hand carrying her through the kitchen to a sitting room with an upholstered chaise. "Let's put her down here for the moment."

Mama Louise came in to inspect the unconscious woman and covered her with a blanket. "She's got a nice gash on her forehead from the steering wheel but I'm not finding any other injuries." She dipped a washcloth in the pan of ice water and gently cleaned the wound.

Katherine's eyes fluttered and she groaned, "Where am I?"

"You're at Spratlin House and you're safe," said Louise.

"What happened?" asked Nellis.

"I was just turning onto the main road when I noticed headlights right behind me. When I came to the stop at Maple Ridge, the truck bashed the car and pushed me into the ditch. I don't remember anything after that." She started to sit up.

Mama Louise held her down, "You took a terrific blow to your head and I think we'd best send for the doctor, just to make sure you don't have any other injuries."

Mr. Charles said, "Things with the unions seem to have quieted down, is there anyone else who might want to harm you?"

Katherine's eyes focused in on Nellis, "Oh my God, it's Hall's buddies from the funeral."

"That wouldn't surprise me," said Nellis.

"If they're after me, they'll go after Maybelle Brown and her kids too. They don't want that truth to come out before the election."

"Who's Maybelle Brown?" asked Samantha.

"She's a black woman who lives in a shanty on the other side of the river with Hall's four bastard children," said Katherine.

"If they'd wanted to kill you, you'd be dead," said Nellis. "Miss Brown's another story. Where does she live?"

"I drove her home from the funeral but I'm not sure I could explain the directions, especially after dark."

"Well, you better figure out how, because you're in no shape to be going anywhere," said Louise.

Mr. Charles interrupted, "I grew up over there and I'm pretty sure I could find her place."

"I counted the roads off the highway, so I could find my way back with some groceries," said Katherine. "It's the third gravel road to the right after the bridge. Follow it around to the 'Y' and bear left, the cabin's at the bottom of the hill next to the creek."

"I know exactly where you're talking about," said Mr. Charles, turning to Nellis. "I can get you there."

"That's all well and good but me standing up to a bunch of drunken honkers is one thing, me standing up to them with a big black guy sittin' next to me is another."

"Just because I serve these white people doesn't mean I gave up my pride in where I came from. Those bastards have been terrorizing my people and my family for generations. It's time for this to stop."

"What if we take two cars, I'll stay and you get Miss Brown and her kids out of there."

"Bring them back here," said Louise. "Those lowlifes wouldn't dare come here."

"You're gonna need help," said Charles.

"I can handle them," said Nellis, turning to Katherine. "You're in good hands here but be a good girl and do as Mama Louise tells you."

"Are you sure going up against them alone is a good idea?"

"No, but it's the only one I've got, at the moment, and I think we're running out of options. Mr. Charles, I think it's time for us to go."

The two men started to leave as Stanton Spratlin hurried into the sitting room next to the kitchen. He glanced around and rushed to Katherine, "You've been injured. What's happened?"

Nellis said, "It's a long story and I'm sure Katherine can fill you in. We've got to be going."

Mr. Charles followed him through the kitchen and produced two umbrellas as they stepped out into the rain. "My truck's over behind the garage. Follow me, I'm pretty sure I know where we're going."

Twenty minutes later, the two men parked in front of the tiny ramshackle house and knocked. The eldest boy, Daniel, opened the door and Mr. Charles asked, "Is your mother home, son?"

"Yes Sir," replied the handsome boy, "I'll get her."

Maybelle appeared, "How can I help you gentlemen?"

"Katherine Kennedy was injured in a car crash and it seems that it was no accident. A witness said a red pickup pushed her off the road. She told us where to find you."

"Lord have mercy, is she gonna be okay?"

"She's probably got a concussion but she should recover. We've sent for the doctor," said Mr. Charles.

"We have every reason to believe they'll come here next," said Nellis, "and I think you should allow Charles to take you someplace safe for tonight."

"I can't leave my house," protested the young woman. "What if they try to burn me out?"

"I'll be staying to make sure that doesn't happen," said Nellis.

"I don't mean to sound ungrateful but why would you get in the way of those white bastards?"

"Because no one else seems so inclined," smiled Nellis. "Don't you worry about me. Get your kids and your stuff and let's get you out of here before it gets dark."

Miss Brown gathered her children and a change of clothing for each and followed Charles out to his truck. She turned around and marched back to Nellis, "I guess I should say thank you, before all this comes down, because I'm afraid I won't get to say it after."

"You take care of your children."

She slogged through the mud to squeeze into the cab of the truck and Charles drove back out towards the highway through a pounding rain.

Nellis settled on a battered chair on the porch, rested his twelve-gauge on his lap, and lit a Winston. He mashed out the stub of the third cigarette, when he heard an engine in the distance and saw headlights flashing through the trees.

Presently, a red pickup wheeled into the clearing, spinning oversized tires that threw up a brown mist. C.W. McCall's 'Convoy' was cranked up on the stereo and the driver was honking the horn in rhythm with the tune. Someone in the back yelled, "It's party time!" as the truck slid to a stop facing the front of the house.

Nellis shielded his eyes to the headlights as he counted five...no, six men jump out of the truck, three on each side of the glaring lights.

"Who the hell are you and where's Maybelle Brown?" yelled one.

"We came to share our sympathies for the loss of her old man."

"I'm the guy who watched that moron put a bullet in his own forehead. Hell of a shot," laughed Nellis.

"You're the one who printed up those damned posters," shouted a voice from the right.

"Yup."

"We oughta string you up!"

"So, where's the lady of the house," called a voice from the left.

"She's out for the evening. Dinner date."

Cat-calls and whistles. "Who'd want that used up piece of trash?"

Nellis stood, the shotgun slung over his shoulder, "Mind your manners."

"Who's gonna make me? You?"

He stepped off the porch and strode directly between the headlights, where he could see the men fanning out right and left. He caught a glint of metal from the second on the right and the one farthest to his left. The click of a rifle being cocked made him drop to a knee to fire a blast into the grill of the truck. The headlights exploded and Nellis rolled right to unload a shot at the sound of the rifle but eased his finger off the trigger. A very large black man had the redneck face down in the mud, with a boot on his neck, and he was holding the rifle in the air. The other five had been jumped and disarmed by a crowd of men with guns and machetes.

Nellis stood up and walked over to shake the very large man's hand, "I don't know where you came from but thanks for the help."

"I'm Johnny Edwards," said the man. "You must be Nellis Gray. We've heard about you from Jazz and, when Mr. Charles called, we invited ourselves to the party. This white trash has been bullying our people for long enough."

"Amen to that," said Nellis, "but I'm damned sure these assholes are just amateurs. The next bunch will be sober and deadly."

"Let 'em come," said another man. "We've had enough."

"I'll stand with you guys anytime anywhere," laughed Nellis. "What do you want to do with these morons?"

"I think we need to have some target practice on this fancy red pickup and then we're going to march them up to the highway, where the Sheriff can haul them off to jail."

"On what charge?" sputtered the Klansman, who was still face down in the mud under Johnny Edwards' size fourteens.

"Being an ignorant bigot, for starters," said Nellis, "but I'm pretty sure we could add attempted murder, inciting a riot, hell, he could add illegal parking too!"

The men all cracked up.

They lined the six drunks up in front of the tiny house and Nellis asked, "Who owns this truck?"

"I do," said the third from the left.

"I'm not sure insurance will cover this." Nellis leveled the shotgun at the driver's door and splattered it with pellets. "Shoulda had one of these other fools drive tonight."

"Hey, you can't do that!" yelled the driver.

"Wanna bet?"

Bits of shiny metal and glass from shattered windows erupted in showers of twinkling sparkles. Tires hissed and withered. Gas cans, stashed in the bed of the truck, went up with mighty whooshes trailing balls of orange flames in a half-dozen small explosions that lit up the forest. Steam whistled from the mutilated hood and oil and fluids floated on top of puddles in the yard. A relentless fusillade of bullets continued until the shattered ruins crumpled into a pile of smoldering metal.

The posse cheered and Nellis turned his shotgun on the invaders, "What do you want to do with these pigs?"

Edwards grinned, "If this was the old days, we'd be finding a stout tree to hang the whole bunch."

"Yeah, but we're better than they are."

"You're right. I called the Sheriff before we came out here."

"You're a good man."

Nellis' truck followed the slow march along the muddy lane, with eight of his rescuers in the bed and two up front, leaving their captives no chance to run off into the woods.

Red and blue lights flashed on two police cars blocking the gravel road at the highway. Sheriff Billings stood between them, with his arms crossed and rain dripping off the flat brim of his hat, as the parade marched out of the woods.

Johnny Edwards jumped out of the cab and pushed the white guys up the final little slippery slope. "Sheriff, we brought you some trash that needs to be cleaned up."

"What the hell's going on here?"

Nellis hopped out.

The Sheriff looked up, "How come I'm not surprised to find your smilin' face in the middle of this mess?"

"Good evening, Sheriff," laughed Nellis. "These morons tried to kill Katherine Kennedy this afternoon on Maple Ridge, about a mile east of the Spratlin place. Then they decided they needed to cause Maybelle Brown more trouble than she's already got but these fine gentlemen had other plans."

"And just what am I supposed to charge them with?"

"How 'bout attempted arson and murder, for starters? I'm sure you've got some laws that apply to terrorizing an innocent young woman for years or how about just charge 'em with being ignorant racist fools?"

The Klansmen were soaking wet and covered with mud but one piped up, "These niggers blew the crap out of my truck. I want them arrested for destruction of property!"

Sheriff Billings swatted the man across the face with his hat, "You're damned lucky they didn't take you stupid rednecks out to string you up from a tree, just like you and your daddy before you did to innocent black people. You're going to jail, so shut up before I take it upon myself to hand you back to these gentlemen, with the offer that they can do whatever seems fitting and I'll just look the other way! Hell, I've a mind to tar and feather the bunch of you just for good measure!"

"You can't do that!"

"Do you really want to stake your miserable life on the mistaken belief that I am sworn to protect you? I pledged to protect the upstanding citizens of this community by putting scum like you behind bars and, if I am not able to fulfill that obligation to the best of my ability, then I have no qualms about letting the good citizens take this matter into their own hands. Do I make myself clear?"

"Yes, Sir."

"Then shut your mouth before I shut it for you!"

Two officers cuffed the men and hustled them into the back of the police cars.

Chapter Seven

It was after midnight by the time Nellis finished giving his statement to the stenographer and headed back to the farm. The truck sloshed through puddles on the gravel road off the highway and pulled up to the gate.

Nellis swore, "Damn it!"

The headlights illuminated Chester's severed head impaled on a gatepost. He grabbed the shotgun and climbed out of the cab, scanning the yard and the drive for assassins. Two sets of muddy tracks ended just outside the gate, formed two 'Y's in the turn, and meandered back out towards the main road. The dogs did not bark but gathered inside the gate with their heads and tails hung low. Chester's empty eyes stared up into the heavens, as if a scream just escaped from his gaping mouth into the storm, and a slow trickle of blood oozed down the post into a puddle next to his headless carcass. He wheeled the fence back and knelt to hug the dogs, "It's not your fault, I'm just glad they didn't get all of you."

Brandy licked his face and moaned and the other dogs joined a gloomy chorus of whines and whimpers, as they brushed against him. He pulled the truck into the barn and returned with a shovel and a wheelbarrow to move Chester's remains to a gravesite next to the vegetable garden.

The tired man dug and swore after each shovelful, until they all gathered around a deep damp hole. Nellis took off his dripping hat, "God bless you, Chester, you were a true friend and we're all going to miss you."

He finished packing the mud back into the grave and hugged each dog in turn. "I promise each of you, those assholes just made a fatal mistake and we're going to set things right."

The pack followed him across the yard through pounding rain to the porch where he dried each dog with a big towel, hung up his hat and slicker, and kicked off his boots. He wandered through the living room and lit a fire under the teapot. He put a teabag in a cup and pulled a tin from beneath the counter that contained several fat buds and some rolling papers. Before the teapot whistled or he could finish rolling the joint, the phone rang.

He hesitated, then picked up the receiver, "Hello."

"Nellis, it's Katherine."

"How are you feeling?"

"I've got one wicked headache but I think I'll live, thanks to you."

"You should thank Samantha and Sissy, first, I just got you to someone who could help."

"Well, it sounds like you helped quite a few people tonight."

"Oh yeah?"

"Mr. Charles brought Maybelle and the kids back to the Spratlin's and those kids are just precious. Then he got a call from a friend of his, who told him the most amazing story about you taking on six armed Klansmen, as cool as Clint Eastwood in one of those movies."

"Having a dozen guys show up out of the darkness, armed with guns and machetes, sure helped. I might have taken out three or four but I'm pretty sure that I couldn't have taken them all. I would have had to reload twice!"

"Either way, I'm proud of you."

"Thanks," said Nellis sipping his tea. "Tell me, what was the name of the guy who's going to run for Curtis Hall's seat?"

"Why do you ask?"

He lit the joint and inhaled deeply.

"I know what you're doing," laughed Katherine.

"I'm stalling," sputtered Nellis.

"Why?"

"When I got home, I found Chester's head impaled on the post by the gate. Someone in the loop left me a message."

"Oh, that's awful, I'm so sorry. He was such a lovely pig."

"He was a good friend and we all buried him together a little while ago in the rain."

"Then I probably shouldn't be giving you a hard time, after all you've been through."

"What was that guy's name?"

"Oh, Miles Brantley. I'm afraid I don't know anything about him."

"Think your contacts could provide another dossier?"

"I don't know whether I'm still privileged but I'll see what I can find out in the morning."

"Thanks, I'd be interested in his inner circle. Let me know what you find out."

"I'll do that."

"Are you still at Spratlin's?"

"Yes, the doctor came by, after you left, and said that I have a concussion and recommended bed rest for a few days. I must admit that it's a rather odd arrangement but Stanton and Mama Louise insisted that I stay the night."

"As I said, do as you're told, remember?" laughed Nellis. "You'll have to tell me about your awkward situation, when there's time."

"I'll take notes," replied Katherine.

"Good night."

Katherine awoke to a gentle knock at the guest room door and Mama Louise peeked in with a big smile and a tray with coffee, "How're you feeling this morning?"

"I've still got the headache from hell but the room doesn't seem to be spinning around anymore."

"Well, let's take things easy. I've brought you some coffee and a robe because I took your dress to see if I could get the blood out of it, before it set. I'll get it back to you in a little while."

Katherine swung her legs over the side of the bed, hesitating before she stood up to pull on the plush purple bathrobe. "I'm still a bit wobbly but I think it will pass."

"The doctor will be by later this morning so, let's let him decide on your condition. You took a nasty blow and you're lucky it didn't kill you."

"From what Nellis and Mr. Charles found out, that seems to have been the point."

"Lord have mercy, I keep thinking that we're all moving forward together and then, we find that a good portion of our society just can't handle all the changes that history has thrust upon us."

"I don't understand how people can use religion to mask hate and bigotry. It's a perversion of everything this country's supposed to stand for."

"I don't have a real education but, from what I've read in the history books, it seems like religion has been manipulated, to control the little people, since the beginning of time," said Louise. "I keep wanting to believe that the good Lord had better intentions."

"I'm afraid it won't change, until something horrible happens that forces people to confront the truth." She took a sip of coffee, "Mmmm, that tastes good. How are Maybelle and the kids?"

"I'm about to serve breakfast to the whole crew, if you've got the strength to join us?"

"I'd like that."

Louise held her arm and they walked slowly through the sitting room to the kitchen, where the Spratlin girls were joking around with Maybelle's kids and feasting on fresh muffins, eggs, bacon, fruit, and pancakes.

Maybelle turned from the stove, "I hope you don't mind me steppin' in but I figured I could keep the kids occupied with eating rather than raisin' a ruckus."

Louise smiled, "I don't mind at all. Actually, considering everything, I appreciate the help."

Katherine took a seat next to Sissy, "I'm afraid I don't remember everyone's names."

Sissy grinned, "Everybody, this is Miss Kennedy, if you didn't already know, and this is Daniel, Hubie, Muriel, and Martin."

The children all giggled and Muriel said, "You're the nice lady who drove us home from church the other day and brought us groceries."

"That's right and I have to say that I'm very glad that we're here together and everyone is safe and sound."

The children cheered, as Stanton appeared in the doorway, "My, we have a houseful this morning and I do hope that you left a little something for me to eat, because it smells wonderful in here."

He sat at the head of the table and Maybelle brought a plate of food and the newspaper. "Thank you."

"No, thank you for letting us stay here last night. You probably saved my children."

Stanton stood up, "I'm glad we could offer you a refuge. Tell me, did you prepare breakfast this morning?"

Maybelle glanced at Louise, "Yes, Sir. Mama Louise was taking care of Miss Katherine and the children were hungry. I hope you don't mind?"

"I don't mind at all and I'd like to offer you a job, helping Louise out in the kitchen. In exchange, all of you can live in the quarters, for the time being, and I'll provide you with a small salary, if you're interested?"

"Are you kidding? Of course I'm interested in getting my kids out of that shack."

"If it's alright with Mama Louise and Mr. Charles, we have a deal," said Stanton, extending his hand to shake. "Now, could I have some pancakes, please?"

"Mr. Spratlin," cautioned Louise, "you know what the doctor said about your diet."

"I know, I know, but they smell so good and this is the first morning, in a very long time, that I've come down to find the kitchen overflowing with the joyous noise of children. I'd like to hang on to this wonder for as long as it lasts. Now, how are all these children getting to school?"

Mr. Charles appeared at the back door, "I could drive them and come back to take you to the plant, if you don't need to be there early?"

"I think we could make an exception today and I might suggest that Miss Brown consider transferring the children to the local school, so the children wouldn't have so far to go."

"Oh, you'll love our new school," said Sammy. "It's a brand-new building and the kids are really nice."

Daniel looked up, "Are they all white?"

"Most of them," said Sissy, "but there are black kids and Indian kids and Mexican kids and even two Japanese kids, who are learning English, so, it wouldn't be like you guys are any different than the rest of the kids in the school."

"Yeah, besides, you'll have us," said Sammy.

Maybelle said, "I'll be happy to ride along and get the paperwork started, if you're serious?"

Stanton looked down the table to Katherine, "Are you up to calling the office to let them know that we'll be a little late?"

"Absolutely."

~

Sibble Savage knocked at the master bedroom door and Stanton called, "Come in."

He was just buttoning his suit jacket and Sibble straightened his tie, "You do look so handsome, when you're dressed for the office."

Stanton leaned over to kiss her cheek, "Your opinion always mattered most. What can I do for you?"

"Mrs. Spratlin would like a word with you regarding all the noise in the house."

"Is she decent?"

"The doctor is coming to see her at ten o'clock, so she hasn't had her medications this morning," replied Sibble. "What's going on?"

"I'm afraid we've just adopted four more children and their mother," replied Stanton, with a grin. "I hope you will treat each of them as if they were our own."

"If I didn't love you and this family as much as I do, I'd have to protest that I'm getting too old to be raising another generation!"

"Are you threatening to retire?"

Sibble placed her hands defiantly on her hips, "Absolutely not! But I had nine-months to prepare, when you and your sister and your children were born. I'm not used to changing everything overnight, especially adding four children all at once!"

"I think you'll find them well-behaved and, if you have any problems with any of them, including Sissy and Sammy, just let me know."

"Those girls are going to turn out just fine. I think the new school is going to be good for both of them. They're already making new friends."

"I hope you're right."

"Better for them to be at the top of the heap than the bottom." She knew all the family secrets and still demanded obedience from her children in critical moments, even if Stanton was the head of the household. "Will you see Mrs. Spratlin?"

"Yes. Mr. Charles is driving the children to school, so I won't be leaving for a little while."

Sibble excused herself and Stanton walked to the far end of the hallway to knock on the heavy door.

"Come in."

Marjorie was propped on a mound of pillows against a carved headboard covered with cherubs and fairies frolicking in a flowering meadow, surrounded by the gloom of opulence, with heavy drapes drawn against the morning light and a world both foreign and frightening. Her hair shimmered in the glow of ornate lamps on the nightstands and her housecoat was arranged to expose scandalous cleavage. She had applied a bit of rouge and some lipstick but her once sparkling eyes, now ghosts peering from dark sockets, strained to focus.

Her voice was barely a whisper, "Thank you for coming to see me."

"I understand that you have not been informed that we have guests."

"Guests?"

"Yes, Maybelle Brown, a young black woman, and her four children. The modern incarnation of the Klan threatened them and would have succeeded, in burning them out of their meager home, were it not for Mr. Charles and our neighbor across the creek, Nellis Gray.

Miss Brown and the children will be staying in the quarters until we can find a better arrangement."

"Until the white trash can be put away, would be a better limit."

"I honestly didn't think you'd approve."

"I might hide away inside this room but I have only fear and loathing for the morally corrupt world out there. We were raised by our black help and I don't think any of us ever thought of them as anything other than family," she said. "As far as I'm concerned all of these children are the only hope for a future without hate."

"How are you feeling?"

"Dr. Selfridge says that my symptoms are very real but they don't add up to a single condition like cancer or heart failure."

"That doesn't answer my question. How do you feel?"

"Seeing you and knowing that you are trying to help these young people makes me feel proud. So, perhaps, today will be a good day."

He walked over to throw open the shades, "It's a beautiful morning and our kitchen echoed with the music of children's laughter for the first time in ages. That should be inspiration enough to make the most of this day."

Marjorie would not be tempted from her despair, "I understand that Miss Kennedy also spent the night."

"Yes, these same criminals ran her car off the road. Mr. Gray rescued her and brought her here. She's suffered a concussion and these men are still out there to threaten her safety. We'll see what the doctor has to say, when he arrives, but I don't quite know what to do about the problem of her security."

"You could put her under guard."

Stanton laughed, "I'm quite sure she wouldn't stand for that."

"Then you should keep her close, until you know she's safe. We both know that you've been seeing her for years, so it shouldn't be much of a burden."

Stanton turned and walked to her bedside, "I have loved you with all my heart, since we were children and, in spite of everything, I'll make sure that you have everything you need."

"You can't magically fill my heart with the fires of passion or repeal the depression that plagues my every waking hour. Just be sure to care for our children."

"The boys are both damaged beyond repair and I'm not sure that either will ever recover, but the girls are another matter. In spite of our failings, they're filled with that joyous sparkle that illuminated the beautiful woman that I married and I honestly hope they survive the family curse to become vibrant and complete human beings."

"Their only hope is to live in the real world instead of all this pretense," said Marjorie, with a wave of her pale hand. "Maybe we would have had a chance, if we'd grown up as normal people, instead of the miserable and lonely children of privilege."

"Unfortunately, we'll never know."

He closed the door gently and padded down the staircase through the central hall to the kitchen, where Brad and Bruce were consuming the last of the pancakes.

"Good morning, boys. How are you this morning?"

Bruce grinned, "Top of the morning to you, Daddy. We're just chipper."

Brad's eyes were bloodshot and three days worth of stubble could not mask his ruddy complexion, "Have we converted the house to a nursery or what? Mr. Charles was leading a parade of noisy children down the driveway, at half past dawn this morning, and Miss Kennedy seems to have taken up residence in the sitting room."

"I'm sure Mother will just love this new arrangement," added Bruce. "Word of this getting out would be positively scandalous!"

"No more than that beautiful boy, who slipped out of the loft and drove off on a scooter at six this morning," said Brad.

"You're right, he is a delicious boy. Maybe I could invite him as my date, if we ever have a really open family dinner, where everyone is invited and all the liaisons are exposed. Better yet, let's make it a costume party and everyone can dress up as who they really want to be!"

Stanton interrupted, "To answer the question, Miss Kennedy was run off the road by a bunch of Klan boys in a pickup, who moved on to threaten Miss Brown and her children. Doctor Selfridge will be here shortly to check on Miss Kennedy's concussion and, if she is well enough, we will find someplace safe to keep her, until all of these thugs are apprehended. Miss Brown has accepted a position as assistant cook and she and her children will be staying in the quarters, until we can be sure the danger has passed."

Brad said, "Tell me who they are and I'll take care of this problem right now."

"Unfortunately, it's not just these guys but a whole segment of society who view hate and bigotry as righteous gospel."

"Hell, in Nam, the Army would round 'em up and shoot every one of them just to make sure."

"That's just as bad," yelled Bruce, "you killed people just for being different, even if they were completely innocent!"

Brad held his head in his hands, "And you wonder why the inside of my head is so fucked up?"

Stanton put his hand on his son's shoulder but Brad twisted away, "Don't touch me. Don't ever touch me!"

"I'm so very sorry you had to witness the worst of humanity."

"Witness? Fuck, I was the guy who pulled the trigger over and over. Most people can't imagine the splatter of a four-year-old's head exploding, or the sound a bayonet makes when it's rammed into a pregnant woman's stomach, or the stench of Napalm burning human flesh, or what it's like when your buddy falls over backwards with a bullet hole between his eyes?"

"You're a monster," cried Bruce. "How can you live with yourself?"

"I can't, you little faggot! I can't!" screamed Brad, backhanding his brother as he stomped out the kitchen door.

Stanton knelt beside Bruce and offered a damp napkin to wipe the blood from his lip, "I'm sorry...I'm sorry for a lot of things."

"That was not your fault," replied Bruce, standing up. "There are lots of things that we can blame you for but the person that Brad's become is not one of them."

"Well, thank you for that but I'm concerned that he might hurt himself or someone else. Perhaps I should go talk to him."

"That's not one of your better ideas. He's off his rocker because he hasn't taken his meds in days and he's drinking again. I'll go catch up with him in a minute, I'm pretty sure I can talk him down enough to eat some pills."

Stanton looked at his son, "How is it possible that I failed you both?"

"You can't blame yourself because you didn't raise us, we were brought up by Sibble and Mama Louise and Mr. Charles and teachers and coaches and tutors, just like you and granddaddy and probably his daddy before him. Our relationship with you was confined to a formal dinner every night and church on Sunday. Neither of you ever attended a game or a play or even a parent-teacher conference. You didn't participate in our lives, so how can you feel guilty for a doing a crappy job of parenting, when you didn't even show up?"

Tears welled in his father's eyes, as Bruce turned and walked out the kitchen door. Mama Louise supported Katherine in the entry to the sitting room as Stanton fell to his knees, weeping with genuine passion. In spite of years of intimacy, he had never revealed the demons behind his carefully constrained disposition.

~

Sibble escorted Dr. Selfridge into Marjorie's room and closed the door.

The doctor approached the bed with grave concern and reached to take her pulse, "How are you feeling today?"

"I'm afraid of dying but I believe I'm more afraid of living."

"Our world becomes more complicated and menacing with every day. Have the Lithium and Valium, that I prescribed, helped with the depression?"

"Not really, they make my world look murky."

He produced a stethoscope and listened to her heart and lungs, checked her eyes and ears, and took her blood pressure. "Everything is normal today and, other than your depression, I must ask whether there are any physical maladies that I should be aware of?"

She took his hand and pressed it to her ample breast, "Tell me, how is Miss Kennedy?"

"I'm hopeful that she'll make a full recovery but she received a terrific blow to the head in the crash and I've prescribed bed rest for the next several days. With any concussion, there is always the danger of further damage from swelling of the brain."

"She has a good brain, make sure you repair it properly." She pressed his hand to massage her chest. "She also fulfills a function, for which I am no longer needed, but that does not mean that I've forgotten the passion that burns in my loins."

"Mrs. Spratlin..." sighed the doctor, as she pushed his hand beneath the covers, "as you know, this is not recommended therapy for your condition."

"Doctor, I think it's crucial to establish whether I am still a functioning female and, besides, your protestations have always been half-hearted at best. The new wing on your clinic will help you treat hundreds of new patients and soothe any guilt you might have for prescribing unconventional therapies."

~

Under threat of the first hard freeze, Nellis finished harvesting the last hard green tomatoes and tore out the wilting vines. He knelt to pick the few remaining squash, when Sissy appeared.

"What are you harvesting?"

"It's supposed to freeze tonight, radio said it might hit twenty-five and that's sure to kill the summer crops like squash and tomatoes."

"Can I help?"

"Sure, I could use a hand covering the greens with this thermal blanket and we can haul these two baskets down to the cellar."

Sissy grabbed a corner of the long sheet of fabric and they lifted it down the bed, securing it with bricks. "That's just like a blanket on a bed."

"Exactly, it holds the warmth of the soil to keep the plants from freezing."

"That's so simple and smart."

"Someone was thinking," laughed Nellis.

Sissy peered up with sad green eyes, "I'm really sorry about Chester. I liked him a lot."

"Me too."

"Don't you want to get mad at whoever killed him?"

He picked up the heavy basket and started towards the cellar door, "Of course, but I don't know exactly who to blame. It seems pretty obvious that they're pals with the men who were arrested and they don't think like you and me."

"I'm kind of glad you and Mr. Charles helped Miss Brown. I like her kids."

"Are they staying with you?"

"Yes, Papa gave Miss Brown a job in the kitchen, with Mama Louise, and the children are transferring into the new school with us."

"What about Miss Kennedy?"

"She's staying in the guestroom off the kitchen, until the doctor says she can start getting around. I went in to talk with her and she's really nice."

"How's that working out with the rest of the family?" inquired Nellis gently.

Sissy stared crying, "Everyone else is still as crazy as always. Geoffrey, the gardener, heard a big argument between my brothers and my father this morning, after we left for school, and the doctor gives my mother pills to make her feel better but I think they make her sleepy. Whenever I try to see her, she can hardly keep her eyes open or understand what I'm trying to say."

"There's a big storm swirling all around you and you're way too small to stop it."

"That's right, I feel like I'm standing in the middle watching it whirl around and around and it's never going to stop."

Nellis knelt down, "You have to believe that none of this is your fault. I've been through a lot of weird stuff in my day and I've learned one thing that always turns out to be true."

"What's that?"

"That behind every storm cloud is a brilliant shot of sunshine." He smiled, "Remember the tornado? Well, when it was all over, I had some new and dear friends and a new barn to boot."

Sissy looked down at the turf, "And so did I."

"So, no matter how bad things seem, there's always something wonderful waiting to be discovered. You just have to believe."

"From all the stories I've read in books, my people are supposed to be the good guys and the bad guys come from somewhere else."

"I don't think that anyone in your family is a bad person, I think they all have problems that they've yet to solve, things that hurt and they don't know how to feel better."

Her green eyes sparkled, "I'm glad you're my friend. You make me feel better."

"Glad to help, girlie, glad to help."

~

Two days later, the black Fleetwood pulled up and honked. Nellis sauntered out of the barn and opened the gate to let Mr. Charles drive through. He closed the steel panel and walked over to the car, as the huge man got out and opened the rear door to reveal Katherine in the back seat.

Nellis shook his hand and patted him on the shoulder, then leaned in to the spacious interior. "Are you supposed to be out and about?"

"No sir, I'm not."

"Then what are you doing here?"

Katherine grinned, "I'm just not capable of being confined with nothing to occupy my brain, so, I've been gathering information on Miles Brantley. I wanted to give it to you in person."

"I appreciate that but I'd have been perfectly willing to come by to pick it up."

"Mr. Charles was kind enough to offer to drive me over here. I think he kind of knew that I had to get out of that house for a while or I'd lose what little remains of my mind."

Nellis climbed in to sit next to her on the broad leather seat, "So what did you find?"

"This one's a doozy. Arrested repeatedly as a teenager for drunk and disorderly and aggravated assault, he barely graduated from junior college with an Associates Degree in something called Business Arts. Then, daddy started buying up little plumbing businesses and, after they bought twenty or thirty of them, the old man hired some pros to run the office and it started working like a real business, in spite of the kid's ignorance."

"Daddy inherited sections of ranchland out east and bought more, when his neighbors got into financial trouble during the recession. The old man's smart and cagey but he doesn't have the background to run for office, so he's gonna buy his eldest son an election. Now, the kid honestly believes he deserves to win the nomination, even though he doesn't know squat about government or history or geography or economics or much of anything outside animal husbandry and plumbing."

"Does he have a chance?"

"Oh yeah, he's working the pious, righteous, evangelical, flag-waving protector of business and small-town America, spouting Second Amendment gun-rights nonsense, declares that abortion is illegal and immoral and any doctor who performs an abortion should be tried for murder, claims absolute proof that the government and the minorities and the immigrants are conspiring to take away everything you cherish, and tops it off with a not so subtle twist on racial purity."

"Gee, sounds like a charming guy."

"And he's got lots of those same weirdoes volunteering to do whatever needs to be done."

"Do we know who they are?"

Katherine grinned, "I've started a list. So far, I've only got sixty-two names and I've got some people doing background on as many as possible. By tomorrow, we ought to have enough to begin figuring out who's where on the ladder."

"Is anybody running against this moron?"

She looked at him curiously, "So far, no one's stepped up."

"And don't look at me. We've already been through this, I'm much better behind the scenes."

"Seems to me, the last time you worked behind the scenes, things didn't turn out so well."

"Not for Curtis Hall."

"You're right about that."

"Give me what you've got and I'll run some other things down while you compile your list," said Nellis, "and stay down, until the doc says you can motivate."

"Yes sir."

"How's Spratlin dealing with all of this?"

"He's muddling through a very trying time at home and at the plant, at the moment, and I'm afraid I'm not offering much help emotionally. On the other hand, having six youngsters around the house seems to brighten him up."

"Lady, that's your business not mine. I was asking about his political thoughts."

"Oh, I'm sorry. He's a staunch Republican but, if they can't come up with a better candidate to challenge young Brantley, I wouldn't be surprised to see him put his money behind a Democrat."

"That's got to be a Cardinal sin!" laughed Nellis.

"Worse," giggled Katherine. "Why is it that I always feel better after talking with you?"

"Because I don't feed you no bullshit, it's all pretty much straight up."

"Yeah, I'm sure that's it."

Chapter Eight

Ned Perkins climbed out of the cab of the battered panel truck and knelt to pet the pack of dogs vying for a rub. He slowly stretched against the side of the van, like a cat waking from a long nap, moaning, "I'm gettin' too damned old to be driving straight through like a teenager on a diet of caffeine, black mollies, and cigarettes. You damned sure better have those ribs smokin' or I'm gonna collapse right here on your driveway."

"Open your nostrils," laughed Nellis. "I guarantee they'll be falling off the bone after nine hours of very slow cookin'."

"I know I'm not worthy, Master, but lead me to them!"

They grabbed his bags and wandered along the side of the farmhouse, where the old Hasty Bake spewed whiffs of sweet hickory. Nellis grabbed two bottles of Olympia from a bucket of ice and popped the caps, handing one to Ned, "Here's to old friends and future profits."

"Amen to that," replied the tired driver, taking a sip and slumping on a bench at the picnic table. "Bring it on, brother."

Nellis darted into the kitchen and returned with steaming baked beans, a fresh garden salad, and warm bread. He opened the lid on the cooker, releasing an aromatic cloud, and removed two racks of baby-backs gently blackened and glistening with a glaze of sweet sauce. "These might be enough."

"We'll see about that," laughed Ned. "You do know how to smoke that meat."

"You bet your ass, I've been practicing since we were kids."

Ned sliced off a rib and tore the meat from the bone, "Now that's the way it's supposed to be! I'm not sure one rack each is gonna be enough, brother, we might need more."

Nellis wiped a slurp of sauce with a paper towel, "Everything go okay?"

"Yeah, no problem. Everyone's chompin' at the bit for the next shipment."

"Too bad it's got to be the last but I lost some of the crop in that storm. We'll see what the New Year brings."

"You just keep working on that hybrid, everyone loves it."

"It is pretty sweet, I'm calling it Jamaican Blue," said Nellis, taking a short break from ribs to sample the beans and salad.

"So, what ever happened with that lunatic who shot himself?"

Nellis shook his head, savoring a succulent chunk of ecstasy, "The Sheriff couldn't charge me with him being a moron, so I got off on that, no problem, but Miss Kennedy, Spratlin's secretary, who got me involved in that whole mess in the first place, was foolish enough to go to the funeral."

"Lemme guess, it had to be one of those old-time Bible-thumping extravaganzas."

"With Billy Joe Hardman on the pulpit warping the Good Word into cosmic justice to validate fear and racism and hatred and all the rest. So, she gets up to leave and the Reverend just can't resist forcing a confrontation. Long story short, a bunch of Klan-types tried to run her off the road and almost killed her. Then they decided to go pay a visit to ol' Curtis Hall's black mistress and their four kids, with every intent of eliminating all the witnesses."

"Holy shit! This is starting to sound like one of those old Thirties movies. I'm seeing it in grainy black and white."

"Worse, I was sitting there waiting on her front porch in the pourin'-ass rain with my trusty twelve gauge, when they showed up."

"How'd that turn out?" Ned grinned, "Seein's as you're sitting here with no visible holes in you, I'm guessin' they got the worst of it!"

"Well, I guess I was fool enough to think that I could take 'em all but, fortunately, a dozen of her neighbors, with guns and machetes, showed up. We absolutely destroyed their fancy pickup, with a half-dozen exploding gas tanks in the back, then marched their white asses through a torrential thunderstorm to be arrested by the Sheriff for attempted arson and murder. Miss Kennedy's got a concussion but the black family has moved into the Spratlin place across the creek, where they'll be safe from these fools."

"So, you're still in it up to your elbows."

"Worse," said Nellis. "Those bastards snuck in here, while I was giving my deposition to the Sheriff, and slaughtered Chester and stuck his head on the post out by the gate. Damned right, I'll find out who they are."

"I'm really sorry, he was a great pig."

"He is sorely missed by all of us."

Ned looked down at his plate, "These aren't...?"

"Chester?" yelled Nellis, "Damn it! I wouldn't cook my favorite pig but I might roast my ex-best friend."

Ned chuckled, "Are you still considering running for office?"

"Stop that! I am not running for any damned office but I am going to make damned sure that the substitute candidate, they're putting up to replace Hall, doesn't get elected."

"Can't be worse than the first guy?"

"Wanna bet?" snapped Nellis. "This new guy has no character, no qualifications, and no knowledge of what a representative is supposed to do. Daddy's literally buying the election. The kid's going to take his salary and a whole pile of money from his sponsors and vote the way they tell him. No doubt, he'll embarrass the local constituency with his ignorance, while he's about it, but that's all he's capable of in the first place."

"I can't believe any intelligent person would vote for him," replied Ned, sitting back staring at the last four ribs on his plate.

"You're allowed to save some for lunch tomorrow," laughed Nellis. "And you're right, no intelligent person would vote for this fool but there are a whole lot of folks who believe the lies, the propaganda about gun rights or abortion rights or gay rights or some other damned thing. Hell, we've got preachers all over this country coaching their flocks on the evils of liberal elitism and the threat of the federal government coming to take their stuff or people of color depleting the genetic stock of the Aryan race or immigrants stealing their jobs. It's all horseshit but ignorant uneducated people believe all that nonsense because their minister wouldn't lie."

Ned laughed, "You've got the passion, brother, you just need to get yourself a shiny black suit and commit to the cause!"

"Damnit! Will you stop that?"

"No, it's way too much fun teasing you, especially now that you're too damned old to do anything about it!"

"I know I could still kick your ass and, besides, I always knew there was something I didn't like about you."

"Yeah, it's called honesty!" roared Ned. "And I know you well enough to know that you can't let go of an injustice or bullying or a stranded kitten for that matter. That's what makes you who you are."

Nellis slugged down the last of his second beer, "Yeah, you're probably right but I, sure as shootin', am not going to run for no damned office and that's final."

"I'd vote for you, if you cooked up another round of ribs."

"You're dreamin' bub, on both counts. If you're foolish enough to stay past breakfast, I'm putting you to work helping repair downed fencing along the south line."

"That sounds too much like work to me," replied Ned. "I'm thinkin' I'll just leave you a pile of cash and take my brown boxes and ease on out of here, so I can turn this around in two weeks."

"That is your function in life, my friend, and we're all thankful for your dedication!"

~

Ned's panel truck disappeared down the lane into a dense fog that rolled through the farm like a sinuous veil parting occasionally to reveal wisps of autumn reds in the oaks and maples and flashes of yellow in the black walnuts and pecans.

Nellis collected the paper and latched the gate, then guided the pack of dogs, cats, chickens, and goats up to the barn for breakfast. He settled in with a hot cup of coffee, a first drag on a Winston, and the paper, as faint patches of blue sky peeking through the gloom and the warmth of the rising sun burned off the mist.

The lead story quoted a brash and totally unqualified Republican primary candidate for president, "I'll build a wall from the Gulf of Mexico to the Pacific Ocean to keep these migrant murders and rapists from crossing the border and then I'll round up every illegal immigrant from every state in the Union and ship them back where they came from! We must defend white America from this influx of black, brown, and yellow invaders!"

An old-school Senator retorted, "Does anyone else have a sense of déjà vu? Adolf Hitler rounded up millions of Jewish citizens and anyone else who dared to speak out against his totalitarian reign or threatened to foul the Aryan bloodline. He shipped them off to concentration camps, where they were slaughtered and their bodies burned in massive furnaces under the banner of 'purification'. Did we learn nothing at the expense of the hundreds of thousands of American troops, who fought and died to put an end to fascism, or are we destined to repeat one of the darkest chapters in history, here, on our own soil?"

Nellis mumbled, "Amen" as the telephone rang in the kitchen. He tossed the paper on the bench, stepped over a sleeping ChaCha, and trotted through the living room the fetch the phone. "Hello."

"Nellis? It's Katherine."

"How're you feeling?"

"I'm better. In fact, the doctor said that I can resume normal activities with a few restrictions."

"Like motorcycle racing or crashing your car or things like that?"

She laughed, "And no roller skating. Listen, I've got that list together and I think you'll find it enlightening."

"Somewhere in there, there's a pack of pig-killing swine and I'm gonna have me a barbeque."

"Not that I blame you, but the Sheriff might frown on another incident."

"Chester was family," replied Nellis. "Do you want me to come get that list?"

"I'm allowed to drive, can I bring it to you?"

"Sure, I'm still trying to get to my first cup of coffee."

"Keep the coffee hot and I'll see you in a few minutes."

He hung up the phone and rubbed the stubble on his face, as his eyes wandered to Ned's duffle full of cash sitting on the dining room table. "Don't have time for a shave but I might make you disappear." He grabbed the bag, carried it outside and down the stairs to stash it in the cellar.

The dogs barked and ran to the gate, as the headlights of the company wagon flashed through the last tenacious puffs of fog. Nellis herded the critters out of the way and let her in. She stepped out of the car dressed for the office in a gray business suit with a yellow scarf draped around her neck. Her auburn hair was carefully combed to conceal as much of the bandage on her forehead as possible but her dark eyes glimmered with that enchanting spark, missing since the accident.

"You look like you're actually focusing again."

"I'm better, thanks to a lot of kind people, including you."

"I'm glad but, the sad part is, we locked up one bunch of vicious varmints, only to find they had replacements ready to roll."

She held out a manila envelope, "I'm betting they're in here somewhere but then, so are a lot of other interesting parties."

"Like who?"

"Well, besides daddy, the biggest contributor is our perennial favorite, Billy Joe Hardman. Second is his cohort, Joseph Jamison, at the Church of Eternal Salvation down in Brimmington, then there's Ely Post, who owns the third largest privately held oil company in the country, a few guys who own refineries, plus a handful of ranchers who, collectively, own about half the state, and, of course, our sad excuse for a governor is rallying the party to back his cause enthusiastically."

"Hell, Brantley makes him look like an intellectual."

"Sad but true," she said, as they walked across the yard and up to the porch.

"Has anyone figured out how all these folk relate to one another?"

"As in?"

"How many of 'em attend Hardman's church? How many of 'em have criminal records? How many work for that oil company or ride herd for those ranchers? Stuff like that."

"No, but that would take some work and access to private lists."

"I'm not above thievin' something vital for a good cause," smirked Nellis, pouring steaming coffee from a carafe.

"Let's start with the material we can get our hands on first, okay?"

He scanned the list, "Here's Ronny Graham, I knew that bum in high school. He was a bully and the dumbest guy in school, but he was a hero lineman on the football team, so he got by with a little help from the teachers, who ignored his mean streak."

"One of those?"

"Yup, your basic low-life. Here's Norman Orinsky, Polish guy with a big schnoz and bad pimples, who made no secret for his hatred of anyone of color. They could have ended up being buds but I haven't seen either one of these weasels in near thirty years."

"Shall we assume that there's no such thing as a coincidence?"

"With these guys? I don't think so. Hatred feeds on hatred, a shared badge of honor in this slimy guild. I'm betting, if we could know everything about each of these characters, we'd end up with a hierarchy of command divided up into several branches of responsibility."

"If it really is constructed like a modern company or even a tiny army, they'd have the main guys overseeing a rank of experts running independent teams who might break up into squads to accomplish specific tasks or goals."

"But, even with strategic layered management, there's always a little group pulling the strings from someplace in the shadows. In corporations, they sit on the board or own the most shares and, in politics, they determine the success or failure of every measure that comes up in a legislature. I can guarantee this group isn't any different."

"I agree absolutely," said Katherine, pouring a second cup of coffee. "Good java."

Nellis raised his cup, "Pure Columbian and I've got an idea."

He disappeared inside and returned with a pack of index cards, several pens in different colors, pushpins, and a large cork board. "Okay, let's transfer what information we've got for every name on the list onto one card for each and we can pin them to the board and move them around as we figure out how they all fit together."

"Great idea," said Katherine. "Let's start with the big contributors, the guys who are probably running the show. I'll print their names in red."

"There you go, we should start with ol' Billy Joe. He deserves a spot near the top along with Jamison, Ely Post, and at least some of those ranchers and wildcatters like ol' man Brantley."

"And we could group the foot soldiers like your buddies from high school in green."

"The middle part's going to be the hardest," added Nellis, "the who's answering to who part. I'd also be interested in who's providing the advertising and PR for the kid's campaign. That's a whole 'nother tangle of money and influence."

She printed 'CAP HARDY' on a card in purple and pinned it on the right side of the board. "We'll use purple for the creatives. This guy does little print promotions for grocery stores and furniture companies, all high volume, low budget, low quality."

"What about television and radio?"

"Here's Chet Clausen, he's a producer over at Channel Eight and moonlights directing Hardman's weekly broadcasts. Glenden Ross, who writes sports reports for the paper, probably handles print editing and speeches."

"See, there is order in this madness."

They worked through the morning, making a dozen phone calls to ask contacts for information about one name or another, and created four distinct layers in three seemingly independent branches. Each working group, under one command, was isolated from what other people were doing in the next.

The creative group was the driving force in the largest branch overseeing all interactions with the public, from ads on the airwaves to sermons on the pulpit. Another bough appeared to be in charge of soliciting large undocumented donations and distributing funds to finance their programs through the accounting firm for Praise the Lord Ministries. The third was populated by most of the fourth-tier recruits, who were trained as obedient and unquestioning foot soldiers, driven by ignorance and hatred that justified their violence. At the top were a pack of cards that could not be tied directly to any of the subgroups or Hardman, Post, Brantley, and Jamison.

Nellis sat back and rocked, rubbing his scruffy beard, "I think we're on to something here. We don't know everything about everybody but we sure know a whole lot more about how the relationships probably work."

She held up a handful of cards, "We don't have any idea of how these fit in. They're certainly not local but their contributions are too large for them not to be important."

"Heck, there's probably another level above these dimwits. We'll figure it out."

Katherine rubbed the bandage on her forehead, "The question is how do we use this to our advantage?"

"Are you okay?" asked Nellis, "Hungry?"

"Yes, I am hungry."

"Great, I've got some leftover roast chicken we can make into sandwiches, if you like?"

"That's sounds wonderful." She stopped and stared at him for a moment, "Do you realize that I completely forgot about going back to the office? I've never done that before."

Nellis laughed, "Maybe a good kick in the head was all you needed to get your priorities straightened out."

"Or maybe just a change in perspective," mused Katherine, following Nellis into the red kitchen.

He pulled a loaf of fresh bread, a chicken carcass, and some lettuce from the fridge and started carving on a well-worn board next to the sink. "You know more about fancy finances than I ever want to know but doesn't it bother you that the same accounting firm is cooking the books for the ministry and these boneheads?"

"If we had more than a suspicion, we could call for an investigation."

"Yeah, but no one's going to bend the laws just because we think these turd-buckets are moving piles of cash around to get their guy elected."

"You know, come to think of it, Brantley's posters and signs are everywhere. Ol' Cap Hardy's been a busy boy."

"Do the Democrats even have a candidate?" asked Nellis, pouring tea from a pitcher and serving up the sandwiches.

"I've heard they're going to run Hal Blaney."

"Who's that?"

"Former judge, clean as a whistle, prominent in the community, and one of the most boring people I've ever met. He can put a room to sleep in nothing flat."

Nellis chewed slowly, "What do you think about your boss running?"

"I think he'd be dynamite. He's got all the right qualities for the job but he's also trying to save the company from bankruptcy, so I doubt he'd volunteer for the campaign, unless he thought it was the last possible hope of keeping Junior out of the House."

"You should, at least, talk to him. Hell, if he doesn't want to do it, maybe one of his rich buddies would rise to the occasion."

"I still like your odds," laughed the brunette. Her dark eyes flashed, "At least you'd be more interesting."

"That may well be but there's no damned way that I'm running for public office now or at any time in the future. Are we clear on that?"

"I'm only teasing," smirked Katherine, "kinda."

"You talk to your boss the next time you decide to show up for work, if you still have a job!"

"Oooo, cranky aren't we? Too much coffee or too little food?"

"Neither. I'd just forgotten how completely impossible women can be."

She put her hands on her hips defiantly, "Are you saying that we shouldn't have opinions or be at least as intelligent as our men or maybe more so, or, God forbid, that we should be subservient to our masters? Haven't you ever heard of women's lib?"

"Yeah, as a matter of fact, I was a charter member, back in the day, when we had quality women leading the charge!" roared Nellis.

"You're just a damned chauvinist pig hiding under a pink blanket!"

He reached to take her in his arms and kissed her passionately. In spite of her warm response, he backed away, "I'm sorry, that was a bit...forward of me."

She pulled him closer and draped long arms around his neck, "Don't be, I enjoyed it so much, I might want to try that again."

~

It was mid-afternoon, by the time Katherine marched up the grand staircase and into her office. Piles of papers and reports were stacked, neatly, into four piles. One might hope they were arranged from most important to least. She hung her coat on the rack and peeked into Stanton's office. Although the desk lamp cast a warm pool across the files on the desk in dim gray twilight, his chair was empty.

She had deflated the largest pile by the time Spratlin appeared, "Do you know what time it is?"

"No, actually, I just started working through all this stuff on my desk and completely lost track."

"It's six-thirty, could I interest you in some dinner?"

"What'd you have in mind?"

"How about a little French?"

"Victor's is always a treat and I'm famished."

"Then grab your coat and let's go. Mr. Charles has a warm car downstairs."

The huge black man tipped his hat and opened the rear door, "How are you feeling this evening?"

"I'm almost, but not quite, feeling myself again and I have you and so many others to thank for that."

"Just so we keep you that way," smiled Mr. Charles. He motored through light traffic to a restored Victorian mansion in a grove of trees overlooking a flowing brook at the edge of town. The driver dropped them at the entrance to the restaurant and parked in the shadows at the side of the building.

Victor, owner and Maitre d', met them with a warm smile, "It's lovely to have you with us this evening. Would you like your usual table by the windows near the fireplace?"

"That would be perfect," replied Stanton, following Victor and Katherine through several rooms, crowded with tables, to a small study overlooking the twinkling brook burbling through the trees.

"Could I bring you a cocktail?" asked Victor, offering menus.

"To tell you the truth, I think I'd like a glass of iced tea with a slice of lemon," replied Katherine, rubbing the bandage.

Spratlin smiled, "I'll have my usual."

"Two fingers of Cragganmore single malt Scotch and two ice cubes," laughed Victor. "I'll be back in a moment."

A waiter appeared with warm bread and cold butter, followed by their drinks. "Before you order, I'd like to offer two specials this evening, Sole Meuniere with a simple lemon-butter-parsley sauce and sautéed vegetables and Beef Bourguignon, a perfect recipe for a cool evening like this."

"I'll have the sole," said Katherine.

"And I'll have the beef."

"Would like an appetizer or a salad?"

"I'd love a little house salad, please."

"Do you have the onion soup this evening?"

"But, of course, this is a French restaurant, even if it is misplaced!" laughed the waiter, retreating to the kitchen.

Stanton took her hands, "I've been worried about you and I'm so very sorry that the ugly underbelly of society has taken it upon itself to attack innocent women and children, including you."

"At first I was scared," she paused, "and I guess I still am, but I'm mad too. The idea that people actually think like that in this day and age is beyond me."

"You were right, we do live sheltered lives."

"Well, I'm sick of pretending and I intend to do something about them."

Amused, Stanton asked, "Like what?"

"I got my hands on a list of the contributors to Miles Brantley's campaign and it's an interesting mix. I took it to Nellis Gray and, together, we broke it down into categories, like who's producing advertising and publicity and who's collecting and distributing donations and who's probably running around the countryside terrorizing innocent people."

"And?"

"It looks like it's based on a simplified corporate organizational structure with several divisions broken into branches to cover specific responsibilities. The financial arm is overseen by the moneymen for Hardman's Ministry. It's all run by the same guys, so who knows where the money's coming from or where it's going?"

"Figure that out and they could all go to jail."

"Unless they own the judge," replied Katherine, sipping her tea.

"I'm glad to see that fire and brimstone in your attitude, it's been waning for a while."

Katherine blushed, "I want to thank you, again, for putting me up at the house and I know it was awkward, at best, for everyone."

"Marjorie actually inquired about your health and suggested that I protect you, until the criminals are behind bars."

"She actually gave you permission?"

"Yes."

"I'll never understand your relationship with your wife."

Stanton took a swig on his Scotch, "That's a long, complicated story that still has chapters to be written before it's complete."

"That doesn't tell me anything."

"As well it shouldn't. You are my reprieve, my safe harbor from the insanity I've made of my relationships with my wife and my children." He looked up with a tear in his eye, "I know that you witnessed my confrontation with the boys at breakfast the other day and I'm embarrassed by the fact that they have every right to feel as they do. I was not an attentive father to either of them."

"What's the old quote, 'Passion isn't proper'? You abide by a code of ethics, a style of behavior that harkens back to the last century, when social status was clear-cut and human interactions within the gentry were prescribed and formal. Everyone knew their place. You might stand for all the right things but you're not one to pour your heart out over your beliefs. They're intellectual not emotional."

"That's true, I'm afraid I'm one of the last local representatives of the Gilded Age but that doesn't mean that I don't feel absolute love for my children or dedication to my principles."

"You do very well with adults but I don't think you remember how to play or the simple joy and wonder of being a child."

He sighed, "I'm not sure I ever was a child. Maybe that's why I enjoy having them around."

"I knew exactly who and what you were, before we ever got involved. I guess I had a fantasy about nurturing the warmth and goodness, that you hide deep behind of your stolid facade, but I'm afraid I've failed at that."

"You've brought nothing but joy into my life."

"I don't think it's enough. I need to decide what my future should be, before I get too old to start a family. The ol' clock's ticking and you're in no hurry to address the problem."

"After all that's happened, can't we just have a nice quiet dinner together?"

"Fine," replied Katherine. "Nellis Gray wanted me to suggest that you run for Curtis Hall's seat."

Stanton's mouth dropped open, "I've never even considered serving in public office and I've got the mess at the plant that needs to be cleaned up, before I commit to anything else."

"I told him that's what you'd say," replied Katherine. "Can you think of anyone else who has the stature and the intelligence to take on young Brantley? The Democrats are running Hal Blaney and we both know he's a born loser."

The waiter arrived with Katherine's Sole and the Beef Bourguignon, "May I bring you a glass of wine or another drink?"

"Just tea for me," replied Katherine, inhaling the scent of the lemon-butter.

"I'll have one more," said Stanton. The waiter disappeared and he continued, "I agree about Blaney but there has to be someone willing to take this guy down."

"Unless a major name shows up, the riff-raff are going to elect another racist nutcase and we'll have no one to blame but ourselves."

Over many dinners, they made a game of offering each other first tastes of their meals and, tonight, each savored the rich flavors on the other's fork. "I might have chosen second best," laughed Katherine, stealing one more morsel from Stanton's plate.

"It's certainly a compliment to chef Rollo that every dish is perfection."

"Can't go wrong in this establishment!"

They were quiet for a while, as they consumed the luscious meals, before Spratlin said, "Mr. Gray won't take on Brantley?"

"Mr. Gray wants no part of public office or the limelight, for that matter, other than when he's onstage playing music. I don't know him well enough but I'm guessing that he hides away in isolation on that farm to deal with his own demons. He's a good man, a righteous man, but he definitely has no interest in anyone else's opinions. He seems to have his own unwritten code."

He wiped his mouth with a linen napkin, "Maybe it's time for a woman to represent the district?"

Katherine smirked, "I'm not qualified."

"Why not? You understand systems and know how to motivate people, you'd be perfect."

"For one, in addition to being a corporate nerd, I've always voted Republican, just like mom and dad, and my sorority sisters, and pretty much everyone I knew, but I never had any reason to question who I was voting for. Somehow, after marching through life with blinders on, I think I'm beginning to find my own values and I find that I have no respect for anyone associated with these people."

"I'm, obviously, a Republican by birth but you know as well as I do that I believe in the welfare of the working middle class. There would be no commerce without their sweat and ingenuity and anyone who thinks otherwise shouldn't be in business."

"I can't argue with that but I'm not your girl. You have the status and the magnetism to make everyone forget about stupid young Brantley, who has no qualifications for anything past animal husbandry."

"You don't mince words when you're mad," laughed Spratlin. "That's why I adore you, you wear your heart on your sleeve."

"Adore…but not love?" replied Katherine, tears welling in her eyes. "Could we get the check, I think it's time to leave."

Stanton raised a finger to the waiter, "Could we have the check, please."

The server started to say, "No coffee or desert?" but noticed Katherine dabbing her eyes and removed their dishes without a word.

The Fleetwood appeared out of the darkness, as soon as they stepped outside, and Mr. Charles hurried around to open the door.

Spratlin said, "To Miss Kennedy's apartment, please."

He pulled out of the parking lot and turned onto Country Lane, heading back into town, noticing headlights coming up fast. Within moments, the glare filled the rear window and flashed in the mirrors. Mr. Charles tapped the brakes but the truck stuck to their bumper. He slowed and waved for the truck to go by, but it tapped the bumper once, twice, then rammed the rear end, grinding back and forth to throw the Cadillac out of control.

Mr. Charles yelled, "Hold on, we're going for a ride," and floored it, pulling away from the truck to roar through the curves along the river. The blue truck pulled along side and bashed the left rear, heaving the heavy car into a spin, but Charles turned hard right before punching the accelerator and swerving left to force the pickup off the side of the road. The Fleetwood pulled onto the highway to cross the bridge and merge into traffic. He called out, "Are you alright?"

"Yes, we're fine. That was a fine bit of driving, Charles. Thank you."

"No problem, Mr. Spratlin, those punks were amateurs."

"But they are persistent," said Katherine.

"I think you should stay at the Manor tonight," said Stanton. "No questions asked, just safe refuge."

"I want to be home with my own things."

"I want you to be alive in the morning. Please accept my invitation as genuine concern."

"Alright but I plan to move home tomorrow."

"Then, I'll hire a guard."

"If you must."

"Mr. Charles, would you please take us home."

"Yes, Sir, Mr. Spratlin. Straight away."

Mr. Charles stopped through the garage before heading into the kitchen for breakfast in the kitchen. The rear bumper was mangled and the front left quarter panel on the Cadillac was scraped up. There were streaks of blue paint running down the side of the car. "I'm bettin' there's a blue pickup with a sight more damage than this. And it shouldn't be too hard to find."

He walked across the courtyard into the kitchen and picked up the phone to dial the Sheriff's office to report the incident and to give a description of the pickup. Stanton appeared, as he said, "Yeah, it's the same bunch, I can guarantee that, Sheriff. Let us know if you find them." He paused, "Yes, Sir, I'll tell him."

He hung up the phone, "The Sheriff said that he'll have his men check the scene and all the body shops around town to see what they can find."

"If you hadn't called him, I was about to."

"No problem, Sir. It's time to put an end to this white trash."

"Amen to that," said Mama Louise. "We're supposed to be civilized."

"Unfortunately, these fools didn't get the memo," said Katherine. "Nellis Gray needs to know about this."

Stanton looked up, "You might tell him that you found a reluctant candidate to take on Brantley."

"Are you volunteering?"

"I don't see anyone else stepping up."

"Oh, you'll be wonderful," said Katherine, hugging him. "I'm very proud of you."

"We'll need to start the ball rolling. Will you come in to the office to attend to that?"

"Of course!"

Samantha and Sissy wandered in to take their plates to the table. "What's everyone smiling about?" asked Sissy.

Mama Louise brought a basket of hot rolls fresh from the oven, "Your father is going to run in the election to become a Representative in the House of Congress."

"Really?" said Sissy. "Would we get to go to Washington if you won?"

"Sure, you'd get to visit, but this would mean that I'd have to spend three or four days a week there and the rest here."

"I'd miss you," said Sammy, "but I'd sure be proud of what you were doing."

"That's reason enough, I guess," smiled Stanton. "It isn't official or anything but it has become a very real possibility."

"Will we have to call you Your Highness or Lord Spratlin or what?" asked Sissy.

"How 'bout you just call me Dad."

"Okay."

~

Katherine's voice buzzed through the intercom, "Dorothy Holcomb on the line."

"Thank you," replied Stanton, picking up the receiver.

Miss Holcomb was the daughter of Ben Holcomb, the last of the old-time political kingmakers in a state that had seen more than its share over the years. Where he and a handful of wealthy associates decided who would run and who would win, Dorothy used her knowledge of the skeletons buried in each candidate's closet to exert her influence over every contest.

"Dorothy, how are you?"

"I'm fine, darling, but you don't call me unless there's juicy gossip or you need a favor."

"Well, maybe this is a little bit of both. I've decided to run for Curtis Hall's seat."

"You do realize that you're taking on Cletus Brantley's boy and that ol' man isn't afraid to haul out the heavy artillery to get what he wants. Hell, I've heard he's stolen one homestead after another, until he owns most of several of counties."

"He represents everything that I detest."

"That's all well and good and, not that I'd disagree with you, but you've got to understand that this isn't the bush leagues. If you toss your hat into this ring, you better be damned sure that you don't have any embarrassing secrets that could destroy your campaign, if they were brought to light." She paused, "And don't say you don't, because none of us is as pure as Ivory Snow. If memory serves, you've got one sitting in the next office."

Spratlin hesitated.

"Don't ever hesitate. Know what the question is going to be before it's asked and have a foolproof answer to every possibility."

"Point made."

"I want you to make a list of all the things that you'd rather keep from the general public - including your relationships, your finances, your addictions and depravities, and those of everyone around you. If they can't find something in your past to use against you, they'll find something about Marjorie or your sons or your partners or best friends or distant cousins. It doesn't matter how far they have to dig, they'll find something and they'll use it."

"Their goons tried to run us off the road last night," replied Stanton. "That was a second attempt on Miss Kennedy's life, in addition to trying to murder Curtis Hall's black mistress and their four children. These animals have to be stopped and I don't see anyone willing to face the challenge."

"You have to understand that those racist bastards have cobbled together a base of zealots who've been brainwashed into believing that the government, or the immigrants, or anyone who doesn't look like you and me is coming to take everything they have. When you're poor, that ain't much, so they're basically buying protection. Elect this nutcase and he'll protect you from all these contrived monsters lurking just beyond the dark horizon."

"How can anyone worry about rights they don't even understand, when they can't afford to feed their children?" replied Stanton. "More than ninety percent of the population has no idea of what's in the Bill of Rights, let alone the Constitution or the Declaration of Independence."

"They don't have the education to take a job that would allow them to feed themselves or their children," said Dorothy. "That's the enigma, isn't it? You know and I know that the Republican Party has evolved into a gentlemen's club with the sole purpose of maintaining the status quo for the very top of the economic ladder. The conservative platform does not benefit the middle or lower classes, or women, or minorities, so they scavenge votes by catering to the poor and the ignorant with a message of fear to solicit the radical fringes on issues like abortion, or gun rights, or taxes, or immigration, or whatever. You've seen it all before."

Now Stanton paused for a long moment, "You're right, I have seen it all before but it was just colorful propaganda to get the voters excited. I never took the time to really analyze the subliminal context and who they were targeting. It was just our guy trying to look better than their guy."

"Modern politics isn't just some rich guy deciding he wants to feed his ego by claiming a need to serve his neighbors. It's a science, it's brutal and very personal warfare, and it's expensive, so, if you jump in, you'd better be in to the bitter end or it'll bury you."

"I've never asked but what party do you belong to?" mused Stanton.

"I'm Swiss! I can't afford to be beholden to either side, if I want to force them to come to me for their dirt," laughed Holcomb.

Chapter Nine

Nellis managed to read through the front section of the paper and reached for the local pages when the dogs sat up on alert, whimpering and whining. He looked across the yard to find Sissy and Samantha and four brown children trotting across the drive. The dogs pushed through the screen door to prance around the girls.

"Good morning!"

"Good morning," replied Sissy, bounding up the steps.

"To what do I owe this honor?" inquired Nellis. "And introduce me to your friends?"

"Oh, I'm sorry," said Sam, "This is Daniel, Hubie, Muriel, and Martin. They're Maybelle Brown's kids and they're staying with us, until all the crazy guys get put in jail."

"Yes, we've met briefly." The old man reached to shake each child's hand, "I'm pleased to see all of you looking so well, and, I guess, I should introduce my friends – Brandy, Mamasan, ChaCha, Gracie, and Cody. They make a lot of noise but, now that they know you, they won't hurt you."

Gracie nudged little Martin and licked his cheek and every child stroked the closest dog.

"So what brings you by so early in the morning?"

Sissy grinned, "Big news."

"And...?"

"Mr. Charles was driving my dad and Miss Kennedy last night and a pickup truck tried to push them off the road," said Sissy.

"And the truck crashed because Mr. Charles was such a good driver," added Samantha.

"Is everyone alright?"

"Yes," said Sissy. "They all came back to stay at the house after the accident. Is it still called an accident, even if it was on purpose?"

Nellis laughed, "We'll just call it an accident, even though we know it wasn't."

"There's more," said Sissy.

"What?"

"My dad's going to run for Congress," said Sam.

"Really? He'll make a fine candidate."

"Would you vote for him?" asked Sissy.

"Even though I belong to the other party, yes. I'll not only vote for him but I'll work for his campaign."

"Oh, good!" said Sissy. "We're going to convince every grownup we meet."

Nellis laughed, "I don't think any adult could possibly deny either one of you."

The girls curtsied.

Daniel leaned in, "We better get going or we'll be late."

"Yeah, let's go," said Sam. "Thanks, Mr. Gray. We'll come by later."

"I'll be around. You children be safe on your way to school."

"We're all stickin' together," said Sam.

The herd of children shimmered through the crisp morning light streaming across the drive and disappeared up the lane. Nellis picked up the local section but the phone rang in the kitchen.

"Hello?"

"Nellis, it's Katherine."

"I'm glad you're okay."

"News travels fast."

"Especially with youngsters!"

"Then you've heard the news?"

"Well, the girls said that a phantom pickup tried to run you off the road, again, but that Mr. Charles repelled the attack."

"The last we saw of the truck, it was spinning off the side of the road."

"That much damage ought to be easy to spot," said Nellis. "They also told me that Spratlin is going to run for office."

"He started the morning with an emotional commitment but, after a very sobering conversation with Dorothy Holcomb, I'd say he's giving it serious consideration."

"As well he should. I take it you still have a job?"

"I think I'm more confused than ever but, if he decides to go through with this, I can't abandon him, even if the whole situation has become…awkward."

"I hope I didn't contribute to your dilemma?"

"I hate to burden you with my problems, but you've become something of a touchstone for me, someone I can count on to keep me grounded, when things start whirling out of control."

"Life ain't easy is it?"

"It's become all complicated and convoluted and that doesn't seem to rile you one bit."

Nellis laughed, "I think it goes back to the Serenity Prayer, do what you can about the things you can, and don't fret the rest of it."

"That's succinct!"

"I like to write short songs that get straight to the point."

"Speaking of getting to the point, I've been doing a little research on our Reverend Hardman."

"Ain't nothin' Christian about that bastard," replied Nellis. "So, what'd you find?"

"I started with the library and it turned out that he wrote an autobiography about his first forty years, a money-making memoir for his parishioners, and they had a copy. I'm only part way into it but he started out as a kid preacher with his father's tent revival, traveling all over the Deep South. His old man went by the name Hannibal Hardman and, it seems, he was part carnival barker, snake oil salesman, and a hypnotic orator with a theatrical flair, and selling religion was easy pickin's. They sold a whole series of self-published interpretations of the Bible, 'authentic' religious relics from the Holy Land, and a medicine chest full of potions and powders. He claimed he could channel the power of God through his fingertips to heal the sick and drive the demons from the mentally ill."

"He got run out of more than one town for screwing the wrong woman and was shot in the groin by an irate cuckolded husband, at one of his meetings down in Tuscaloosa. The kid didn't miss a beat, kneeling to cradle his dying father and, covered in blood, he gave a sermon that had everyone in the tent weeping and wailing long before the cops showed up. Oh, and the assailant was found trussed to a cross suspended from the tent posts."

"Natural born shyster."

"He realized that he could make people do his bidding through the power of suggestion," said Katherine, "but that's just the beginning of his journey to bigger and more outrageous theatrical productions that draw tens of thousands to outdoor services around the world. He reaches out to millions of true believers every Sunday night, through his television and radio broadcasts, to solicit donations that come rolling in to his own private post office."

"So, money to run Brantley's campaign is just a drop in the proverbial bucket?"

"Bad pun, but you're right."

"We need to focus on our immediate concerns, like making sure the kid doesn't get elected, but I'd be real curious about who or what else those funds are buying?"

"I'm betting those tentacles reach into some interesting places."

"For sure. I've been talking to some old friends about old man Brantley. He was known as 'Clete' back in high school, where he had a reputation as a bruising fullback. Inherited the family spread from his daddy, who was fourth or fifth generation to run the homestead. Ol' Clete's been taking the family appetite for gobbling up land to the extreme, buying up every foreclosure he can find. Now he's trying to pull off a deal that would extend his property from Kansas, continuously, all the way to Texas."

"That's truly astonishing!"

"Farming and ranching take second place to the drilling that's sprouted up on most of the land he's bought in the past ten years. It was a minor part of his holdings before, now he's a major player."

"Who handles his money?"

"I heard he's hooked in with a couple of international banks in New York but I sure wouldn't be surprised if he wasn't financially involved with the good Reverend's people. They're both white supremacists and ultraconservatives out to protect their own from government interference on any level."

"Did you find out anything about how he went after the properties that he bought?"

"I talked to one guy, who mentioned a black farmer who suffered a wild fire that burned everything. He had to file for bankruptcy and Brantley got the property for taxes. The guy said he'd heard other stories like that."

"I'll see what I can find out," said Katherine.

"Good, I'll keep looking too. There's something useful buried in here someplace and we need to find it."

"I'll call you back, if I learn anything new."

"Call me back anyway."

"Okay."

He started back to the porch, ready to give up on the paper and get on with his chores, when the phone rang again.

"Hello?"

"Nellis, it's Sheriff Billings. Do you have a minute?"

"I guess I could squeeze an extra one in."

"I assume you've heard about the mash-up last night between Spratlin's Cadillac and another pickup?"

"Yeah, and I'm thankful that Mr. Charles is a good driver and the clown in the pickup wasn't."

"Well, the truck got sideswiped by a tree as it flew off the road. We found it, abandoned and submerged, in Turkey Creek. The tags had been removed and someone made a feeble attempt to scratch out the VIN number. Anyway, we traced it to Merlin Mathews and his buddy, Bobby Lynn Hawkins, who showed up at the hospital with a broken arm. We're holding both of them, until we can investigate further."

"I sure appreciate you sharing the information, Joe. I'm guessing these guys were in league with the first bunch of numbskulls?"

"Praise the Lord seems to be the common denominator but these two work for Russ Russell up at Triple Creek."

"How come I'm not surprised? We've got to stop these lunatics before someone actually gets killed."

"I can't arrest folks for having bad intentions, I need more than that."

Nellis hesitated, "Sheriff, it seems fairy obvious that this is a broad conspiracy that stretches from the open range through the pulpit all the way to Washington, D.C. What would it take to get a grand jury investigation?"

"I'd need detailed information about the connection between those who orchestrate everything to those who act on those orders, preferably from reliable witnesses or original documentation."

"How long would it take for a jury to be called?"

"You give me what I need and I could have them convened in two weeks."

"Thanks, I'll get back to you."

He leaned the tackboard up against a post on the porch and stared at the four cards across the top. "I'm bettin' those four have some buddies."

∼

It was after midnight, when Ned's panel truck eased through the gate and parked behind the barn. The dogs pranced around and nuzzled him for a pet, as he stretched his lanky body, grinning, "This is the best part of my work, bringing home the bacon! What're you cookin' for me this time?"

Nellis clapped him on the back, "I've got some beautiful chickens that I stuffed with a little rosemary and a whole head of garlic each. They've been smokin' for 'bout four hours, so I'm thinkin' they oughta be just about perfect."

"Hell, I'll give you two hundred grand for that meal."

By the time Ned showered, Nellis had platters with plump chickens reeking of garlic, roast potatoes, savory butternut squash, and peasant bread waiting on the table.

"Oh my, that smells so good! All I've had for the past two days is road food."

"Want a brew?"

"Sure."

Nellis brought two bottles of Coors, "A friend brought me a case from Colorado. It's got the consistency of piss-water but you can't buy it anyplace east of the Rockies."

"Yeah, it needs to stay cold but I'm pretty sure they invented refrigerated trucks a long time ago, so what's the big deal?"

"Who knows, maybe it's the novelty or something," replied Nellis holding up his brew, "Peace."

"Amen, brother. It's good to be here to enjoy some of your fine cooking." He sawed off a leg to gnaw on, "Oh, man this is fantastic. Did you smoke a bunch? One might not be enough!"

Nellis grinned, "I get a kick out of folks enjoying my cookin'."

"Speaking of cooking, what's happening with your candidacy?"

"Old man Spratlin's thinking about running and he's a much better choice than some ornery ol' dirt farmer. He's got social position and a bank roll to back his run."

"Yeah, what about his politics?"

"He's an old-time Republican but he's lined up against the last wealthy remnants of the Klan. A cranky old country Democrat like me has no chance in hell of beating a Republican, even one with no qualifications."

"So, you're backing a Republican? That's blasphemy!"

"Yeah, I know it's kinda strange but the alternative is downright scary," replied Nellis, passing a basket of hot bread. "Say, I've got a question."

"Yeah?"

"Weren't you an accountant in a previous lifetime?"

Ned smiled, "Yeah, I loved the work, I just couldn't sit behind the same desk all day every day. It made me more nuts than I am normally."

"Well, I'm working on some research about the Praise the Lord Ministries and a gangster rancher who's running his ignorant son for Curtis Hall's seat. There's a shitload of money washing through the accounting firm that's handling both of them. Hell, it's gotta be like a private bank and ol' Billy Joe's even got his own personal post office to keep the receivables private. I've got a hunch that there's way more to all of this than they want known but I don't know enough to know what I'm lookin' for."

Ned relished a bite of squash, "That's like eating a spoonful of butter."

"That's why they call it butternut!"

"Accounting firms are starting to move everything over to computers but most still have paper copies of everything because they're paranoid."

"In this case, their scared of the government and their clients!" laughed Nellis.

"Exactly. So, there's probably lots of files full of raw data that get consolidated down to a working set of books for the rancher. Actually, if you really are on to something illegal, there are probably two sets of books, one for the rancher to see the real numbers and another sanitized version for the auditor. They're both locked away in a safe in some bigwig's office."

"What about the Ministry?"

"That's a bigger kettle of stinky fish because they get huge piles of cash donations from all over the world and that's hard to track. It's like the money I brought to you tonight, if someone was tracking serial numbers on some of those bills and you deposited them in the bank, they could connect everything together but there's no way to know which individual bills are going where in an enterprise the size of the Ministry."

"I see what you mean."

"On that income level, cash becomes a problem of mass. They can't just pile it up in a warehouse somewhere, they have to use it, circulate it, run some through the banks or a stock broker to make everything look legit, but it would be very easy to scrape money off the top to be used for just about anything from gambling to hookers to illegal enterprises."

"Like a political campaign and the muscle behind it?"

"Sure, that'd be easy."

"Would there be a record somewhere?" asked Nellis.

"Knowing accountants, I'd say absolutely but I also know that they would bury that information, so only the need-to-know crowd could be privy."

"If you had those accounts in hand, could you tell what they were doing?"

"Sure but I kind of doubt that they'd just hand them over," said Ned, leaning back for a swig of his Coors. "That was one fine meal."

"Glad you enjoyed it."

"You're not thinking about thieving the files are you?"

Nellis grinned, "The thought had crossed my mind but it'd take a bit of reconnaissance and I'd need you to go with, to make sure we get what we need."

"No shit? No way! I take my chances on the road but I am not breaking into offices that are probably guarded by big dogs or wired for security, at the very least, and risk going to jail on a burglary charge!"

"Hell, it'd be shorter than conspiracy to distribute," laughed Nellis. "How long can you stick around?"

~

Nellis had the animals fed, the front section of the newspaper read, and was pouring a second cup of coffee before Ned rambled through the kitchen and out onto the porch in a dazed stupor.

The phone rang and Nellis picked it up, "Hello?"

"Nellis, it's Jazz, man. I'm in town for a few days and wondered whether we could get together to jam. We're doing Friday and Saturday at the Juke Joint. I've got the whole crew staying at my mom's and I brought along Jose, a Mexican percussion guy, who'll knock your socks off."

"Cool, I'm really glad you're back. We need to talk. Can you come by today?"

"Sure, man. I'll motor over after lunch."

"Okay, see you then." He paused, "Oh, what are you doin' awake at this hour of the day?"

"Haven't been to bed yet, it's the ol' 'miles to go before I sleep' thing," laughed Jazz.

He carried a cup of java out to Ned, "Would you consider helping figure out the dark secrets of the accounting firm, if I could guarantee you a safe entry and exit?"

"You can't, so don't ask."

"I don't know brother, I think maybe I can."

~

A bright yellow Volkswagen bus, a brilliant sunflower blooming in an otherwise dank gray afternoon, pulled up to the gate and honked. Nellis followed the dogs out of the barn to greet Jazz, who parked next to the panel truck and untangled himself from the cab to give Nellis a hug. "That's not Ned's ol' truck, is it?"

"Yeah, he's staying with me for a few days of R&R. Only problem is that he eats like a horse and I've got to keep meals comin' or he gets cranky."

"Sounds like the same old guy. Hell, I remember him eating four large pepperoni pizzas by himself one night in high school. I thought I was going to puke just watching him."

"And he's still no bigger than either of us."

"So, what'd you think about jammin'?"

"I think we ought to put on another concert to benefit Spratlin's campaign for Curtis Hall's seat, if he actually signs on."

"How come I know there's more to this than just playing a gig?"

"I'll explain it all to you when we get inside. Suffice it to say, I want to hold it in Town Square, right in front of the Praise the Lord Ministries building on a Saturday evening. We can get the Sheriff to call it a block party and close down the streets for a few hours."

"I know you better than that...so, there's an 'And' coming."

"And I need your skills with locks for a few minutes during our intermission, while the politicos give some speeches."

"What are we after?"

"Adjoining the Ministry is an accounting firm tht handles the books for Billy Joe and for young Brantley's old man and his gang of big spenders. I think it's really their private bank and I need some documentation to prove it."

"So you want to stroll in there and ransack the place, hoping to find a set of books that's probably locked up in a safe in the head guy's office?"

"No, we'll need some folks, who nobody knows, to do a little reconnaissance for us before the concert."

Jazz scratched a straggly goatee, "I've got that new percussionist, Jose, and a cool Mexican named Maria chick doing vocals, who could definitely play a part."

"Come on in and I'll buy you a cup of coffee to go with a really bizarre tale."

~

Katherine answered the phone, "Mr. Spratlin's office, this is Katherine. How may I help you?"

"Darlin', I need all the help I can get."

"Nellis? I'm starting to agree."

"I gotta know, is he in or is he isn't?"

"Still nothing definitive but I think a final decision is close. He's talking it over with his kids tonight."

"Good, because I'm putting together a little promotional concert in Town Square for publicity, donations, and to get people signed up to vote. Think a marching band and lots of flags, a little rock-n-blues music, maybe a big barbeque cook-off, and some fireworks and fiery speeches to get people excited."

"Knowing you, there's more to this than you're saying."

"Well, of course but I don't think this is the time to talk about all that."

"I could come by after work."

Ned and Jazz wandered in to the kitchen to collect a cold brew, chortling over some joke.

Katherine asked, "What's all that noise in the background?"

"I've got a couple of old friends over and they're entirely too noisy and they eat too much food."

"Did you invite them?"

"Foolishly."

"I think I need to meet them."

"You already know Jazz, the guitarist who played at the Armory. My friend Ned's in from Atlanta for a few days of tellin' lies and making up memories that didn't happen. I'm ashamed to admit that I've known 'em both since junior high."

"Then they probably know the unvarnished truth about the mysterious Mr. Gray," laughed Katherine.

"Maybe, if I threaten not to cook, they'll protect my secrets but I'm not puttin' much faith in that assumption."

"I'll see you in a couple of hours and...what's for dinner?"

Nellis found Ned and Jazz bantering on the porch, surrounded by the dogs. "Listen, Miss Kennedy's coming by and jokingly invited herself to dinner. If you two want to eat, I could use some help getting things straightened up and some veggies harvested for a salad, while I crank up the smoker."

"Hell, I made the mess inside," said Ned, "least I can do is clean it up."

"Cool, you can set the table for four while you're about it."

"And I'm definitely harvesting some greens but I need to call my Mama to let her know I've been hijacked by you two desperados, so she can look after my crew."

"Yeah, she's got that fabulous garden and the orchard behind."

"It's always provided just about everything we needed and none of the kids minded helping out, because we got to sample while we worked," said Jazz.

~

The last tinges of gold and crimson etched puffy clouds building in the west reflected in the windshield of the company station wagon, as it pulled up to the gate, followed by a black sedan. Katherine got out and marched back to speak to the driver. She drove through the gate and the other car turned around in the lane and headed out to the main road.

Nellis opened the door, "What was that all about?"

"I got fed up with staying in the guest room at Spratlin's, so Stanton hired a guard, who follows me around wherever I go. I told him I was in good hands, if he wanted to go find some dinner."

"I can't vouch for my friends, they're rather unsavory and just barely housetrained."

"That just makes them more interesting," laughed Katherine, kicking off her heels to stroll across the drive to the house barefoot. "I'm looking forward to meeting people who actually know you."

"I'm not all that mysterious, lady. I've just got some privacy issues."

"I'll say!"

They walked through the parlor into the kitchen and Jazz reached to shake her hand, "I'm Jazz and this heathen is Ned, who now lives in Atlanta. You must be Katherine and I've got to admit that I'm completely charmed. What could you possibly see in crusty old Nellis?"

"He's been a good friend, when I needed one," replied the beautiful brunette, accepting a glass of Merlot from Ned.

"All kidding aside, he's the most straight up guy I know," added Jazz. "He showed me that tackboard with all the lowlifes arranged according to duties and status but I just have to know how you're tied up in this whole political quagmire Nellis is trying to drag us into?"

She glanced at Nellis, "I'm Mr. Spratlin's personal secretary and I got to know Nellis when he proposed putting on your concert. Then, we collaborated on producing the infamous poster of Curtis Hall. I made the mistake of attending the funeral, out of guilt and curiosity, and got into a confrontation with dear, sweet Billy Joe Hardman. I was ambushed by his hit men, who demolished my car and left me in a ditch with a concussion. I probably wouldn't have survived, if Nellis hadn't dragged my unconscious body back to Spratlin House for medical attention."

"And you want me to believe that he's been the absolute gentleman, through all of this, with a beautiful, intelligent woman like you?"

"Yes, unfortunately," laughed Katherine, leaning to kiss Nellis on the cheek. He blushed and the boys cracked up.

She took a sip of her wine, "So, what are you planning or do I want to know?"

"Okay, well, if he decides to run, then I propose that we put on a concert at Town Square, right directly in front of the Praise the Lord Ministry building. During the speeches, we'll break into the accounting firm next door and Ned, who's also an ace accountant, will help us find that little nugget to spur a grand jury investigation."

"And how do you plan on getting in, finding your prize, and getting out without anyone in the crowd noticing?"

Nellis grinned, "Diversions, and…we've got Jazz, who's handy with locks. Harvey, his pianist, has a way with safes. His sound guys know more about electricity and alarm circuits than the mojos who install the systems, and Sunny Lynn and the backup singers are going to put on a little all-American medley with the marching band, followed by fireworks to keep everyone distracted."

"And you expect Spratlin to go along with this?"

"No, I expect you to arrange for him to talk for eight minutes and then introduce the high school band and the trio, who will sing for another eight, with the pyrotechnics overlapping for an additional four. That gives us twenty minutes to get in and out. By the time they're through, we'll be back on stage ready to rock."

"How are you going to know what you're looking for and where to find it?"

"Oh, we'll have some scouts check it out long before we go in," said Jazz.

"So, you're all in on this?"

Ned grinned, "He didn't really give us much choice, either we're in or we don't eat and, with his cooking, I'm pretty much putty in his hands."

~

Stanton knocked and peeked into Marjorie's bedroom. She was propped up against a bank of pillows in the glow of lamps on the night tables. Her eyes were clear and focused, "Come in. I've been waiting for you."

He walked to her bedside and took her hand, "And why is that?"

"Because, I know you have something important that you want to discuss with me."

"And how do you know that?"

"I am still the mistress of this house. It's my business to know things."

Stanton laughed, "Well, of course, you're right." He paused, "I would like to ask your opinion about my running for Curtis Hall's Congressional seat in the election."

"I think you would make a superb candidate but I have two questions. The first is how will this distraction affect the recovery at the plant? The second is what motivated you to take on this challenge?"

He sat on the edge of the bed, feeling like a young boy seeking the approval of his mother for some outlandish plot. "We're not out of the woods, by a long shot, but we have turned the corner on rebuilding the pension funds. I got new financing, while I was in New York, which cuts our interest rate and extends our credit line for operations, and the sales staff have brought in several new contracts. Little by little, we'll restore the fund completely and I truly believe that Jules Schreiber has convinced the union guys of our sincerity."

"Just so you're on top of things."

"We've got good people working on every aspect of it and I have faith in them. The second question goes back to those same people who terrorized Miss Brown and her children, ran Miss Kennedy off the road, and tried again the other night. I have every reason to believe that they're being directed by Billy Joe Hardman and Cletus Brantley, the father of young Miles, who's also running for that seat."

"How can you suggest that Reverend Hardman could possibly be involved?" demanded Marjorie.

Stanton stood, "You know, as well as I do, that the man is a charlatan, at best, with the morals of a snake-oil salesman. It's also become obvious that the one thing that all these goon squads have in common is attending his services."

"I just won't believe that of the man," replied Marjorie, dabbing her nose with a silk hankie.

"Our society ought to have conquered racist hate generations ago but there's always going to be a group of ignorant people who fear anyone different. Men like your dear Reverend feed those illiterate minds with twisted scripture that reinforces their feelings of superiority and privilege, while stoking their paranoia about 'those' people who are going to come and take everything. From there, it's easy to justify hate and violence, because it's turned into us against them and we are the anointed."

"You're not afraid to show your conviction, I haven't seen this Stanton in years."

"It's come down to a rather simple calculation, first, there is no one willing to stand against this young man or all that he represents…and, after considerable consideration, it's become obvious to me that this is the right thing to do."

"Then you have my blessing."

He stood, "You do realize that this could get nasty, that our family secrets could be spread all over the front page of the paper?"

"We both know that's part of the price of celebrity and good gossip is hard to come by in a small community like ours."

He kissed her hand, "Thank you."

"No, thank you for standing up for what's right. It's about time."

~

The children, summoned to attend dinner, were surprised to find the table in the kitchen set with everyday China instead of linens, silver,

and crystal in the formal dining room. Sissy wandered over to the stove
to hug Mama Louise, "Why are we eating in here?"

"Because that's what you father requested. He'll be down in a
few minutes."

Maybelle added a half dozen pieces of fried chicken to the
platter in the oven and started another batch. She turned to Louise,
"You're sure he won't mind my kids sitting in?"

"No, he said all the kids."

Brad opened two cold beers and handed one to Bruce, "Here's
to family dinners."

Stanton appeared in the doorway, "Why don't you open one
more for me?"

The eldest son grabbed another bottle and handed it to his
father, "What's so important that we all have to sit down together?"

"I'll get to that when we're all here."

With that Daniel, Hubie, Muriel, and Martin trooped in the
kitchen door. Maybelle gave each a hug in turn, "Now everyone wash
your hands, we'll be serving up fried chicken with mashed potatoes and
green beans in a minute."

"We've got fresh squeezed lemonade for you youngsters, so
wash up and find a place at the table," added Louise.

Platters were passed and the children chattered through dinner,
until Stanton tapped a spoon against his water glass. "The reason that
I've asked all of you to have dinner with me is because I need your
opinion and, perhaps, your blessing. I want to run for Curtis Hall's
Congressional seat but I will not commit unless every one of you
approves."

"Why is it up to us?" asked Samantha.

"And do you mean to include us too?" asked Muriel.

"I mean all of you," replied Spratlin. "If I decide to do this, we
will all be under the scrutiny of the press and I am absolutely positive
that Brantley's people will use anything that they can find to embarrass
us and, if they can't find anything, they'll make something up."

"They're not good people," said Mr. Charles, who entered from
the courtyard.

"I think my...lifestyle might hurt your chances," said Bruce.

"You are my son and I love you just the way you are but, at the same time, I don't want to put you in the limelight, if you might be hurt or embarrassed."

Bruce stood up and walked over to hug his father, "I can't believe you just said that."

"It's what I believe."

"Don't worry about me, I'll try not to embarrass you."

Stanton turned to Brad, "What do you think?"

"I'm actually proud of you for even considering taking on those...bad people, especially when no one else seems to have the guts. I chased that fat phony off the property the last time he came by to bless Momma and, if you need some dirt on him, I've got something that will make the censors blush. I'm definitely in."

He looked to Sissy, Sam, and the other children, "And what do all of you think?"

"You saved my Mom from those men and gave all of us a chance to feel safe and to go to a good school," said little Martin. "You're our hero."

Stanton blushed, "So, am I to interpret all of this as your approval for me to run in the election?"

"You just let us know what we need to do and we'll be there for you," said Bruce, scanning the younger children.

"We'd vote for you, if they'd let us," said Sissy.

"Then it's decided," said Stanton hugging all the children at once.

The children wandered off, after thanking the ladies for a wonderful dinner, and Spratlin retired to the library to make a few phone calls. The first, to Katherine, went unanswered. The second rang through to Nellis Gray. "Mr. Gray, this is Stanton Spratlin. I've decided to run for Congressman Hall's seat and I'm hoping that I can count on your support."

"That's wonderful news," said Nellis. "I'm here with Miss Kennedy and two of my friends. We've been planning a benefit concert for two weeks from now, if you did decide to jump in. We'll provide the crowds, you provide one hell of a speech."

"I can do that and I appreciate your enthusiasm. Might I speak with Katherine?"

"Oh course, hang on."

Nellis handed her the phone, "I'm delighted to hear the news!"

"I tried to call you earlier but I'm glad that you're among the first to know."

"I'll be at the office in the morning, raring to go."

"This could get ugly," said Stanton, "and I don't want our relationship to become public fodder."

"We're grown ups who knew the dangers, when we started our affair," replied Katherine. "If they want to play rough, I think we've got the right people on our side."

"I hope you're right."

"Have you talked to Dorothy Holcomb yet?"

"No, she's next on the list."

"If you can get her blessing, I think we can win this thing."

"We'll see what she has to say. I'll see you in the morning."

"Count on it."

Chapter Ten

Nellis, Jose, and Maria sat in the old pickup across Towne Square from the offices of Paisley/Hatch Accountants, located in a traditional red brick building with black shutters and doors against white trim, nestled in like a dollhouse next to the base of the grand staircase to Hardman's gaudy cathedral.

"It might be a while," said Nellis. "We don't have any idea of whether or when ol' Cletus might show up."

"We can be patient," said Maria. "I'm looking forward to playing my part."

"You know what we're looking for."

"Yeah, who Brantley visits in which office and where the Ministry honey pot is buried," replied Jose.

"Hey, look!" said Maria, pointing to a long black Cadillac pulling up in front of Paisley/Hatch. "Is that him?"

Nellis lifted binoculars, as a heavyset man in an expensive leather coat climbed out, slicked back his silver hair to hoist a gray ten-gallon hat, hitched up his pants, and marched up the sidewalk. "That's him! Go! Go!"

The couple ran across the lawn, past a fountain of angels, to follow Brantley into the building just as the door was hissing closed.

He greeted the receptionist, "Morning, Janet, is Ted in today?"

"Good morning to you, Mr. Brantley. I'll just ring his office."

She spoke quietly into her headset, "Mr. Riley, Mr. Brantley is in the lobby. Fine, thank you." She hung up the phone and looked up, "Mr. Riley will be here in a moment, if you'd care to have a seat."

"Why, thank you, Ma'am." Cletus settled into a leather wingback chair and picked up a National Geographic.

Jose guided Maria, who was wearing a deep burgundy shawl over her hair, up to the desk and the receptionist smiled, "How may I help you?"

Maria pulled the scarf around her face, nervously, "My mother sent me to make sure that the donation she sent to you got here."

"Why are you asking here?"

"Because the Ministry's all locked up and the post office box on the contribution envelope is registered to the Ministry at this address. The name on the application is Trevor Hatch," replied Jose. "I believe he is one of the principles in your firm."

"Praise the Lord Ministries is one of our clients but I'm not sure we could track an individual contribution. What is it you want to know?"

"Well, I knew my mother had scrimped and saved her money for years and years and she always watched the Reverend Hardman's broadcasts. So, when he said the good Lord was going to take him, if he didn't collect enough money to feed the starving children in Ethiopia, she sent every last penny," said Maria sincerely. "She got a confirmation from the Post Office that her letter had been delivered but she never heard anything back from the Ministry, so she asked us to find out what happened to her money."

She started to cry, "Without that money, I don't know how we'll afford her hospital bills."

The receptionist looked sympathetic, "I'm so sorry."

"This is her dying wish, making sure that her hard-earned dollars are going to be used to save those children, if they can't be used to save her own life," said Jose. "We'd like to speak with Mr. Hatch, if that's possible?" He glanced at Brantley following Riley up a circular staircase, into a hallway on the right and, from the flash of shadows, into the first office on the left.

The receptionist looked frazzled and dialed a number. She waited a moment, inspected the impoverished couple, "Yes, Margie, I've got a Mr. and Mrs....?" She looked up expectantly.

"Ortega," whispered Maria.

"Ortega, here, and they have a question for Mr. Hatch about what happened to their mother's donation."

She listened, "Yes, I realize this is unusual but a few moments of his time with concerned contributors might be useful for everyone. It seems that the woman who made the donation is terminally ill and wants some assurance that her contribution will go to help the children in Ethiopia."

"Thank you, I'll bring them up." The receptionist stood, "If you'll follow me, Mr. Hatch has just a moment in his schedule."

"Oh, thank you," gushed Maria. "Mama will be so relieved to know that her gift is appreciated."

They followed her up the curving stairway to a balcony, noticing plush offices off the hallway to the right, as she punched a code into a panel next to double doors on the left. While the lobby and public areas were furnished in heavy fabrics, crystal chandeliers, and traditional antiques, this wing was ultra modern with recessed lighting, industrial gray carpeting, and brushed stainless accents. Glass block walls formed a blurry tunnel, above a giant room filled with workers in cubicles, that opened to a circular reception desk in the center of an atrium, surrounded by executive offices.

A matronly brunette stood to greet them, "Mr. and Mrs. Ortega, I'm so glad that you took the opportunity to stop in the see us today. Mr. Hatch is expecting you."

"Gracias," said Maria, following her into the office directly behind the desk.

Trevor Hatch, a heavyset sixty with salt and pepper hair accenting dark beady eyes under bushy brows knotted across a permanent crease in his brow. He winced a smile and reached a beefy hand to Jose, "Mr. and Mrs. Ortega, thank you for coming. How can I help you?"

Maria curtsied, "My mother sent her entire life savings, when Reverend Hardman said that the good Lord was going to take his life, if he didn't find a way to feed all those starving children in Ethiopia. As it turned out, she's in the hospital with no money to pay the doctors or the bills, so she asked us to come here to make sure that her donation was being used to feed those kids."

Jose added, "We know that we're intruding on your busy schedule but how could we deny her dying wish?"

"I don't see how you could," said Hatch. "Will you please have a seat? Could we get you anything - coffee, tea, a glass of water?"

"No, thank you," replied Maria. "We just need some way to prove to her that her good intentions are being fulfilled."

"Well, I'm not sure that it's even possible to track down an individual contribution, once it's been processed and placed in the fund. If there's a note or letter with instructions on how it is to be used, then our tellers make sure that those gifts are applied to an individual account for that particular project. In this case, they would have gone into the Ethiopian Children's Fund."

"Would there be any record of that?" asked Jose.

"Well, we receive so many contributions from donors all over the world, it would be difficult, if not impossible, to extract one transaction. How much was her contribution for, if I might ask?"

"Five-thousand two-hundred and eighty-six dollars," replied Maria, gazing around at the sleek Scandinavian furniture, splashy abstract art, and an expensive golf bag full of clubs, leaning in the corner. "I'm sure that's not enough to even cause a ripple in your accounts."

"We treasure every contribution from the piggy bank, that one little girl sent in, to people like your mother, who send in their savings to help our brothers and sisters in need."

"So, you're saying that you can't offer any proof that you received her donation or what happened to those funds?"

"I'm saying that every donation is applied where it is intended to go but we are not required to keep individual records of amounts less than one hundred-thousand dollars," replied the accountant brusquely. "I can only offer you my assurance that our people are trained to treat every transaction with care and respect. Everyone on our staff is dedicated to fulfilling the mission of the Ministry."

"I guess that will have to do," replied Jose, standing to leave.

"Mama will be so disappointed," cried Maria, burying her face in her hands.

"Now, now, dear," said Hatch, offering an embroidered handkerchief. "Let me see if we can arrange for a certificate that you could take back to her."

The matronly secretary appeared at the door, "Miss Hancock, would you be kind enough to have someone fill out a personalized document made out to…what was your mother's name?"

"Marcia Sanchez," sniffled the young woman.

"Yes, Mrs. Sanchez contributed five-thousand dollars to the Ethiopian Children's Fund and I'm sure an official reply would help ease her doubts."

"Five-thousand two-hundred and eighty-six dollars," whimpered Maria.

"Yes, Sir." She backed out of the Hatch's office and reappeared moments later waving a flashy form letter with the Ministry Logo floating in billowing clouds, a hand-lettered acknowledgement, and Hardman's signature stamped at the bottom. She handed it to Hatch, who inspected it and offered it to Maria.

"I know this is completely insufficient but I hope it will help your mother believe that every penny of her hard-earned money is going to help the needy. That's the whole purpose of Reverend Hardman's Ministry, helping the needy, the sick, and the helpless to a better life. I know he prays for every donor every day."

"Well, thank you for your time," said Jose, lifting a weeping Maria out of the chair and escorting her out of the office.

She turned, "I assume there's no chance of getting some of that money back to pay the hospital bills?"

Hatch frowned, "I'm sorry but I don't see how that could be accomplished."

She stared for a long moment, before they followed Miss Hancock through the glass tunnel, out through the double doors to the balcony, where Riley and Brantley were just emerging from the first office in the other hallway. The rancher was saying, "You make sure to get Billy Joe on board, so we can move when we need to."

"I'll take care of it," replied Riley.

Jose turned to the secretary, "Thanks for your help."

"I wish we could offer more," replied the woman, as the couple slowly descended the circular staircase behind the two men.

Jose and Maria walked slowly down the path to the sidewalk and around the square to the pickup truck. They climbed into the cab just as Brantley's black Cadillac pulled away from the curb and exited down Second Street in the opposite direction.

"How'd it go?" asked Nellis.

Maria grinned and handed him the form letter, "Those bastards don't keep records of contributions less than a hundred thousand dollars!"

"And we know exactly where they keep their secret files," added Jose.

"Where?"

"There's a giant walk-in safe behind the bookcase in Hatch's office. Someone didn't bother to close the door all the way. The only problem is that the executive offices are buried upstairs in a secure wing."

"Damn," said Nellis, "are we going to have to crack the code?"

Maria giggled, "Nope, I watched the receptionist punch in 2-4-4-9."

"You're terrific," said Jose, hugging her. "I couldn't see her fingers."

"You have to walk through a long hallway with glass bricks on either side that reveal a huge workspace with lots of cubicles."

"We couldn't tell but I'd guess there could be a hundred, maybe a hundred and fifty," added Jose.

"What about Brantley?" asked Nellis.

"His guy is Ted Riley and his office is the first on the left off the right upstairs hallway. If the secret books aren't kept in his safe, I'll bet they're in Paisley's office and I'll bet his office is at the end of that corridor."

"And there's something brewing," said Jose, "because Brantley told Riley to get Billy Joe lined up for something."

"He said, 'Get Billy Joe on board.'," added Maria.

"Great work, you guys. This will help a lot!" said Nellis, cranking up the engine to pull into thin traffic.

~

A rat-a-tat of sticks slapping snares, over the 'um-pa' of mallets pounding bass drums, set the tempo for a trill of flutes and horns as the

Cameron High School Band marched up First Street and around the square to the tune of 'Good Times are Here Again.' They stopped in front of a stage constructed of two flat-bed trucks covered in red, white, and blue bunting facing the Ministry building, so the background for the audience included the cityscape rather than Billy Joe's garish edifice.

The first Halloween decorations were obscured by a forest of American flags lining the edges of the plaza, behind two-dozen giant smokers wafting licks of sweet hickory and ready to serve up a feast for hungry patriots. The marching band finished a rousing rendition of 'America' to cheers and applause from a growing crowd slowly packing the quadrangle around the fountain.

Nellis stepped up to the mike and grinned at Sam and Sissy and the other children, who were planted front and center. "I'm Nellis Gray and y'all know the band, Jazz Taggart and his band of Merry Men!"

The band played a few bars before Nellis cut in, "We'd like to welcome you to a celebration of our community, of all that we've survived together because we believe in each other. So, we're gonna play some music for ya' to give everyone time to visit each and every one of our celebrity chefs, who made sure to have plenty of everything. Get a tasting ticket at one of the booths, they're only five dollars to sample locally grown beef and pork from each of the vendors. I promise you, you won't be disappointed!"

Cheers.

"Oh, I almost forgot, for those so inclined, there are two wagons serving liquid refreshments at opposite corners of the Square but don't tell, because some people frown on such behavior." He pointed across the commons with a grin and a laugh. "If anyone has not registered to vote, please visit the booth over here to the right of the stage and these fine people will get you set up."

The drummer pounded out a few bars of a marching beat.

"So, as I said, we're going to play you a few tunes, then we'll turn it over to Dorothy Holcomb, who has an announcement she'd like to share with each and every one of you. Then the silver voices of the Satin Sisters, featuring Mazy Jane, and our own Sunny Lynn, team up with the

Cameron High School Marching Band for a medley of patriotic songs and some fireworks! After all that, we'll be back to boogie. Y'all enjoy!"

The band kicked in to a roaring rendition of 'For All That's Right and True' as streaks of crimson brushed passing clouds and the streetlights flickered and flashed through a thin haze of barbeque smoke, illuminating a jovial milling crowd. The Praise the Lord Temple glowed with ecclesiastical excess but the brick building next door remained dark. Two of the band's roadies appeared out of the crowd next to the mixing board and Jerry grinned, as he held up a thumb.

The sky was dark by the time the band finished the set. Nellis said, "We'd like to thank all of you for coming! We hope you're enjoying the chow and stay tuned for Cameron's own, Dorothy Holcomb!"

A stout little woman tottered across the stage to the microphone. She wore a red and white shawl over a blue dress and styled salt and pepper hair framed a pale round face with piercing blue eyes that did not smile with her pouty lips. "Ladies and gentlemen, y'all know me and, if you don't, then I'm sure you've heard of my daddy, Ben Holcomb. My family has been involved in local and state politics for more than a century and, in all that time, we have never publicly endorsed a candidate for any office…until now."

The crowd settled down to listen, "Now, you may or may not know that I am an independent, which means I don't have to prove my loyalty or take any sass from either political party. I am for the most qualified candidate for the office they are seeking, period." She paused, "But this election is different. As reported in the Gazette, there have been several racially motivated attacks over the past few months and I have to ask myself, how is it possible that people can be that cruel and ignorant in this day and age? When our founding fathers wrote that government was to be of the people, by the people, and for the people, that includes everyone, no matter their race, color, or their religion. We are all equal under the law of this great land!"

The crowd cheered.

"I'm here to tell you that the current candidate for this seat has no qualifications what-so-ever. Sure, we're seeing lots of expensive posters with his smiling face and there are endless ads on radio and television showing him working with his daddy on the ranch but you never hear him actually speak. What they don't tell you is that he barely graduated from high school, couldn't get into a real college, and was turned down by the Army and the Coast Guard as unfit. All of which means that it's quite possible that an illiterate racist, whose only expertise is in animal husbandry, will represent our district in the next session of Congress. You can bet he'll be taking orders from daddy and his cronies, who ponied up the money to pay for the kid's election!

My daddy'd tan my fanny, if he could hear me talkin' today. He'd say, we don't tell people who to vote for, we try to get the parties to put up candidates who are worthy of the honor of serving." She gazed across the sea of faces and grinned, "You know, he might actually approve of this because someone needs to tell the voters the truth about what's going on behind all the splashy advertising and clever patriotic mumbo-jumbo. Unless you're a racist sexist bigot who wants to turn the calendar back a hundred and fifty years, Miles Brantley's candidacy is a sad joke!"

She watched ripples of applause consume little eddies of catcalls and boo's. "Washington does not need another ignorant hot-head spewing fanatical rhetoric and claiming to be fighting for God, the Constitution, and the American People. God. Really? I'm fairly sure that he can take care of himself and, besides, we have plenty of preachers in this country to remind our citizens about their moral shortcomings. But that's good advertising, it sounds good, in spite of the fact that our founding fathers were God-fearing men who fought and argued to ensure that church and state would remain separate. As to the Constitution, I'd be willing to wager, even though that's illegal in this state, that Candidate Brantley's never even read the document, let alone has a clue what it all means. And then there's the promise to defend the American People...which people? From what? Is he going to stand up for every one of us or just some of us? What about black people and brown people and red people? And what if we don't believe or support his policies or his sham religion, will he defend our right to disagree? I think not!"

Murmurs.

"In spite of what the talking heads on the television tell you, it is our responsibility, every one of us, to dig a little deeper to really understand who we are voting for. Far too often, our system presents the dilemma of choosing between two distasteful choices and there is no 'None of the Above' box to check on the ballot, if we don't like either one. Despite your disagreement with one candidate's stand on something that's dear to you, if the person you vote for is not qualified, that affects the whole country. Don't be duped into voting for the wrong person for the wrong reason! Every vote counts!"

The crowd was silent, "So, considering that a vote for young Brantley is against everything we stand for in our wonderful little town, I would like to propose another candidate for this office, a man that you all know as a philanthropist, a community leader, and President of Stanton Oil, Mr. Stanton Spratlin!"

Polite applause rolled across the plaza but few, if any, turned away. The Spratlin children cheered. Stanton hugged Dorothy and stepped to the microphone. He wore a dark blue pinstripe suit with a plain red tie and a little American flag pin on his lapel. "Ladies and gentlemen, I grew up here, just like most of you, and my family put down roots, generations ago, by building the refinery into what it is today and employing your parents and grandparents and many of you. I'm proud to say that we're a community that, through celebrations and natural disasters, has always stood together for the common good. It's our custom to protect and care for each other, when we need each other most."

He paused to look out at the crowd, "Recent events, in our city and in my life, forced me to take a long hard look at what grounds my ethics and my principles. As I discovered, it's far too easy to become isolated and comfortable, oblivious to racism, hatred, and violence happening right here in our little village. Even worse is allowing that sense of security to excuse our own responsibility to stand up and shout at the top of our lungs, 'We will not allow this to happen in our town...or the next town or the one beyond that. This is where it stops!'"

The vast majority of the audience burst into rowdy applause.

Shielded by a wall of flags and the glare of lights on the stage, Nellis, Jazz, and a crew of six slipped across the street and into the unlocked back door to the offices of Paisley/Hatch. The two roadies, Matt and Jerry, took up posts at the front and back, while Jose and Maria led the charge up the curved staircase to dart into Ted Riley's office. Harvey, the pianist, inspected a heavy safe hidden behind a double-door cabinet. He pulled out a stethoscope and knelt next to the steel box, "This one's a beaut, I'll have to use my special talents."

"You guys stick with him, I'll take the rest of the posse across the hall," said Maria, leading Nellis and Jazz across the balcony, through the security doors and the darkened glass hallway to the executive offices surrounding the atrium.

"Holy Shit!" said Jazz. "If these guys get to hang out in digs like this, I'm changin' my profession!"

"Yeah, man, I can see you doin' a pious James Brown thing with the cape and the limp," whispered Nellis. "They'd be throwin' wads of cash to save your ass!"

Jazz picked the lock to Hatch's office and Maria padded around the desk to pull a panel in the bookcase revealing a far larger, walk-in safe.

Jazz whistled quietly, "Now that's a safe!" He checked the hinges and the seals, then the locking mechanism. "This thing might be big but it's ancient technology, I could probably open it, if I had Harvey's stethoscope or a crystal wine glass."

Ned and Harvey burst into the room, "We found Brantley's books and I've got Jose photographing them."

The pianist walked up to the safe with a grin, "I haven't seen one of these in years, this is definitely old school!"

"Hell, I could open that sucker," said Jazz. "Get on with it, so we can get the fuck out of here, before someone comes snooping around."

Harvey leaned close to the mechanism and twisted the dial gently, noting the clicks. "Fuck, really?"

"What?" asked Nellis.

"The combo is 07-04-17-76, can you believe that?"

He heaved the door open and Ned pointed a flashlight to scan across several dozen binders stacked on two shelves. Finally, he said, "Ah, here we go!"

He reached in and pulled out two heavy black books, which he opened on the floor, placing the light in his mouth to use both hands to flip through the pages. He picked up the second book and scanned the entries. Several loose sheets dropped to the floor as he pulled the flashlight out of his mouth, "This is dynamite."

Ned pulled a Minox camera with a tiny flash from his pocket and Nellis turned the pages as he snapped one frame of each.

He was four pages from finishing the second book, when Jerry ran into the room, "We've got company!"

Jazz looked up, "What's cookin'?"

"Security guard from the Ministry strolled over to look around, probably wondering why all the lights are off. No doubt he's going to call for help."

"Is Matt keeping an eye on him?" asked Maria.

"Yeah, he's around back but I don't think he's got keys to get in, he's been jiggling the doors." He glanced at his watch, "And the girls have been singing for seven minutes."

"That means we've got five to get out of here and back on stage," said Nellis.

"I'm done," said Ned, "Let's go."

They replaced the books in the safe and Harvey locked it up, leaving it set exactly as he found it. The crew ran through the glass tunnel and across the balcony as Jose was coming out of Riley's office.

"I didn't touch the safe."

"Great, I'll take care of it," said Harvey, putting the binder back on the shelf and securing the door. "Let's hit the road."

They tiptoed down the staircase, freezing against the wall as the beam of a powerful flashlight traced through the lacy curtains on the windows, then moved to the other side of the front door. Jerry led them down a hallway to a utility room and the back door. Matt held them up, "Is he still around front?"

"Yeah," replied Jerry, "I think he's coming around the far side."

"Then, let's head the other way," said Nellis, leaning out to peer up and down the alley. "Let's go!"

"Wait," said Ned, pulling him back inside, as the beam swept across the pavement outside. "Lock the door and hide."

Matt latched the door and everyone ducked down. The guard ran the light through the window to inspect the entire room, before he wiggled the door handle and wandered away.

"We can't just bust out of here, man," said Jazz. "We need a diversion with some style."

"Like what?" asked Ned.

"Well, like we were out here smokin' a reefer, man. That'd give that pig something else to think about, besides someone breaking into this place."

"You know, he's on to something there," said Ned. "Anybody got a spare joint on 'em?"

Nellis grinned and pulled a fat joint out of his pocket, "I've got just what we need, I was saving it for after the gig."

"This is the moment," said Ned.

"Okay, someone see if he's gone around the corner and I'll fire it up."

Matt opened the door to peer out. The alley was vacant and the crew slipped out, securing the door just as the guard popped around the corner.

He pointed his flashlight, "What are you folks doing out here?"

Jazz stumbled over to him, waving the joint, "Ah, man, you ain't gonna arrest us for tokin' a little weed are you? We've got to keep these folks entertained for at least another hour or two and we're were just getting in the groove, if you know what I mean? We ain't doin' nobody no harm, Officer, honest. We're just getting' high."

"First, that's illegal, and, second, this is private property. You guys clear out or I'll call the real cops and have them arrest you for possession or trespassing, at the very least."

"Yes sir, officer. We'll be moving right along, right along," said Jazz, doing a little jig, as the rest of the crew ambled out onto the street. "You have a good evening now, ya' hear?"

The crowd cheered as country singer Sunny Lynn and Mazy June and the Satin Sisters belted a rousing acappella rendition of 'America the Beautiful' and rockets exploded over the plaza in dazzling glitters. Nellis glanced over at the massive stairway rising up to the entrance of the Ministry where three men, accompanied by two uniformed deputies, stood watching the festivities. He mumbled, "Oh, shit!"

The rest of the crew followed his gaze and Harvey said, "We've gotta get on that stage before those assholes try to talk up this crowd."

"Let's go!" said Jazz, prancing along outside the line of flags, overwhelmed by whiffs of hickory-smoked beef and pork and the sweet tangy scent of barbeque sauce.

They stopped at the corner of the stage to look back across the commons, where Billy Joe Hardman and both Brantley's, escorted by the security cops, were charging through the crowd. Jazz grabbed Nellis, "Gotta go!"

Before the ladies scooted off the stage, the band was plugged in and cranking through the opening bars of an irreverent protest song, 'Meager Minds'.

The five men stopped at the front of the crowd to stare up at Jazz and Nellis, who were trading guitar licks and oblivious to their arm-waving and hollering. Twelve-thousand watts of power through the PA system was barely enough to overpower Billy Joe Hardman's screechy tenor. When the jam finally faded, the Reverend yelled, "I'd like a word with these fine citizens."

"Who invited you?" asked Nellis. "And, oh yeah, the political part of this party is over. We're just here to entertain our neighbors."

Jazz started a Jimi Hendrix version of the 'Star Spangled Banner' and the crowd roared.

Not taking 'No' for an answer, Billy Joe led the Brantleys to the stairs at the far end of the flatbed and marched up to a microphone. He held up his worn Bible, "It's nice to see so many brothers and sisters gathered together for this celebration, in the shadow of our chapel, and I look forward to seeing you at services in the morning. It's too bad that only some of the candidates were invited to speak and, considering this is a free and democratic society, I do believe that the front-running candidate should have been included!"

He held his Bible above his head, "With your votes, Miles Brantley will join a legion of candidates, who are about to rise up to defend millions of oppressed Christian citizens. These candidates are dedicated to taking back our rights and our government from the liberal clique, who have tried to cram their socialist agenda down the throats of God-fearing Americans for far too long. The future of our country depends on the unity and determination of White Christian America!"

Modest applause.

"I believe you've been told by Stanton Spratlin that there have been numerous racial atrocities in our fair city. What he didn't tell you was that, according to the stories I heard, there was a confrontation when a landlord tried to evict the riff-raff who wouldn't pay the rent. If the fact that the landlord was white and the tenants were black means that it was a racial incident, well, then so be it."

Nellis stepped up to the mike, "Actually, Reverend, I was there that night and I tell can you and these fine folks the truth about what actually happened, just so there isn't any misunderstanding about terminology here."

"That won't be necessary," replied Billy Joe. "The Good Book tells us all we need to know about our place in the world and sinners like you."

"Well, if you call a truckload of drunken bigots out to rape defenseless women, bully and abuse fatherless children, and attempt to burn down their house in the middle of the night, righteous or patriotic, then I guess that's your right...even if your version is an outright lie! And, last I heard, those good ol' boys are still in County jail for their 'misunderstanding'. I believe the charges include aggravated assault, attempted murder, and attempted arson but we can ask the Sheriff, if you doubt my story."

"I believe he's up for re-election too and a dramatic yarn about defending the less fortunate is always good for a few extra votes, but these folks know a crook when they see one and I'm sure they'll turn him out, as soon as they understand that bribery and lying to a federal grand jury charges are about to be brought against him."

"You don't say? Is your little advertising agency working on a new political campaign based on more concocted lies?" Nellis turned to the crowd, "You do realize that young Miles' campaign is being funded by donations that true believers send in to the Praise the Lord Ministries. Reverend Hardman and Cletus Brantley want to buy themselves an election."

"That's a lie," yelled Hardman.

Young Brantley took the mike, "My campaign is funded by contributions from donors just like all of you. After the election, our books will be open to anyone who wants to check the facts."

Jazz could not contain himself, "After the election? Really? Who do you think you're kidding? These people understand a sham when they see one, brother, and you're it."

"I'm running to stop the pointy-headed liberals from destroying everything our sacred country stands for, everything our veterans fought and died for. They're trying to take religion out of our schools, they're proposing outrageous new gun laws to restrict our Second Amendment rights, and they're taxing all the common folk, so they can feed and care for a whole population of immigrants and scum who are sucking the life out of our society. It's time for us to stand up to demand protection for our rights and to save the purity of our heritage. It is our patriotic duty to stand against everything liberalism stands for before it's too late!"

Nellis raking a finger across his throat and the roadies killed the mike, "I believe that concludes the comedic portion of our program."

Cheers and applause.

"Let's get down and boogie!" yelled Jazz, as Jose counted off 'Praise the Children'.

In frustration, Miles stepped away from the microphone, turned to Nellis, and spat on the stage, "I'll take care of you, you nigger-lovin' piece of shit."

Nellis stopped playing and used his Strat to herd the Brantley's and Billy Joe towards the stairs. "Sonny, you don't have a clue who you're threatening."

~

Nellis finished feeding the critters and wandered into the dining room, with a cup of coffee and the paper, to find Ned pouring over stacks of pages gleaned from the binders at Paisley/Hatch. Nellis counted three empty glasses, two empty beer bottles, a large coffee mug, and an ashtray overflowing with butts and roaches, "Long night?"

"Yeah, fascinating stuff," mumbled Ned.

"I don't suppose you need another coffee?"

"Naw, I think I filled this mug up two or three times and I need to pee."

"Well, don't let me keep you," laughed Nellis, unfolding the Gazette, as the accountant stumbled to the bathroom.

The front page featured a smiling photograph of Stanton Spratlin making his first speech as a candidate at the rally. The banner headline read, 'Spratlin for Congress' and was accompanied by a three-column story about his achievements and qualifications.

The telephone rang in the kitchen and the Sheriff's voice said, "Nellis?"

"Yes, Sir."

"I have some bad news for you."

"What's that?"

"I had to let those varmints out of jail. The judge set bail and Trevor Hatch showed up at the courthouse to pay it within an hour of the ruling."

"Who do they work for?"

"They're roughnecks for Post Oil."

"When's the trial?"

"Next month, lemme see…the fourteenth."

"I'll mark my calendar," said Nellis. "Think they'll stay out of sight until then?"

"Yeah, but, even if they jump bail and hightail it outta state, we both know there's always another pickup load of drunken rednecks just waiting to be told where to go and who to abuse."

"Speaking of which, Billy Joe doesn't seem to like you much."

"Well, the feeling's mutual but I'm a public servant, so I will protect those who need protecting."

"He claims that there are charges being filed on you for bribery and lying to a Grand Jury, said so in front of a thousand people the other night."

"Yeah, I was there and heard his spiel."

"He's got a judge in his pocket, doesn't he? It's gotta be Judge Fredrickson."

"I'm not at liberty to respond," said Joe. "They can trump up anything they want but proving it is another matter."

"Yeah, but that's a big hassle for no good purpose."

"That's how they work."

Nellis snickered, as Ned tiptoed back into the dining room to sit at the table, "Two can play that game."

"I don't even want to know," sighed the Sheriff. "Say, did you hear anything about someone rustling a dozen prime heifers and a slew of hogs from ol' man Brantley's spread up by Taylor Lake?"

"No, can't say I have. You know me, I'm a homebody and don't get out enough to pick up on the latest gossip. Hell, I can't remember the last time I was up to the lake."

"Yeah, right, but you keep showing up right in the middle of every mess that crops up in this county," chuckled Joe Billings. "I was just wondering, because Jimmy Cobb smoked up some of the finest ribs I've ever tasted, at the festival the other night, and he told me that all the meat had been anonymously donated to all the chefs."

"Really? No shit, that's wonderful. We do have some thoughtful and generous citizens in this little burg. That's what makes it special."

"You don't think the two incidents relate to each other?"

"Well, now that you mention it, I guess you could draw that conclusion or, maybe, it was just a coincidence. Either way, a whole lot of people enjoyed a terrific evening and the event raised money for Spratlin's campaign and the rest is going to be donated to the food bank."

"Things do work themselves out in wondrous ways, sometimes, and I guess it would be foolish to doubt the wisdom of the gods. Either way, I've still got to investigate the theft, which means I get to spend a day driving up there and back."

"Take your fishin' pole, brother.

"Oh, I do have one more question for you."

Nellis hesitated, "What's that?"

"Seems the power and security system at Paisley/Hatch was disabled during the rally on the Square. Do you happen to know anything about that?"

"Why do you ask?"

"Well, the security guard from the Ministry noticed that the building was dark. He claims that, when he went to check, he found the whole band hanging out in the alley behind the offices."

"Well, I guess I can't incriminate myself, now can I? We were smokin' a little weed and that was the only place around that wasn't filled with people," replied Nellis. "Was there a burglary or something damaged?"

"They can't find anything missing or out of place, other than a single ledger sheet under Hatch's desk that should have been in the safe."

"Hell, someone could have dropped it."

"I'd buy that if the cleaning crew hadn't been through those offices on Friday night and no one entered that suite until Monday morning."

"Okay, that's pretty weird."

"Yeah, that's what I thought too."

"Wish I had an answer for you but I honestly don't. Let me know what happens with the judge."

"I will. You stay out of trouble now, ya' hear?"

"Yes, Sir."

He hung up the phone and Ned looked up, "I'm guessin' the Sheriff got a complaint about cattle rustling?"

"Yeah, seems someone absconded with a dozen head and some hogs from Brantley's spread up by the lake."

"Well, a lot of folk benefited and, from these records, I don't think it's going to hurt the old man's bottom line one bit."

"What'd you find?"

"Well, for starters, he's been buying up properties left and right but the whole thing's cagey. He's got a little investment company that deals in troubled mortgages and they buy the paper on a piece of property that he's interested in and force foreclosure. He buys the land for pennies on the dollar and turns around to sell the mineral rights to a trust that leases them to Post Oil, where he's on the Board of Directors. So, in the end, he makes money two or three ways before the ink's dry on the title."

"That's ingenious," said Nellis. "Is it legal?"

"Yeah, just barely. Ethical it ain't."

"What else?"

"I'm not far enough into it yet but I'm seeing hints that his whole empire is a house of cards with money being shuffled around from one corporation to another. Sure, every one of his enterprises is making money but they're carrying huge debt at eleven plus percent. This thing has grown so large, so fast, that it could all just collapse under its own weight, if they can't cover the notes."

"That's greed, that's what that is, and it's going to bite that bastard right in the ass."

"I'm sure Paisley/Hatch is covering their part in all of this in the primary books but they're right in the middle of all these deals."

"And they're taking a fat percentage too. What did you find in the Ministry books?"

"That's going to take a while. If Brantley's future is sketchy, Billy Joe's is the exact opposite. Theirs is a problem of too much cash coming in too fast and no one having a handle on who's doing what with it. Billy Joe doesn't draw a salary, which is great for public relations, but his living trust pulls twenty cents out of every dollar sent in by tens of thousands of people, who can't afford to be ripped off by this evangelical con artist. That's before the Ministry pays all his expenses, which are many."

"That trust has got to be huge," whistled Nellis.

"Huge enough that most of it has to be invested and guess who's handling that job for the Ministry?"

"Paisley/Hatch."

"You betcha."

"And they're investing Billy Joe's money into Brantley's acquisitions!"

"Exactly."

"Oh, this is just too sweet," said Nellis, sipping his second cup of coffee. "It sure seems like a good ol' farmer and his wife might ask their preacher for prayers, if they were in a bind, and, if that information was passed through the chain, Brantley's company could help jack their misery index in a hurry."

"There's also a connection to Post Oil but I haven't had a chance to look into it."

"Did you find an account that might have paid bail for the midnight riders?"

"There are so many, sprouting from every division of the corporation, that I don't think they even know where the money's going but I haven't found the smoking gun, yet."

Nellis leaned back in his chair, "They nabbed Al Capone for tax evasion, where do these guys stand?"

"Technically, Praise the Lord is exempt," replied Ned.

"For what comes in from donations but what about what happens after that? Like, if they invested in some shady land deals that made a fat profit?"

"Depends on how all those trusts and corporations are set up and how the profits are allocated. It might be easier to go after Billy Joe, himself, because his trust is moving funds around to cover everything that isn't funded by Church accounts. Those details are definitely not in these records but I'll bet a peek under those covers would sink his ship."

Nellis wandered into a back room and returned with the breakdown of personnel and responsibilities. "This is the organizational chart of Brantley's campaign. Most of these characters at the top – Hardman, Brantley, Post, and Jamison – don't connect directly to any particular branch but they probably oversee everything that's going on in this little financial universe they've created. The rest are arranged in our best guess at a hierarchy for PR, donations, and all the rest of it but, as you can see, it all ties back in to the financial wing of the Ministry."

Ned studied the cards on the board and grinned, "If you're right, then all of this ought to fit together somehow. What's with this little stack pinned at the top?"

"Oh, those were names of big donors who didn't seem to fit into the organizational charts."

"I'll bet they show up in the books."

"I think you're on to it." Nellis grinned, "We've got to share this with Katherine."

Before he could reach the phone, the dogs started yelping outside, so he padded out through the porch to find Sissy, Sammy, and the four Brown children on the stoop. "How are all of you this fine crisp morning?"

Little Muriel piped up, "Cold!"

"Well, it is early winter," laughed Nellis. "Are you on your way to school?"

"Yeah, Mr. Charles had to drive my dad and Miss Kennedy to the Capital to sign the papers for his candidacy, so we get to walk," replied Samantha.

"Are you still enjoying the new school?"

"I like the fact that we're expected to learn, instead of being treated like we were too stupid to understand anything at our old school," said Hubie.

"What's your favorite subject?"

"Math."

"Why?"

"Because it's like learning how to solve puzzles," replied the boy, with a big smile, "and there's always an answer."

"You stick with it," laughed Nellis. "We don't have enough youngsters who are interested in math and science."

Sissy tugged on his jacket, "My brother, Brad, told me to tell you that he knows some things that might be helpful."

"Why, thank you for delivering that message. Does he have a phone number?"

"Just call the house phone and Louise'll connect you," said Samantha.

Nellis looked at the girl, "And how's his rehabilitation coming along?"

Samantha looked down at her shoes, "He's better than he was but he still drinks too much beer and gets crazy sometimes."

"He's lucky to have family to help him recover."

Sam looked up with sad eyes, "I know he can be the person he was before he went to war…again…someday."

"I'll call him this morning."

Little Martin interrupted, "We better get going or we'll be in trouble again."

"Alright, alright," said Sam, hugging Nellis. "Let's go."

Mama Louise answered the telephone, "Spratlin House, this is Louise. How can I help you?"

"Louise, it's Nellis. How are you?"

"I'm splendid this morning and every morning, but you already know that."

Nellis laughed, "You are a splendid woman and we are all blessed to call you our friend."

"Are you always smooth with the ladies?"

"I try to be but I can guarantee I'm not always successful!"

"I love ya', just the way you are! Now, what is it you want, besides tellin' lies to a fat ol' black woman who isn't buying any of it?"

"I was wondering whether Brad was around. Samantha told me to give him a call."

"Let me transfer your call to the pool house. He might still be sleeping, because he didn't come down for breakfast."

"Thank you."

The line buzzed four times before a deep groggy voice answered, "Hello?"

"Brad, it's Nellis Gray. Samantha told me to call you."

"No one should have to be awake at this hour," mumbled the veteran. "Are you going to be at your place in an hour?"

"Yeah, I've got plenty to do."

"I'll come find you."

"See you then," replied Nellis. The line went dead.

The deep guttural thump of Brad's Harley announced his arrival long before the bike pulled up to the gate. Nellis wandered out of the barn to let him in and he pulled around next to Ned's truck. "So this is the barn my daddy built! It's a beaut!"

"I'm in his debt," replied Nellis.

"Naw, you got a barn, we got Sam and Sissy."

"Can I offer you some coffee or a beer or something?"

"I'm fine, thanks," replied Brad, leaning against the bike. "Listen, I was at the rally and saw what Cletus Brantley and Hardman tried to do and I've gotta say that you handled that pretty well."

"I've got no respect for either."

"Me neither but we both know that those guys will do just about anything to get that punk kid elected and they're definitely going to go after my father."

"We all see that coming."

"Well, I've got an ace in the hole for you, in case you really need it."

"What's that?"

"The good Reverend Hardman is a blubbering faggot."

"How do you know that?"

"He propositioned me."

"Really?"

"Yeah," replied the veteran, his ruddy skin flushed, "I'm all for my daddy winning this election for all the right reasons so, I'd rather not have to explain how it happened, unless we're up against the wall, if you know what I mean."

"I'll keep that one in my vest pocket," said Nellis, "but there is something that you need to contribute to your father's campaign."

"What's that?"

"Remember what it felt like to wear your dress uniform, the fearless pride in yourself and your men and your country. That's the man the public needs to see." He paused staring into Brad's bloodshot eyes. "You can go back to being crazy when all this is over but, in the meantime, clean up your act and be who you're called to be."

Spratlin straightened up, wavering between shame and anger for a long moment, before he snapped to attention and saluted smartly, "Sir! Yes, Sir!"

"I didn't serve and I wouldn't have served if they'd called me up. My beef isn't with you guys, who faced hell on earth, it's with those bastards in D.C., who trumped up a phony war so big corporations could show big profits. Bastards should all be in jail for treason."

"We agree on that."

"Fine, you have your assignment and I'll keep your information private. If we have to use it, you'll be the first to know."

"Fair enough," said Brad, extending a hand. "You're rock steady, man, and a lot of people are leaning on you, whether you know it or not."

"I just do what I've gotta do, simple as that. There's right and there's wrong but I don't mind twisting that gray part in the middle a little bit, when it's the right thing to do," smirked Nellis. "Go get cleaned up and see who needs you to do what."

Brad climbed on the bike and pumped the starter. The engine rumbled to life and he saluted, as he drove out the gate.

Chapter Eleven

Katherine took Stanton's hand, "I'm very proud that you want me to witness your papers."

"I trust and admire you and, even though things have…changed between us, I still think we make one hell of a team."

Katherine blushed, "I'm not sure that either of us knows what's going on with our hearts, at the moment, but we will defeat young Brantley in the primary together."

"Are you sure you're ready for the fight? It might get rough."

"I'm tougher than you think," laughed the brunette, her dark eyes glimmering as she raised her fists. "No matter what happens, they could never tarnish our time together. That will always be very special to me."

"Me too." He squeezed her hand, gazing out the window at passing fields, bristling with golden stubble as affirmation of a bountiful harvest. He called to Mr. Charles, "How far do we have to go?"

"Oh, about thirty miles," replied the driver, glancing back and forth between rearview mirrors.

"What are you looking at," inquired Katherine.

"There's a black pickup that's been following us for miles. Stays about a half a mile back, no matter whether I speed up or slow down."

"Well, there's not much out here. Maybe he's just going where we're going."

"Yeah, well, now he's coming fast."

The truck whizzed past and spun sideways, blocking the road. The Fleetwood screeched to a stop, as two hooded men jumped from the truck and ran to the car. The stocky guy on the left pointed a pistol at Mr. Charles, who kept his hands on the wheel. "Unlock the rear doors or I'll put a slug in your ear!"

Mr. Charles glanced in the mirror. Stanton said, "Do as he says."

The locks clicked and the man on the right opened the door and leaned in. "I've been sent to deliver a message. Do not sign your candidacy papers."

"Why wouldn't I do that?"

The man reached into a pocket to retrieve a Polaroid photograph. He handed it to Spratlin, who gasped. It portrayed the six children, bound together and gagged with tape, in the back of a panel truck.

"If you want them back, you'll do as instructed. Don't get stupid and call the police, if you want to see them alive again. We'll call you at your residence and we will be watching."

He backed out and slammed the door. The two men climbed into the truck and sped away.

"Did you get his tag number?" asked Katherine.

"There were no plates, I looked." Mr. Charles leaned over the seat, "I'm sorry I couldn't stop them, are you okay?"

"We're fine but the stakes just went up," said Spratlin.

"Shall I turn around and head for home?" asked the driver.

"No, we've got an appointment and I intend to keep it."

The Highway Patrol was happy to provide the new Republican candidate for Congress with an escort back to Cameron, after learning from Miss Kennedy that attempts had been made against their lives. There was no sign of the black pickup, as Mr. Charles followed the cruiser back across the state.

Katherine clutched Stanton's arm, "I don't know whether to think you're brave or foolish but I'm proud of the fact that you stand by your principles, even in the face of catastrophe."

"Without the official papers, we have nothing to bargain with. We can choose not to campaign, if it comes to that, but it's a point of negotiation, which buys us time."

"We can't go to the police."

"No, but I might ask Mr. Gray if he would consider adding his considerable talents to our think tank, when we get back."

"I was going to suggest the same thing," said Katherine. "There's something I need to tell you."

"Is it something a candidate should know?"

His secretary hesitated, "Probably not, so suffice it to say that we might have access to some very interesting information that could change the balance of this whole thing."

"I don't want to know...yet."

The State Troopers pulled over beneath the arch over the drive leading into Spratlin House, opposite another squad car. The window rolled down as the Cadillac eased between them and Stanton leaned out, "Thank you very much for the escort."

"No problem," said the Trooper. "Someone from your house called the police to report six missing children but they refused to talk with the detectives until you arrived home."

"Thank you. I've been advised that, if I contact the police, my children will be killed, so would you instruct everyone to stay away from this property until we hear from the kidnappers?"

"Yes, Sir. We'll be invisible, starting right now."

"I'll be expecting my neighbor, Mr. Nellis Gray, to stop by. Please do not interfere with him."

"Yes, Sir."

The window rolled up and Mr. Charles pulled along the drive and through the portico to drop Stanton and Katherine at the kitchen door.

An hour later, Nellis drove the old Ford across Maple Ridge and into the Spratlin property. Katherine's phone call was desperate and short on real information, just, "Something terrible has happened, can you come by Spratlin House immediately?"

He parked behind the kitchen and knocked on the door. Mama Louise appeared with tears glistening on her plump cheeks. "I'm so glad you're here."

"What's happened?"

"Someone's taken the children."

"But I just saw the whole pack of them this morning on their way to school."

"The principal called to find out why they were all absent."

"I'm so sorry," said Nellis, giving her a hug. "Is Mr. Spratlin at home?"

"Yes, he's in the study, if you'll follow me." She led him through the kitchen into a hallway that opened into the foyer and knocked gently on a tall door.

Katherine opened it and wrapped her long arms around Nellis' neck, "I'm glad you're here."

"From what I hear, I wish it was under better circumstances."

Stanton was sitting on the front edge of a large desk with Bruce, Bradley, Mr. Charles, and Maybelle Brown. Brad shook his hand, "If I knew where to find these bastards, I'd take care of this in a hurry."

"Let's figure out what's going on, then we'll work on strategy. Tell me what's happened and don't leave anything out."

Katherine started, "Mr. Charles was driving us to the Capital when we were stopped by two gunmen in a black pickup with no plates. They showed us a photograph of the children, who were bound and gagged in the back of a truck."

"The obvious message was that they could move them anywhere anytime," injected Bruce.

"Exactly," said Stanton. "The man told me not to sign the formal papers or they'd kill the children."

Nellis stared at his eyes and found stark fear and uncompromising determination. "You signed them anyway, didn't you?"

Spratlin stared back, "Yes, it seemed good strategy at the time, something to bargain with, if nothing else."

"I'm no lawyer but that makes this a Federal crime," said Katherine.

"Which means they're willing to gamble everything to keep you out of the race," said Maybelle, dabbing at the tears spilling from her dark eyes that could not wash away the panic. "What could possibly be that important?"

"That's a great question," said Stanton. "I've been thinking about it all afternoon and I can't think of a reason why they're so desperate to get the Brantley boy elected."

"Money," said Nellis. "It's always about money."

"Who profits?" asked Brad.

"Well, them obviously," said Bruce. "The question is how?"

"Katherine and I, and a few other folks, have been doing some research into the structure of the kid's campaign organization, as well as the connections to Hardman's church, Cletus's ever-expanding holdings, and Eli Post, who's got lots of money tied up in all of this. We haven't put all the pieces together, yet, but there's no doubt that this is way deeper than just getting Junior elected to an office, for which he has absolutely no qualifications." Nellis smirked, "And it's all running through Paisley/Hatch."

"They must hope that he'll get put on a committee that will benefit their scheme," said Katherine.

"I take it that your information is not suitable to be handed over to a grand jury?" inquired Stanton.

"Let's just say that a judge might consider it inadmissible," replied Nellis. "Have you heard from the kidnappers, since you were hijacked on the highway?"

"No, and that worries me," said Stanton.

"My guess is that they'll keep the children alive, until they get what they want," said Nellis.

"What I don't get is why today? They've got two more weeks until the primary election. What are they going to do with the children until then?" asked Maybelle. "That's a long time to keep the kidnapping a secret."

"Today was the last day to register, so, if they'd scared Stanton off, they could have dumped the kids and cruised through the general election. By the time an investigation could begin, their boy would be elected. Hal Blaney might be qualified but he's no competition in this district," said Katherine.

"I'll get my folks to start thinking about how a rancher, an oil company, and world-wide evangelical circus barker turn a profit on the election of an ignorant kid," mused Nellis. He stared at Katherine intently, "Unless…"

"What?"

"Unless, someone much higher up is cherry-picking elections, like this one, to stack the Congress with radical robots?"

Katherine looked up, "Those extra cards, that's how they fit in."

"I'll make some calls," said Stanton, "as soon as we get through this next step."

"Next question is where are the kids and how are we going to get them back?" said Bruce.

"Anyone good with stereo gear?" asked Nellis.

Brad grinned, "Yeah, I've got a pretty awesome rig in the pool house."

"Think you could get a decent recording off the phone?"

"It'd be better to wire it into the line than try to get it on a mike," said Bruce.

"Why not just rig a connection between the speaker in the phone and the input?" said Brad. "I had to hotwire the radios out in the field all the time. At least this time, I won't have flak exploding over my head while I'm working."

"Get on with it, they could call any time," said Nellis.

"Wish we could trace the call," said Maybelle.

"We don't have the gear for that but maybe we'll pick up something on the recordings," said Nellis. "Mr. Spratlin, I want you to take your time on the phone. Let them hear a little bit of your panic before you demand proof that all of the children are alive and well. There is nothing to negotiate, if they aren't."

"I can do that," replied Stanton.

"Once that's been established, then we get to the 'what do you want' part. They'll probably threaten to kill or harm one or more of the children unless you concede to their demands. Make small concessions, nibble at the edges, ask questions, and keep them talking."

"Oh, my babies," cried Maybelle.

Katherine took her in her arms, "We'll get them back but we're all going to have to be completely silent during the call."

The door creaked opened and Marjorie stood silhouetted in the hall light and, with just a hint of hesitation, stepped into the study. She was dressed in a gray wool sweater over beige slacks, her hair was brushed into a loose bun, her face pale without the pasty makeup, but her eyes were cold and hard. "Who the hell stole our children and what are we doing to get them back?"

Stanton rose and walked over to take her hands, "Are you well enough to be up?"

She glanced at Bruce, "None of that matters when our babies are threatened, that's a mother's instinct."

"Then welcome aboard," said Maybelle. "We need all the help we can get."

The telephone rang and everyone jumped. Nellis held a finger to his lips and said, "Wait until the fourth ring and let's hope Brad's got the tape machine wired up."

Stanton picked up the receiver, "Hello?"

"Dad, it's me, Brad. I was just testing the equipment. It works."

"Thank you," said Spratlin, hanging up the receiver. Everyone was staring at him. "That was Brad testing the equipment."

"Good," said Nellis. "The next time it rings, we'll be ready."

The phone jangled again and Stanton almost picked up the receiver to yell at Brad, when Nellis grabbed his hand. "Wait."

On the fourth ring, he answered, "Hello?"

A muffled voice said, "Spratlin?"

"Yes."

"You were instructed to not sign those papers."

"Had I not completed that step, I would have nothing to bargain with and, before this goes any further, I want proof that our children are alive. All of them!"

"You take orders, you don't give them."

"Then I'm afraid there is nothing further to discuss," replied Spratlin, slamming the phone on the cradle.

Maybelle whimpered.

"That was perfect," said Nellis. "They'll call back in a minute. Don't back up and don't give in."

The phone rang again and, again, he let it ring three more times before he answered, "This is a negotiation. You won't get anything from me until I know the children are alive and well."

A chorus of young voices screamed, "Daddy, come save us!"

"Satisfied."

"For the moment. What do you want?"

"We want you to withdraw from the primary."

"Scared you can't get your boy elected, if he actually has to show up in public?"

"You're in way over your head and we hold all the cards. Do as we say or we'll send you a body a day, starting with the youngest."

"I don't believe you, because we both know that it's a matter of hours before the Feds get wind of this and open an investigation into the kidnapping and the election. I had nothing to do with that, the principal at their school called the police when she realized the kids were missing."

"Little Muriel started wailing and the other children screamed, "Leave her alone! Don't hurt her!"

Stanton clenched his jaw and inhaled slowly, to keep his voice steady, "I have no assurance that you will return the children, if I refuse to campaign."

"You can be damned sure they won't come home if you do," replied the voice. The line went dead.

Maybelle sobbed, "What have you done?"

Marjorie wrapped an arm around her shoulder and turned to her husband, "You played that exactly right. You've thrown them off their game and they need time to adjust their plan."

"She's right," said Bruce. "They thought they could scare you off."

Stanton replaced the receiver and withdrew his hand from the side pocket of his jacket. He held out the Polaroid of the children, "I really don't remember putting this in my pocket."

Katherine squeezed his arm, "I don't remember you handing it back to that man, either."

Nellis took the print and held it under a lamp on the desk. The children were bound together, their mouths taped, and the glare of the flash showed the terror in their eyes. The rear doors of a green panel truck were open wide above a rusty chrome bumper with no license plate and oil-stained concrete underneath. The edge of something dark and angular showed under the right-hand door and a hanging shop lamp reflected shiny silver glimmers on the left. "I wish there was more detail."

Bruce leaned over to inspect the print, "I've got a copy stand set up in my studio. I might be able to copy that in black and white and play with the contrast a little bit."

"How long would that take?"

"Maybe an hour," replied the artist.

"Get on with it," said Nellis, "but don't damage the original."

"I won't, I'll just make a copy of it."

"Let's see what Brad got," said Nellis, leading the group out of the study and down the hallway to the kitchen.

The veteran had a large reel-to-reel set up on the big table between two speaker cabinets running off a stereo receiver. "This is a fairly simple rig but we might be able to use the Dolby to cut down on some of noise and the tone settings to tune things up or down."

Nellis took a seat, as everyone crowded around and Mama Louise brought a tray of coffee, tea, and a big pile of pastries.

"Let's hear what you got."

Brad hit 'Play' and the reels turned slowly. A loud click preceded Stanton saying, "Hello."

"Spratlin?"

"Yes."

"You were instructed to not sign those papers."

"Had I not completed that step, I would have nothing to bargain with and, before this goes any further, I want proof that our children are alive. All of them!"

"You take orders, you don't give them."

"Then I'm afraid we don't have anything further to discuss."

There was a loud click before a hiss that lasted several seconds, interrupted by a man's voice in the background asking, "What happened?" The recording ended.

Nellis said, "Back it up to the very end, I want to hear that voice again."

Brad hit the rewind, then play. Stanton said, "Then I'm afraid we don't have anything further to discuss," before the hiss filled the speakers.

"Stop."

He punched stop, "Okay, just this section. Turn up the volume, turn down the mid-range and the bass about twenty-five percent."

Brad made the adjustments and pushed 'Play'. In the gap between the click of the call ending and the voice, there was a faint noise in the background.

"Do it again, only louder. Turn the mid-range up a little and take the high down fifty percent."

The few seconds of noise blared through the kitchen and stopped. "Did you hear it?"

"Yeah," said Brad, "but what is it?"

"Do it again, but this time, close your eyes and pretend you're standing outside on a cold night."

Everyone in the room stood perfectly still and closed their eyes. The tape played and no one reacted for a moment, after it stopped.

"I heard something like a train clacking over a crossing, way in the background," whispered Marjorie, "and maybe a horn far away."

"And there was an echo, like the noise was bouncing around a big empty room," added Maybelle.

"I think you're exactly right," said Nellis. "Now, if we knew the exact time of the call, we might be able to figure out which crossing."

"It was eight minutes past seven, when the telephone rang the first time and seven-fourteen for the second," said Katherine.

"And how do you know that, dear?" asked Marjorie.

"I'm a secretary. I have to keep track of schedules and appointments. It's developed into an obsession."

"One we're all glad you have," smiled Stanton. "Why don't you call Ben Silverman over in Shipping? He knows the schedule for every form a transport that comes through this city. You can use the office line in the study."

Katherine left and Nellis said, "Okay, let's review the second section."

The next bit of tape revealed the slamming of two doors, after the children yelled, "Leave her alone! Don't hurt her!" followed by the rapid thud of something hammering against metal. There was a faint, 'Damnit!' between the voice's final threat and the receiver clunking on the cradle.

Maybelle said, "The guard's trying to lock the kids up in the truck but they're kicking at the metal doors."

"Those guys'll have a problem, if those kids get loose," laughed Brad. "They're all smart and tough."

"I think they can hold their own for a little while," said Nellis, as Katherine returned with a small piece of paper.

"Ben said that there was only one train in the area at seven-eighteen, an MKT from St. Louis, and it would have been approaching the outskirts of town from the northeast."

Bruce returned with a small stack of dripping prints and laid them out of the counter. "Here are the best blow-ups I could get from a Polaroid, which is soft to begin with."

He pointed to the first black and white image, "Here's the whole shot, which doesn't show much, but I enlarged the right side and the dark thing under the door is a crate of some kind. It looks like it's made of wood but there's nothing distinguishing about it. The same on the left, maybe a shop light reflecting in the glass in the window...but I made an enlargement of the window and pulled the contrast down a little and I think that's the reflection of the handlebars of a motorcycle."

Nellis leaned over the print, "I'm guessin' it's a Harley but Brad probably knows more than I do."

Brad held the print up to the light, "Yeah, man, that's an old-style Sportster for sure."

"Then I got interested in the rearview mirror," said Bruce, pointing to the final print, which showed a dark smudge with a white hole in front of something bright and angular. "I think the dark thing is one of the kidnappers wearing a black hood with eye holes."

"That's good," said Katherine. "If the children can't identify them, maybe they'll be inclined to let them go."

"Maybe," said Nellis, "What's the bright angular thing?"

"I think it's a piece of a neon sign. See the way it glows around the edges? It was pink in the Polaroid."

"Yeah, and I know exactly where that is, it's the Homeless Shelter sign over on Fourth Street. There's a bike repair shop across the intersection."

"Do you think they're still there?"

"Only one way to find out," said Nellis, "but, before we go off half-cocked, let's make sure. Can I use the phone?"

Stanton replied, "Certainly."

Katherine followed Nellis into the study and closed the door, "Do you really think we can get them back?"

He held up one finger, "Yes, but let me make a call and we'll know for sure."

"Okay."

Nellis dialed and waited, "Constance?"

"Yes."

"I believe that everyone should have shelter during the holidays."

There was a long pause, before she whispered, "Are you?"

"Yes, Ma'am, I think we're talking about the same person. Now, I was wondering whether I might ask a favor of you?"

"Of course, anything."

"I was wondering whether you and Hank Garrett might round up some of our friends to scout that motorcycle repair shop across the street?"

"The boys who used to run that place were so courteous and kept the place up but these new guys are a bunch of thugs. What are we looking for?"

"We believe that six kidnapped children are being held in a panel truck inside that warehouse."

"Oh, my!"

"At this point, all we want to know is whether that truck is inside but we don't want to endanger the children under any circumstances."

"I understand."

"Okay, call Louise at 555-2719 when you know one way or another but, to save time, we'll assume that we have a go."

"I can do that."

"If your people can keep them contained for thirty minutes, we'll have time to send in some reinforcements."

"I like your plan," replied Constance. "You can count on us."

"Oh, and it would be better if no one knew about our special relationship. You know how people talk."

"Honey, I ain't never going to tell anyone about my sugar daddy."

Before they stepped into the kitchen, Marjorie asked, "What did you find out?"

"We're not sure, yet, but Nellis has some people looking into it," replied Katherine.

"I think we should assume that it's game on," said Nellis. "So, Mr. Charles, would you ask Mr. Edwards and his buddies to take up positions around that building very quietly? Brad get your guys together for an invasion..."

Before he could finish, Bruce interrupted, "Don't forget me, I've got a crew that can create a spectacular diversion and I've got the perfect little outfit for the occasion."

"Cool," said Nellis. "Go for it. Meanwhile, no one in, no one out, and no one gets hurt. If we're right, there should be a bunch of civilians hanging around keeping the bike shop buttoned up. Be aware that they're on our side and we all want to get the kids out safe and sound, that's our only objective."

Stanton said, "I'll call the Sheriff and keep them in the loop but out of the way, until we get the children out."

～

Sissy reached behind Samantha to untie her hands and whispered, "They just used a stupid cinch knot, pull on the tail and you can slip your hands right out."

One by one, the other children wiggled free, except Muriel, who sniveled in frustration until Daniel untied her.

"Okay, this is just to prove that we can do it, but we can't let them know."

"We can't just go busting out of this truck. We don't know how to get out of the building," said Sam.

"Yeah," said Daniel, "It's all for one and one for all. We all get out of here together or we don't go."

"Agreed," said Sissy.

"I keep hearing the clink of bottles," said Hubie.

"Yeah, they're drinking beer," said Daniel. "I could smell it on that guy with the beard."

"Good," said Sam. "They'll get drunk and fall asleep and we can sneak out."

"There's a plan," said Daniel.

"I'm hungry," said Martin.

"Me too," said Muriel.

"Okay," said Sissy. "Let's tie each other up again and start making a racket, until they feed us and let us go to the bathroom."

"If they do, we should run around and make as much noise as we can," added Daniel. "Maybe someone will hear us."

"That's great," said Martin, "but can we wait until after we eat?"

"We'll see," said Daniel.

They slithered down the slick floor to hammer on the panel doors, hollering and howling until they flew open and two burly men reached in to untie them. The stinky fat man with a red beard and tattoos on his hands said, "We brought you some burgers and fries and Cokes. You'll need to eat up, we'll be leavin' soon."

"I need to go the bathroom," said Samantha.

"Me, too," said Muriel and Hubie at once.

"Okay, form a line and you can take turns using the can," said the burly man. He was wearing a leather vest with a big pink rose embroidered on the back and pointed to a small dark closet with a toilet. "It ain't all clean and pretty but it works just the same."

Samantha took Muriel into the stall and closed the door, just as little Martin picked up a piece of scrap steel and started banging on the metal leg of a workbench with all his might. Tattoo man raced to grab the boy but Sissy, Daniel, and Hubie darted around the shop, screaming and yelling as loud as they could manage.

Sam and Muriel emerged to find the three men chasing after elusive children, scurrying in every direction, and joined in the chase. The kids tossed any metal object that might make a loud noise onto the concrete floor, dumped over chairs and tables, and the three drunk bikers stumbled after stampeding children tearing through the warehouse, until tattoo man grabbed little Muriel and held her above his head, shrieking, "Stop or I'll drop her!"

The children froze in place.

The bearded biker with beer breath pointed to the truck. "Get inside and don't make a sound, if you want to eat."

Samantha sighed dramatically and marched across the shop to help Muriel and Martin climb inside. Rose man brought four white bags and a cardboard tray full of drinks. "Eat up."

The door closed but reopened a few minutes later. Tattoo man brushed all the sacks and wrappers onto the ground and climbed in to tie each child in turn. "Get comfy, you're gonna be in here until we hit the road."

"When's that?" asked Sissy.

"As if it's any of your business, little Miss Busybody, we should be hearing about your next stop anytime." He backed out and slammed the doors.

"That's not good," said Daniel.

"The longer we stay here, the drunker they get. We still might get a chance," said Samantha.

"I scoped out the exits, while we were running around, and tried all the doors. The only one that isn't locked is on the far wall next to the rollup door," added Sissy. "If they settle down, make a run for that door and keep going!"

"I'm scared," said Muriel. "Do you think anyone's looking for us?"

Samantha leaned close, untying the rope from her little wrists, "I think there's a whole posse looking all over the city but they haven't found us, yet. If we can escape, great, if not, then we need to help them find us by raising a ruckus until someone notices."

~

Life on the street had changed over the past few years. Sure, there were still old-time rummies and druggies emulating the bums of another era but, now, the faces of the homeless were younger, kids who struck out on their own, only to be battered by life's harsh realities that extinguished their dreams and drove them to the farthest margins of society. Whether young or old, each appreciated the kindness of those who provided food and shelter during the rough patches and volunteered without hesitation.

Aging cross-dresser, Sara Jane and her youthful boyfriend, Michael, wandered over to lounge on a grassy patch, in a warm splash of light firing between the buildings from the setting sun, just outside the steel roll-up door of the motorcycle shop. A group of teenagers in the alley giggled and laughed as they shared a joint and three old birds down on the corner passed a bottle in a brown paper sack, raucous voices rising into an argument over some tall tale. One or two at a time, folks wandered through the intersection to take up positions around the building, until more than a hundred were casually hanging out with the neighbors on a cool autumn evening.

Everything remained calm and quiet, until Uncle Milty, a confirmed drunk who had been absolutely sober for the past twenty years, stumbled across the broken sidewalk to hammer on the corrugated door screaming, "Lemme in, I need some money to feed my granddaughter and you're my last hope."

A voice from inside yelled, "Go away, you old bum!"

"No man, you've gotta help. Please, let me in!" He hammered again, only louder.

The crowd on the street stifled grins and giggles.

Milton pounded and yelled until, finally, the door rolled up enough for a hand to toss out a crumpled up five-dollar bill. "Now, get lost!" The door slammed to the pavement.

Sara Jane sat up to scan the street for Constance, who was standing with her arm around Sammy's shoulders on the sidewalk in front of the shelter. She held up her right thumb and walked over to whisper, "Green panel truck with the rear doors closed but there was stuff on the floor all around it."

"What kind of stuff?"

"White bags, like food bags."

Constance hugged the girl. "I think tonight's going to provide enough good gossip to last for years. I'll be right back, I have to make a call."

Within minutes, two-dozen armed black men appeared, quietly taking up positions on the corners and rooftops to surround the building. They were followed by a white van rigged with gigantic speakers on the roof, blasting 'Jive Talkin'" at sonic levels, and swirling lights splattering the neighborhood in pulsing streaks of pink and purple. Twenty chopped Harleys roared down Fourth Street in formation and lined up to block the door to the shop, as fifteen circus clowns erupted from the music van and danced into the street to fire dozens of Roman candles exploding in brilliant splays of red and yellow and screamers streaking across the pavement in streams of silver sparks. Astonished locals clapped and cheered, joining a gyrating kanga line dancing around the building.

The black Fleetwood pulled to the curb in front of the shelter and police cars blocked the streets to prevent an escape and to contain the loud chaotic street party in front of the repair shop.

Brad climbed off his bike and hammered on the rollup door. "Open up, asshole. I want my sisters back."

A muffled voice yelled, "I don't know what you're talking about."

"Then open up and let's have a look."

"We're leaving and you're not going to stop us, if you want to see them alive again," cried another voice.

"Okay, c'mon out."

The door rolled open to the thunderous growl of two motorcycles revving their engines to lead the truck to freedom, only to slam on the brakes to avoid the tangle of bikes lined up outside, dazzled by circus clowns dancing into the building, fireworks exploding, brilliant lights spinning blinding colors, blaring music, and crowds of homeless people, dancing reinforcements behind a dozen bikers and a squad of armed black men. Brad grabbed the first rider in a chokehold, relieved him of a revolver, and dropped him to the pavement, then spun to land a heavy boot under the second biker's chin, as the mob stormed into the garage.

He ran to pull the bearded driver out of the truck, which slowly crunched the two bikes into gleaming scrap metal, and knocked him out with a straight right. By the time he raced to the back door, Bruce was pulling on the latch. "Here, let me!"

The doors popped open, revealing the children in a tangle of arms and legs. The brothers hopped inside to free Sissy, Samantha, and the rest of the kids. Sissy hugged Bruce, "I love this outfit and the nose, but couldn't you find anything else to wear?"

"Oh, I asked a bunch of my friends to help out and we decided that it would be far more entertaining if we transformed it into performance art, so we danced our way in to save you!"

Before the children could climb out of the truck, Stanton and Marjorie appeared, with Maybelle and Mr. Charles, to hug each child in turn.

Samantha looked up at her mother, "I can't believe you're here."

"I've been absent through most of the living that's been going on around our home, through celebrations and crisis, and I think it's high time I stood up to defend my family and make amends for my sins."

Sissy and Samantha snuggled into her embrace, as Katherine leaned out the window of Nellis' old pickup to wave, as it rolled past the warehouse and disappeared around the corner.

~

Ned looked up from the dining room table, as Katherine and Nellis appeared through a cloud of sweet smoke. "Success?"

Nellis laughed, "Yeah, the folks down on Fourth Street are going to be talking about the invasion of black guys with rifles, circus clowns dancing through the street to blaring music, and a couple dozen heavy looking guys on Harleys invading the repair shop."

"Someone should have filmed it," smiled Ned.

"One of Bruce's friends actually proposed that but we nixed it."

"How are the kids?"

"They're all safe," said Katherine, hugging Nellis' arm, "and on their way home by now."

"Mission success."

"So, considering you've been sitting on your ass, raiding my fridge and smoking up all my dope, while we were out trying to save a pack of innocent children, did you accomplish anything? Wait, before you answer," said Nellis turning to Katherine, "do you want anything?"

"A glass of Chardonnay and a joint. I've only smoked pot a couple of times with Nellis, since I was in college and we're not going to discuss how long that's been."

"That we can do," said Ned, strolling into the kitchen, while Nellis sat down at the table to roll a tidy joint.

The accountant reappeared with a glass of wine and two cold beers on a silver tray with a white towel draped over his wrist and offered the glass to Katherine, "Mademoiselle."

Nellis took a slug of beer and lit the joint, passing it to Katherine. "Go easy, darlin'. I promise this is stronger than the crap you smoked in college."

The beautiful brunette grinned, exhaling without coughing.

"So, what'd ya' find out?"

Ned walked over to his pile of papers, "Well, I keep going back to why these guys are in cahoots and what they're after, so I plotted out every property that we know old man Brantley has acquired over the past five years, plus all the properties owned by his buddies." He pointed to a large map of the state, hanging from the bookcase, with a pink geometric matrix running, almost continuously, from border to border.

"That's incredible," gasped Katherine. "How could one man buy up that much property and what does he want to do with it?"

"Ah well, he's had some help but that's the question, isn't it? First, I considered natural resources, and most of this isn't suitable for farming, so I'd include grazing, oil, mining, and water rights, among others. Most of this land is desolate oil country but it's just not enough to warrant buying elections."

"No matter how screwy his finances, he already owns all that stuff," said Katherine.

"So, someone else wants to do something with that land and these guys are setting it up to cash in," said Nellis, puffing on the joint.

"Now you're on to it," laughed Ned. "The guy who's making the most out of all of this is Post, because he's picked up the mineral rights to all of this but there's a problem."

"How to move the oil to refineries."

"There are a few small operations in the state but, if you ran a big fat pipeline down the middle of this property, you could collect from this whole area and feed directly into a system on the other side of the state line that would carry it to the Gulf."

"And charge for every drop that runs south, that's big money," said Katherine. "But how's our favorite preacher hooked up in all of this? He doesn't need the income."

The corners of Nellis' bloodshot eyes crinkled, "It's all smoke and mirrors. His whole pious shtick is guilt and salvation transformed into a theatrical extravaganza. I wouldn't be surprised if there's a whole lot more going out than coming in."

"Why would Post and Brantley need him in the first place? They could have pulled this off without his help."

"It's Paisley/Hatch," replied Ned. "That's his private bank and they're financing this deal."

"Which isn't regulated by the government," said Nellis.

Ned held up the six cards from the organizational board, "I also figured out where your mystery names fit in."

"Where?" asked Katherine.

He held his bottle up to toast Nellis, "Your phone bill's going to be a tad steep next month because I made a bunch of long-distance calls."

"You damned well better have found something mighty interesting or you're going to be working it off out in the fields."

"Oh, I did, believe me, I did," said Ned, turning over one card at a time. "Ford – evangelical minister from Milford, sponsoring another young under-educated white-supremacist candidate for the seat in District Four. Pratt – right-wing oilman from Bailey in cahoots with Post, also funding a candidate for the seat in District Nine. Ballantine – heavy construction, things like highways and pipelines. He's putting his money into yet another upstart in District Two. Hammond, he's got a refinery up in Duncan and he'd like to run his product directly to market. Fitzpatrick in MacIntosh, owns mineral rights for most of the northwest part of the state. And, Rumsted, yet another preacher with ambitions to make his tent as big as Billy Joe's. He's started his own television station to broadcast his sanctimonious sermons across the globe and wants to open a university to brainwash faithful and gullible students to go out on missions to spread his twisted version of religion to the truly desperate."

"They'd need Congressional approval for an interstate pipeline," said Katherine. "It makes perfect sense."

Nellis rolled another joint, "All of this makes sense, except for Hardman."

"Why?"

"Because, our minister might be a fat pig and a shyster but he's obviously an astute businessman. He built an empire from nothing, so, much as I loathe the man, I keep wondering what leverage they have on him?"

"You mean like blackmail?" asked Katherine.

"Yeah, even if he was flat broke, he could make a plea to the congregation and have millions flowing into his accounts within days."

"You've got a point," said Ned. "If we knew that, maybe we could turn this whole conspiracy on its head."

"I've got an idea," said Nellis, the corners of dancing eyes curling into a wicked grin behind a cloud a blue smoke.

Chapter Twelve

Bruce glanced up at his mother, took a deep breath, and dialed the phone. "Reverend Hardman, please."

"Yes, this is Bruce Spratlin calling on behalf of my mother, Marjorie Spratlin." He hesitated, "Thank you."

"Hello."

"Reverend, this is Bruce Spratlin, I apologize for bothering you at this hour, but my mother asked me to call to see whether you might stop by to offer a blessing. I'm afraid she's not doing very well tonight."

"Has she seen the doctor?"

"I'm surprised he hasn't just moved in," replied Bruce.

"I have to be honest with you. The last time I was there, your older brother, Bradley, physically accosted me and threatened to kill me, if I ever visited your home again."

"Well, I'm afraid he's had some drinking problems, since he got back from the war, but I'll make sure that he's gone when you arrive, if that will help?"

"I'm a man of the cloth and violence is against everything I believe in," sniveled the preacher. "You understand that this is rather awkward, considering your father's candidacy and all?"

"I'm sure my mother has always made it worth your while. Are you going to deny her in her time of need?"

"Fine, I'll be there in a hour, if that's convenient?"

"Absolutely. I'll see you then," said Bruce, hanging up the phone. "That wasn't as hard as I thought it would be."

"He likes those checks," said Marjorie.

"Alright, places everyone," said Nellis.

The lights of the black Lincoln flashed up the drive and into the courtyard. A very large man in a dark suit got out and walked around to open the rear door eyeing Bruce and three friends, who were still dressed in their clown costumes and struggling not to fall into character.

Bruce stepped forward to offer a gloved hand, as the Reverend rolled out of the car and straightened up with a start. "I'm sorry for the outfits but we were having a party this evening that was interrupted by my dear mother's request to summon you. I do apologize for the inconvenience."

Hardman sneered, "I'm here to serve my flock. Take me to her."

The four clowns marched the portly preacher through the kitchen and up the back stairs, their oversized shoes flop-flopping along the plush carpeting of the deserted hallway to Marjorie's suite at the far end. Bruce knocked gently and opened the door to step inside, "Reverend Hardman is here to see you."

"Please send him in."

Bruce stepped back to allow Hardman to enter and closed the door behind him. He turned to the clown posse, raised a finger to his lips, and shooed them down the corridor, before tapping lightly on the next door. He eased inside to find, Elgin and Shelton, who worked production at the local television station and brought along a video camera, microphones, and a little black and white monitor that displayed a grainy, contrasty view of his mother's bedroom.

The picture was adequate to identify Billy Joe, as he waddled over to the bedside to take her hand. "You wouldn't have summoned me, if things weren't dire. How can I soothe your anguish?"

Marjorie settled comfortably into a bank of pillows with the covers pulled up to her chin and lifted her eyes to take in the cultured concern on his perspiring face, the tiny drop of drool at the corner of his pudgy mouth, and the faint whiff of fine Bourbon on his breath.

Before she could respond, he realized that the pasty skin was flush with color, her lips curled into a knowing smile, and her eyes, long dulled by handfuls of medications, were focused and glimmering blue.

"Quite the contrary, my dear Reverend, quite the contrary."

"How is that?"

"Haven't you heard? I got my children back tonight! They're safe and sound in this house!"

Billy Joe fumbled, "I…uh…I didn't know they'd gone missing."

She clutched his hand to her breast, "I think it's more likely you didn't have time to learn that another gang of your renegade redneck enforcers got busted tonight."

"I'm afraid I don't know what you're talking about," replied the preacher, pulling away. "I came here to help a dear friend, not to defend myself against the false and insulting accusations of an over-medicated hypochondriac."

"That may be, but it didn't take Dick Tracy to find out who pays the rent for the motorcycle repair shop over on Fourth Street, where we retrieved my children."

He stepped back, as she tossed back the comforter, swung her legs out of bed, and stood up, fully clothed. "I have no idea."

"Of course not, it's just another real estate investment, isn't it? Tell me, I've always wanted to know, what percentage of the millions of dollars in donations actually go to help those starving children in Calcutta or to build schools in Africa or to provide clean water to the destitute residents of the slums of South America? What percentage actually goes to help people and how much goes into your pocket?"

"I have an accounting firm that runs everything and, as everyone knows, I take no salary."

"But everything you could ever want is paid for by the church. You forget that I've been to your palace and I know antiques, so I appreciate your treasures. I come from old money but you have artwork and furniture pieces that are beyond even my budget. You have a lake house, another in Palm Springs, and I heard a rumor that you've just closed a deal on a lovely little chateau in Pebble Beach. Oh, and let's not forget your hideaway in the Alps. I must assume that they're all furnished in the manner to which you are accustomed?"

"I must ask you, dear lady, why have you asked me here?"

"To give you the opportunity to tell your side of the story, before it all hits the press in the morning paper and the Federal Prosecutor begins convening a grand jury."

His jaw dropped and his jowls ballooned like a blowfish in distress, "What do you mean?"

The bedroom door opened and Brad marched in, still wearing his biker leathers and carrying a capped bottle of beer. "She means we know that, in spite of your racist subversive hateful spiel, you're being used by Post and Brantley, and all the rest of those bigots, to steal the rights to vast properties so they can build a major pipeline through the state. They're blackmailing you, so they can run their business through your private bank, Paisley/Hatch."

"Protect me from this ruffian, he threatened to kill me!"

"That's true, I did, and I'm still holding that out as an option, unless you come clean right here, right now!"

Hardman stepped behind Marjorie for protection. "I still don't know what you're talking about."

"Of course you do, you lying sack of shit," said Brad, leaning close. "You and I both know that you like boys with big dicks and by tomorrow, your fan club is going to know all about it too."

"Liar!"

"Oh, bullshit! I might have been half-stewed and completely out of my mind, during our little dance out on the driveway, but I distinctly remember you staring at my erection and drooling all over yourself, as you blubbered about how you could help me recover from my torment. When I grabbed your miniature cock, it was as hard as a little pickle."

"No one must ever know," mumbled Billy Joe, clutching Marjorie's shoulders.

She reached up to pat his hand, "It's all going to come out, one way or another, dear. You would be smart to get ahead of the curve on this one, before it takes you under. I'd suggest your topic for Sunday's sermon might be about confession and forgiveness, if you still have a congregation."

The bedroom door opened, again, and Stanton walked in with a big grin, "I've just finished a long chat with Harry Thomas, the Federal Prosecutor, and he's expanding his inquiry to include all the contested seats in the State. The governor will announce the unprecedented decision to postpone the election for thirty days to allow a preliminary investigation to determine whether a prosecutable conspiracy exists."

"But that's illegal," stammered Hardman.

"So are money laundering, intimidation, attempted murder, and kidnapping, just to name a few."

"I think I need to speak to my lawyer."

"As a matter of fact, I took the liberty of setting up a meeting with the prosecutor, as soon as you leave this property. There are two patrol cars waiting at the gate to escort you to his office," said Stanton. "I would suggest that you cooperate."

"There will be a squadron of Harleys patrolling the neighborhood, just in case your troublemakers decide to stop by for a little chat," said Brad.

Stanton turned to his son, "Would you show Reverend Hardman out?"

"I'd be glad to," said Brad grabbing the collar of his suit to heave him out into the hallway, which was jammed with clowns blowing horns and tossing streamers and confetti, husky bikers patting him on the back, and a chorus of black men singing 'For He's a Jolly Good Fellow', as he stumbled through a gauntlet that extended down the stairs, through the kitchen, where Mama Louise, Maybelle, and the rest of the household staff hammered pots and pans with metal spoons, and out the back door. A large white van with giant speakers on the roof and pink and purple searchlights spinning in all directions blared the Rolling Stones 'Sympathy for the Devil' to the delight of a small crowd that cheered as the rotund Reverend rolled into the car and the huge driver eased the Lincoln out through the portico, followed by a pair of thundering Harleys.

~

Sissy moved her white king's pawn two spaces and Nellis brought the black queen's knight to the front. "I guess I underestimated you, back when we started playing checkers."

"You should have figured it out, when I beat you every time we played," laughed the little imp.

"I'd guess Mr. Charles taught you classic chess."

"You responded to my opening with an Alekhine defense, from a game between Aron Nimzowitsch and Alexander Alekhine in the Semmering Tournament in 1926."

"How could you deduce that from the first two moves?" inquired Nellis.

"Because it's a common opening in modern chess."

"And you just had to know where it came from, right?"

"Right," replied Sissy, advancing her queen.

"I don't mean to be nosy but have things settled down at home?"

"Yeah, I guess it took us getting kidnapped to make everyone else realize what's important."

"I'm sorry it came to that."

"Me too. Those guys, who snatched us, were really stupid and, if you hadn't shown up to rescue us, we would have snuck out when they fell asleep."

"But you were tied up."

"We'd already untied each other a couple of times, so we knew we could get out of the truck. They let us out to pee and we all started running around trashing the shop, so I could find a door that wasn't locked, and, the way they were drinking beer, we figured they'd pass out sooner or later."

"Your brothers rescued you."

"Yeah well, knowing how things happen since you saved us from the tornado, it was your idea."

"Credit where credit's due."

"Okay, they both claim to be straightening up their acts. Brad claims he's quit drinking and is taking his medicine and Bruce is going to see a head doctor and wants to go to film school in California."

"What about Samantha?"

"She's tough and brave. When I got scared, she made me believe that we were going to get out of there together."

"She's the one who's going to need time to heal and a whole lot of support from you. My wife was like that, tough as nails, ready to face any challenge from anybody or anything…until it was over, and then she'd collapse. What about your folks?"

"Daddy said that the governor thinks there were guys like Brantley running in seven other districts, so they're going to hold up the election until they figure it out."

"And I heard that Reverend Hardeman and his cronies are going to be indicted for fraud and money laundering."

"What's that?"

"That's taking money that was supposed to help starving children and using it for something else."

"Like an election?"

"That's exactly right," replied Nellis, pushing a pawn. "What about your mother?"

"I don't think she's taking those pills anymore because she was in the kitchen for breakfast this morning and made us all put on nice clothes, so a photographer could shoot a family portrait in the living room. I think they're going to use it for my daddy's campaign." She reached into her pocket and pulled out a slightly crumpled black and white Polaroid. "Here, he gave me this to look at until he can make some prints."

Nellis took the photo and put on his reading glasses to find Stanton and the children surrounding a smiling Marjorie. He grinned, "Y'all look like the well-heeled all-American family."

Sissy sat back, pondering the board, "I think we're a lot closer to being a family today than we were yesterday…but no Spratlin is normal."

"Wouldn't it be boring if they were?" snickered Nellis, as Sissy slid her bishop across the board. "What's that?"

"I'm sure someone's done that before but I don't know what it's called and, oh yeah, you're in check!"

"You're sneaky, but we already knew that," said the old man, pushing a pawn.

She ran the king's bishop to the far side of the lattice, "Check."

Nellis moved a knight to protect his king. "You're relentless, young lady."

"You were getting ready to attack my flank, so I interrupted your plan and gained the advantage."

"Did you figure that out on your own or did Mr. Charles share that wisdom?"

The little blond blushed, as her rook took his king's knight's pawn to set up a blockade for her final offensive. "Mr. Charles has lots of those sayings."

"I'll bet he does."

Gracie cocked an ear to an approaching car and a gentle honk roused the other dogs, who ran yelping down the drive. Sissy jumped up to follow, "It's Katherine!"

They pulled the gate open and shooed the dogs out of the way to let the station wagon ease across the yard and up next to the house. Sissy ran to hug Katherine, as she got out of the car. "I haven't had a chance to thank you for saving us."

"Oh, you don't have to thank me, your brothers were the first ones in the door."

"Yeah, but I know who dreamed it up and it wasn't anyone from my family," laughed Sissy, scanning the packed wagon. "Are you moving?"

"Well, yes, sort of…it's kind of hard to explain but Nellis offered me the spare bedroom, until things settle down and I can feel sure that a pickup full of rednecks isn't going to show up in the middle of the night." She glanced at Nellis and grinned, "I guess we're going to see whether we can stand being roommates."

Sissy raised an index finger to her chin, inspecting Nellis, "He is kind of crusty on the outside but I'm pretty sure he's a creampuff underneath."

Katherine leaned to whisper, "We both know he's devious, so I might need your help keeping him on the up and up."

"Up and up?"

She laughed, "That's on old saying that means that he'll behave himself."

"We both know that's not going to happen!"

"You're probably right. Do you think he's trainable?"

"It might take some patience," snickered Sissy. "He's kind of stuck in his ways. That's why I always beat him at checkers and almost always at chess…he's predictable."

"Really?" inquired Nellis, with a cocked eyebrow.

"How many times have you won at checkers since we started playing?"

Nellis pondered, "A few."

"You usually start the game with the same move but you only win when you change the opening."

"How old did you say you are?"

"I'm going to be nine in January."

"Nine going on twenty-five!" laughed Nellis. "I thought I was dealing with this sparkling little cherub and you were playing me the whole time! You're a chess shark impersonating a little girl."

"Only when we're sitting at your game table."

"How 'bout 'our' game table?"

Katherine opened the back hatch, "If you two have settled your little tiff, maybe you could give me a hand with some of this stuff?"

She turned away to lean against the fender and bury her face in her hands, weeping. Nellis wrapped his arms around her and Sissy hugged her waist.

"I'm sorry, I guess actually moving in with you made me realize that this is the first time that I've felt safe in a long time. Is it really over?"

"It won't be over until people learn to listen to each other with their hearts and accept each other for who they are. It won't be safe until the bigots finally figure out that they don't deserve any more rights or privileges than anyone else and no one has the right to tell the rest of us what to believe, that's up to each person to decide for ourselves."

"I won't hold my breath."

"The only thing more powerful than hate is love," said Nellis, hugging the girls, as the dogs gathered around. "I lost my roots out on the road because I allowed myself to believe that I was that performer in the spotlight. That personality was what the audience expected to see, not who I really was, but I couldn't get enough adulation to satisfy my ego and there was always another town, another gig, and another crowd, even if they all looked just like the last and the next."

He kissed Sissy on the forehead and, then, Katherine, "The two of you made me realize that my roots are bound up in the dirt under our feet, and all these critters, and the few people I allow inside that gate. My only significance is governed by who is foolish enough to love the real me."

The Characters

Nellis Gray — cranky, craggy, lives alone in an old farmhouse in a garden wonderland with five dogs and six cats, chickens, a few goats, and a pot-bellied pig named Chester, plus raccoons, fox, bunnies, squirrels, possum, and lots of birds.

'Lucy' — Nellis' 1959 Goldtop Les Paul six-string electric guitar.

Nanny - his wife, who died of cancer and haunts the house, son (Nathan) took off when he was 17 and hasn't been heard from since, daughter (Ashley), a nurse, married to a college professor in Boston — no children, doesn't come home.

Chuck Stern — runs cattle on the Gray property

Nellis' nephew — Henry, and his buddies — Jamie (black kid), Mikey, & Marty hand out posters the state fair to finance a student film project

"Sissy" Shirley Ann Spratlin — 3rd grade, blond curls, pug nose with freckles, big green eyes - spritely, giggly, inquisitive, determined, and frightened.

"Sam" — Samantha Spratlin — 8th grade — slender, pale skin with dark eyes and auburn hair, late in maturing, dying to be popular in the new school, and anxious to build another life away from the stress at home. Consoling Brad during his attacks and tending to his needs, while trying to protect Sissy from him.

Brad Spratlin — oldest brother wounded in Vietnam, post-traumatic stress, angry, violent, alcohol, drugs, flashbacks — hanging with bikers — hulking, burr cut, shrapnel scar on his right cheek, a dragon tattoo to chase away his demons on his right shoulder. Lives in the pool-house next to a perfectly maintained pool that hasn't seen a swimmer or a party in years.

Bruce Spratlin – brother – gay artist / musician and activist, lives in a renovated loft in the barn where he paints giant depressing abstracts and male nudes to purify his rebellious soul, wild parties, sleeps all day, alcohol and drugs, drives baby-blue VW bug.

Stanton James Spratlin – father – distinguished, aristocratic, proper, hanging on to a time gone by, white hair – broad shouldered, always impeccably dressed, closet alcoholic, depressed and desperate, failing business / disappearing fortune. Oblivious to the turmoil brewing in his model family.

Marjorie Murray Spratlin – mother – needy bedridden alcoholic hypochondriac, blind to impending financial disaster and the demons that possess her children, who reluctantly visit her bedside for monologues about her latest disease or how her children neglect her and are the cause of her anguish…except Bruce, who was sexually trained by his mother

Ruth – Stanton's sister

Stately Spratlin House in disrepair, spring annuals didn't get planted…the trim's in need of paint, dead branches hang in the trees, the Cadillac that Mr. Charles drives the family around in is shiny but it isn't new, the children are attending the local public school instead of the Academy, and the horses and ponies have been sold. Mama Louise has been harvesting vegetables out of the first vegetable garden since the end of WWII.

Dr. Selfridge – dour and arrogant, stately manner, quack / pill pusher – Valium and Lithium for calm and sleep

Rev. Billy Joe Hardman – Evangelical preacher who pumps Marjorie with fire and brimstone and never leaves without a donation for the church – bigoted, homosexual, money grubbing, self-indulgent, ministers to Marjorie Spratlin by laying hands between her legs. Rotund, thinning slicked back died black hair, pudgy pale face that he trained to mirror the emotions of his parishioners.

Hannibal Hardman - Billy Joes' father - preacher

Mama Louise – cook – the good-humored backbone of the staff and the family, lives in renovated servants' quarters over the garages. Originally from southern Georgia.

Sibble Savage – nanny / housemaid – slender, aging waif, who looked after this generation and Stanton and his sister before them…more parent than their real parents and knows all the family secrets, which guarantees her place in Spratlin House until she joins her husband, who was killed in the Korean War.

Mr. Charles – houseman / chauffer – distinguished overseer - everything on the property must meet his approval, things were done as they had always been done and the honor and social graces of the family were to be protected.

Geoffrey – 18-year-old gardener – pot smoking, black kid who knows a lot about plants and even more about getting into trouble. Hot for Sam.

Gametable – Louis XVI – late 18th Century, walnut & tulipwood, lifting top with inset game-boards inside, traverse drawers, tapered legs terminating in sabots.

Stanton Enterprises – his father ran it for his grandmother's family, thriving example of management and worker rights and benefits, but the decline in the market dive sopped up two-thirds of the funds invested for pensions and benefits and the company does not have the resources to cover the difference.

Katherine Kennedy – Stanton's secretary, mistress – long, lean, thick auburn hair, dark piercing eyes, high cheek bones, strong jaw, wide smile – intelligent, organized, and safe and secure inside her bubble.

John Malcolm – Treasurer of Stanton Enterprises

Fred Jamison – VP of Stanton Enterprises

Dobie Johnson, Roy Stiles, and Mitch Mitchell – rough union representatives

Jules Schreiber – union lawyer

Jason (Jazz) Taggart – guitar player – Jazz Taggart and his Band of Merry Men
Matt & Jerry - roadies
Jose – percussion
Maria – background vocals
Harvey - keyboards

Joe Billings – Police Chief – wife – Sally

Curtis Hall – Congressman

Maybelle Brown – Curtis Hall's black mistress and mother to his four bastard children – Daniel, Hubie, Muriel, and Martin

Miles Brantley – young Republican running for Curtis Hall's seat

Cletus Brantley – Miles' father – owns an enormous ranch and is planning to buy his son an election

Eli Post – Post Oil – third largest privately held oil company in the nation

Rev. Joseph Jamison – the Church of Eternal Salvation down in Brimmington

Chet Clausen – producer at Channel Eight and moonlights for Hardman's weekly broadcasts

Glenden Ross – writes sports reports for the paper and handles print editing for the ministry and the political wing

Ronnie Graham and Norman Orinsky – racist bullies from Nellis' high school days

Hal Blaney – Democratic candidate

Dorothy Holcomb – political Grande Dame

Paisley/Hatch Accountants – for Brantley, Billy Joe Hardman, and Praise the Lord Ministries.

Trevor Hatch – accountant for the ministries
Ted Riley – accountant for Brantley

Sister Gwen – the St. Francis Orphanage

Hank Garrett – runs the soup kitchen
Benny Fisher – baker

Constance Calhoon – matron of the homeless shelter

Sammy Smith – brain damaged youngster who helps around the shelter

Harry Thomas – Federal Prosecutor

Victor – maitre d' at Victor's French restaurant
Rollo – chef

About the Author

Rick Stiller is a novelist, an award-winning commercial photographer, an educator and advocate, and a Master Gardener.

Nellis Gray is the first novel in a trilogy that explores bigotry and racism, a brewing revolt by those rendered destitute and helpless through the revocation of our rights, liberties, hopes, and dreams by a tyrant and a fanatical fraternity of tycoons who acquired the presidency as the ultimate investment. Watch for the publication of SunnyBreeze and Storytime.

If you enjoyed this story, please give it a five-star review on my Amazon page and like my 'Eric T Stiller – Author' page on Facebook.

More novels by the author

The Morgan's Knot Serial Fantasy
(a continuing adventure for all ages)

Morgan's Knot (vol. 1)
Island of the Children (vol. 2)
Ice Island (vol. 3)
Islands of Glass and Steel (vol. 4)
Islands in the Sky (vol. 5)
Islands of the Mind (vol. 6)

Dealer - A brash young entrepreneur recognized the financial potential in 1967's counter-cultural revolution and built a robust and illicit chain, importing from the Caribbean, South America, the Middle East, and Asia to supply a budding market from coast to coast.

For more on my novels, photography, & music, please visit:
www.rickstiller.com.

Made in the USA
Columbia, SC
13 October 2021

46830740R00130